A PERILOUS JOURNEY OF DANGER & MAYHEM

BOOK 2:
'THE TREACHEROUS SEAS'

By Christopher Healy

A Perilous Journey of Danger & Mayhem Series:
Book 1: A Dastardly Plot
Book 2: The Treacherous Seas
Book 3: The Final Gambit

The Hero's Guide Series:
The Hero's Guide to Saving Your Kingdom
The Hero's Guide to Storming the Castle
The Hero's Guide to Being an Outlaw

A PERILOUS JOURNEY OF DANGER & MAYHEM

BOOK 2:
'THE TREACHEROUS SEAS'

Christopher Healy

WALDEN POND PRESS
An Imprint of HarperCollinsPublishers

Walden Pond Press is an imprint of HarperCollins Publishers.

A Perilous Journey of Danger & Mayhem: The Treacherous Seas
Copyright © 2019 by Christopher Healy

ISBN 978-0-06-234201-0

Typography by Joel Tippie
20 21 22 23 24 BRR 10 9 8 7 6 5 4 3 2 1
❖
First paperback edition, 2020

To my Aunt Jo Ann,
who first introduced me to travel

A PERILOUS JOURNEY OF DANGER & MAYHEM

BOOK 2:
'THE TREACHEROUS SEAS'

PROLOGUE

From the Journals of Alexander Graham Bell

September 12, 1883

Dear Diary,

There's nothing like the feeling of the wind in one's beard! As I write this, I am speeding southward on my newest creation, the *AquaZephyr*—an oceangoing vessel unlike any other. Our destination: Antarctica! Our objective: ~~Ambr~~ The South Pole! And, yes, also Ambrose Rector. Apprehending that diabolical genius is the part of this mission I prefer not to dwell on. But we know that the villain is also sailing for the uncharted southern continent and we must stop him before he obtains more of the supernaturally powerful "space rocks" that fueled the strange and terrible machines he used to take over the World's Fair last May.

Darn you, Rector! Why must you ruin everything?

September 15, 1883

Dear Diary,

How I wish I could turn back time and reverse my decision to send Rector on his first fateful expedition to the Antarctic years ago. In my defense, however, the man was just a hapless, lack-talent lab assistant back then. He managed to ruin every project he touched. He once caused an explosion that destroyed half my workshop. And all I'd asked him to do was polish a spoon!

I had to do something before Rector ended up burning my lab to the ground. But firing the son of the Inventors' Guild's founder wasn't an option. So I sent him on a long boat ride to Antarctica. How was I to know that, while he was down there, he would find a magical meteorite, be transformed into an evil genius, murder the entire crew, and then return to New York in my stolen ship to exact revenge? Seriously? Who could have seen that coming?

September 21, 1883

Dear Diary,

The *AquaZephyr* is operating at record-breaking speeds! Eight days out and we've already left the Florida coast in our wake! Not too shabby for a ship constructed in a mere six weeks. I daresay that despite Rector's two-month head start, we stand a chance of overtaking the scoundrel before he reaches Ant-arctica.

My word, this Caribbean weather can change in a heartbeat. In the time it has taken me to write this, the skies have shifted from bright blue to slate gray. And the wind! I can barely hold down the page to write. Best to head belowdecks before the rain makes my ink run.

September 21, 1883

Dear ~~Diary~~ WHOMEVER FINDS THIS:

SEND HELP! WE'VE BEEN BOARDED BY PIRATES!

PART I

Pick a Peck of Pepper's Pickles . . . Please
New York City, September 12, 1883

"*BOOP! BOOP! BOOP!*"

Emmett Lee screamed and fell off his bed, accidentally tearing down the sheet that hung between his cot and Molly Pepper's.

"Emmmmmmmmett," Molly moaned, wrapping her pillow around her head. "What are you doing?"

"What am *I* doing?" Emmett sputtered. "Robot's the one making the noise." Beside his bed stood a tall metallic man with a scuffed oil-barrel chest, clunky aluminum-tube arms, and a rather dapper straw hat. The automaton's handlebar mustache spun like a pinwheel as he continued to *boop*. "Robot, please stop," Emmett moaned. "Why are you doing this?"

"I was trying to anticipate your needs," Robot said. His trap-hinged jaw sometimes clicked as he spoke, but,

3

as he'd been originally created to sing at parties, he had a delightful tenor voice.

"And you thought we *needed* to be startled out of a deep sleep?" Emmett asked.

"I thought you needed to be awakened," said Robot.

Molly squinted at the clock on the wall and, giving up, slipped on her eyeglasses. "Oh, bother beans! It's seven twenty!"

"That is what I was going to say," said Robot. "Except for the 'bother beans' part. Should I start saying 'bother beans'?"

Emmett double-checked the clock. "The shop's supposed to be open already! And we're going to be late for school! Okay. Okay. Don't panic. We can figure this out. The walk to school takes, what, a half hour?"

Molly leapt from her bed. "Robot, lights!"

Robot began igniting the gas lamps that sat atop teetering piles of books, while Molly shook her mother, who lay snoring on yet another cot only two feet away. "Mother!"

"Was somebody booping?" Cassandra mumbled.

"The booper was I, Mrs. Pepper," said Robot.

Molly ripped the blanket from her mother and shouted, "We were supposed to be up an hour and twenty minutes ago! We're late for everything!"

"Oh, yes, I almost forgot! We're late!" Cassandra bounced from her bed onto her tool-strewn workbench (for the bedroom was also the Peppers' workshop) and ran across the tabletop to a counter stacked with pots, mugs, and cans (for the workshop was also the Peppers' kitchen). Cassandra often took this route to avoid tripping over the half-built inventions littering the floor of the cramped little room. There were plenty of benefits to living with a brilliant inventor like Cassandra Pepper, but uncluttered living space was not one of them.

Cassandra hopped down and flipped the toggle on her Brew-Master 1900, which instantly began spouting steam.

"I'm still doing the math, but I don't think we have time for coffee," Emmett said from behind the sheet that Robot helpfully held up for him while he changed into school clothes.

"There's always time for coffee," said Cassandra.

"Well, let's see," said Emmett, misbuttoning his shirt. "If we leave right now and take Bleecker Street to— no, at this hour, we should probably go up West Third, unless—"

"Robot, can we make it to school on time?" Molly asked, squeezing into her ankle-length black dress.

"Your average walk to school takes eighteen minutes," said Robot. "You should arrive for the morning bell if you leave within the next eleven minutes, thirty seconds."

"See, plenty of time for a hearty breakfast," Cassandra said cheerily as she dropped a full loaf of rye into the Mega-Slicifier. With a grinding noise, the device began shooting thin squares of bread onto the table like a river-boat gambler dealing cards.

"There's one thing I don't understand, though, Mother." Molly climbed over an open crate of nails while weaving her dark hair into a long braid. "What happened to the clock you built? The alarm didn't go off."

"That's because I didn't set it," Cassandra said, passing a hot mug of coffee to her daughter.

"You, um, you did this on purpose?" Emmett said. He fell over in a frantic attempt to pull his pants up. "Can I ask why?"

"Molly said mornings were boring, always the same old routine," Cassandra explained. "So I decided to spice things up!"

"Congratulations, you've succeeded," Molly replied as she fed bread slices through the Toastinator with one hand and buttoned her dress with the other. While she didn't want to say so in front of Emmett, she was genuinely enjoying the frenzy. It wasn't that she wanted to return to the terror and chaos of last May, when Ambrose Rector and his henchmen, the Green Onion Boys, were constantly trying to kill them, but she had been longing for a little chaos to be thrown back into their lives. Emmett, however . . . Well, Molly was pretty sure that, after years of living on the streets, hiding from Jäger Society goons who wanted to deport him back to his birth country of China, Emmett was fond of finally having a "same old routine." Moments like these, Molly hoped her friend wasn't regretting his decision to stay with the Peppers.

"Get over here and eat, Emmett!" Molly called, sliding aside some loose screws to make space at the worktable (which was also the dining table).

"I really just want to get to school." Emmett, fastening his brown tweed vest, stumbled over a partially constructed Multi-Broom PowerSweeper. "It took an escort from government agents to get me into that school in the first place. I'd rather not risk it."

"I understand, Emmett, but you'll be fine as long as we abide by the contract," Cassandra said as she launched dollops of butter onto the toast with her Pat-a-Pult. "In the meantime, you children are twelve years old—I can't send you out without a proper morning meal." She cracked three eggs into the coffee maker and held a bowl by its spout to catch the coffee-speckled yellow mush that spewed forth.

Molly wasted no time digging into her bowl of slop. "This is surprisingly un-awful," she said. She flipped open a folded copy of yesterday's *New York Sun*. Emmett gave her a sideways look. "Just because we're late doesn't mean I can't be informed," she said. "Don't worry, I'm only scanning."

She took off her glasses, slid them surreptitiously under a napkin, and began reading.

President Calls Off Search
for South Pole

In the sixty years since a Russian vessel first spotted the mysterious "Seventh Continent of Antarctica," many intrepid souls have set out in search of the fabled South Pole—which scientists believe to lie deep at the heart of Antarctica's forbidding, snowcapped landscape. But most are thwarted by the miles-thick ice shelf that surrounds the continent and turn back before even reaching shore. Those who manage to make landfall fare worse. Many expeditions do not return at all.

Tragically, this appears to be the fate of the research vessel *Slush Puppy*, America's most recent attempt at victory in the race to the Pole. The wreckage of the ship washed onto an Argentine beach last week. All crew members are presumed dead.

The fate of the *Slush Puppy* signals the end of our Age of Antarctic Exploration, as President Chester A. Arthur today signed an executive order forbidding further attempts to locate the fabled Pole. "Too many fine American lives have been lost," Arthur said. "It's not going to happen. We might as well try reaching the moon!" The president then turned his attention to the new set of bronze mustache combs presented to him by the king of (continued on p. 5)

"Hey, Molly," Emmett said, wiping his mouth. "I know you like to recap the news for me on the walk to school, but we're probably going to be running today, so—"

"That's okay! Nothing interesting, anyway." Molly quickly refolded the paper. There was no need to share what she'd just read with a boy whose father *died* on a failed mission to Antarctica. It was Ambrose Rector who was responsible for Captain Wendell Lee's death too—though not in the way that Emmett or Cassandra thought he was. They believed that Rector had outright murdered Captain Lee along with the rest of the crew of the *Frost Cleaver*, but Molly alone knew otherwise. Rector had revealed to her that he'd actually marooned Emmett's father in Antarctica, leaving the poor man to slowly die of starvation and frostbite. It was, honestly, a much more gruesome death, which was why she'd never told Emmett about it. She struggled over that choice daily, but always came to the same conclusion: Why fill Emmett's head with images of his father suffering a lonely, painful demise? Emmett's feelings about his long-gone father were complicated enough as it was. It was better to spare him. She hated Rector for burdening her with this secret—among a million other reasons.

Molly shivered. There hadn't been a day since the attack on the World's Fair that Ambrose Rector hadn't wormed his way into her head. It didn't matter that the villain had been spotted fleeing New York Harbor in the *Frost Cleaver* months ago; she knew he'd return eventually. And with more of his deadly "Ambrosium."

Bam! Bam!

Molly jumped. "Robot, is that you?"

Robot tilted his head. "That is not me. I am me."

"No, the knocking," Molly said.

Somebody was pounding on the front door, beyond the tall folding screen that separated the Peppers' living quarters from the actual pickle shop.

"We have a customer!" Cassandra announced.

"I'll get it!" Molly said.

"But—*school!*" Emmett sputtered.

Molly ducked under the table and squeezed around the screen.

Unlike the messy rear half of the Peppers' pickle store, the front half, where customers entered, had not a mote of dust on the floor, nor crumb on the counter-top. Not a single drop of brine meandered down the side of a jar. Keeping the shop neat, however, wasn't diffi-cult when there were generally no pickle purchasers to wait on.

Molly threw up the sashes and squinted as sunlight burst in, revealing the morning buzz of Thompson Street outside. Jasper Bloom, a stocky, stubble-cheeked young man in gray coveralls, waved at Molly as she unlocked the door. Jasper was a friend—and the Peppers' only regular customer, which was why she felt bad about the unenthusiastic nod she greeted him with that morning.

"And a howdy-do to you too, Molly Pepper," Jasper said, tipping his cap. "I must say I was not expecting to see your charming self here at this hour. Not that I'm displeased, mind you. Although you do have what appears to be muddy eggs on your face. Anyhows, I'm surprised because I was under the impression that you and Emmett left for your daily jaunt to school at seven. Then again, I was also under the impression that this store *opened* at seven, and yet there I was at 7:27, standing pickle-less in the sun. And doing far too much door knocking. Do you know what all that knocking does to a man's knuckles, Molly Pepper? It chafes them. I got chafed knuckles now. That sorta thing never used to happen to me when I was an ashman. I've gone soft, Molly Pepper. Soft like a puppy's floppy ear. Do you know what Balthazar Birdhouse would say about these soft, chafed knuckles of mine? No, you don't—'cause you still never met the man. And that's a good thing. So, why is it you're not at school? You're not sick, are you? 'Cause if you're sick, I'm not sure you should be handling my pickles."

"We're running late!" Molly blurted, grateful to get a word in before Jasper rattled on for another twenty minutes. "So take your daily pickle and go. No offense." She plucked a fat garlic dill from a jar and handed it to him in a piece of wax paper.

"Hmmph, 'no offense,'" Jasper echoed. "Do you know what I think whenever Balthazar Birdhouse says 'no

11

offense'? That was a trick question—Balthazar Bird-house never says 'no offense.' He just offends you and takes full credit for it. Emmett Lee! You're here too?"

"Yes, Jasper." Emmett had come running from behind the screen with his and Molly's schoolbags. "And if we don't leave in the next four minutes, we're going to miss the bell."

"I made them late on purpose," Cassandra said, poking her head out while she got dressed behind the screen. "To make morning more fun."

"Okay, Jasper, pay up so we can get going." Molly held out her hand.

"Well, you see, Molly Pepper, that brings up another question," Jasper said, dropping a nickel into her palm. Molly braced herself. He was going to ask for a job. Every day, he would come in, buy a pickle, and ask for a job. "As you know, I used to be an ashman—probably the best in New York City, if I'm being honest. You might hear differently from Balthazar Birdhouse, but seriously, which of us are you gonna trust? Anyhows, I was relieved of that job after I missed several days of work helping some certain children deal with a certain diabolical madman, and I am now among the unemployed. Although I did keep the uniform—please don't tell anyone."

"Jasper, we've told you we can't afford to pay another worker," Molly said.

"Come back tomorrow, Mr. Bloom," Cassandra said,

stepping into the front shop area. Her button-down black dress was askew, but her hair had been pinned up into an almost-neat bun. "Here, Molly, you nearly left without your spectacles again."

Jasper perked up. "Tomorrow it is!"

"Nothing's going to be different tomorrow," Molly grumbled as her mother slipped the round wireframes onto her face. "Except maybe I'll do a better job of misplacing these glasses."

"What makes you so certain nothing will change, Molls?" Cassandra grinned coyly.

Molly narrowed her eyes. "Is there something you're trying to tell us, Mother?"

"To hurry off to school?" Emmett tried, nodding hopefully. "That's what you're telling us, right? To go to school now?"

"Oh, I can't hold it back any longer: *Everything* is going to change!" Cassandra gleefully exclaimed. "Today is the day the Guild votes!"

That brought Emmett back from the door. "Wait—the Inventors' Guild? They're voting *today*?"

"To finally change their membership policy?" Molly asked.

"Yes!" Cassandra bounced with excitement.

"How do you know?" Molly asked, flabbergasted.

"Yes, how do you know?" asked Jasper. "I have no idea what you're talking about, but if a conversation takes place in my presence, I *will* be part of that conversation."

"The Inventors' Guild—you know, the fancy club where all the most powerful inventors work and never have to worry about money because the Guild seems to have endless resources?" Molly said. "Well, they have a strict 'No Girls Allowed' policy."

"And they've never seemed keen on changing it," said Cassandra. "Until the World's Fair, that is, when their stodgy old hides got saved by a bunch of brilliant scientists who happened to be ladies. Alexander Graham Bell and Thomas Edison promised us a vote after that. And they're finally having it!"

"That's amazing, Mrs. Pepper!" Emmett said. "But how do you know it's happening today?"

Cassandra giggled devilishly. "Bell told me weeks ago. He and Edison have both promised to sponsor me for membership as soon as the Guild changes their charter to allow women."

"You kept this from us? For weeks?" Molly gaped. Keeping secrets was something they'd all gotten better at after three months of being forced to pretend the World's Fair fiasco never happened, but still, this was *big news* for her mother to keep quiet about.

"I wasn't even going to tell you now," Cassandra said. "I wanted to surprise you when you came home from school."

"School?" Molly blurted, wrapping her arms around

14

her mother. "Who cares about school?"

"I do," said Emmett. "Not to, you know, bring down the mood or anything, but . . ." He gestured toward the clock.

"No, Emmett is right," Cassandra said. "As much as I'd love to be there as the results are announced, you two probably shouldn't get caught skipping school right when we've finally gotten the Jäger Society's truancy goons off our back."

Molly scoffed. "And all we had to do to make that happen was save the world."

Cassandra ushered the children toward the door. "The vote is just a formality anyway," she said. "Bell and Edison run the Guild; the others will do what they say. Don't worry, though—as soon as you're home from school, we're closing the shop early and heading straight to the Guild Hall!"

Emmett glanced at a clock behind the counter. "Ugh, the morning bell's in eleven minutes."

"We're fueled by good news!" said Molly. "We'll run fast!"

"Well, actually, we might tire out if we run the entire way," Emmett said. "We should probably alternate. Run the first block, walk the second—no, wait, walk first. Or—are there an odd number of blocks or—"

"I'm running." Molly dashed outside. She didn't know how she was going to concentrate in class today. Not that she was particularly good at that on a normal day. But today, it was going to be impossible to stop daydreaming about her mother striding up the Guild Hall's golden staircase, about her grand new office with a telephone and electric lights and tools so new they shone, about Alexander Graham Bell fetching her coffee and Thomas Edison humbly pleading for her help on his latest—

Molly stopped. There was a man across the street, a man in a long, dark coat. His bowler hat was tilted down to shade his eyes, but he seemed to be staring right at her. All thoughts of Cassandra's news left Molly's head, replaced by nightmare memories of Ambrose Rector.

Emmett dashed past her, saying, "I thought you said *run* first!"

Molly looked back across the street. The man was gone. She gripped the straps of her bag and ran to catch up, but not before checking over her shoulder one more time.

2

Cassandra the Guildswoman

I JINXED MYSELF, Molly thought, while ignoring her teacher's lecture that morning. She'd planned to day-dream about her mother as a Guildswoman, not about the mysterious stranger across the street. *But, no, I just had to go and wish for more excitement in my life.*

It was true, though, that in the three months since the World's Fair Affair, her day-to-day life had devolved into a dull, repetitive routine: boring breakfast, boring chores, boring school. (The only time school wasn't dull was when Molly got in trouble, which was why she tried to get in trouble as often as possible.) After school, it was time for Molly to run the boring pickle shop while Emmett and Cassandra worked together on new inventions. And she couldn't even chat with Robot while she worked the counter, because no one was allowed to

17

know Robot existed. Boring.

Even so, it wasn't the running from gangsters, staging jailbreaks, and fighting murderous madmen that she missed. Well, maybe she missed that stuff a little. But even so, she hadn't been asking for a mysterious stranger. Most mysterious strangers she'd met tried to kill her at one point or other. And even if Ambrose Rector himself wasn't a threat at the moment, several Green Onion Boys had evaded arrest after the Fair. And those guys were ruthless criminals. Any one of them could be out for revenge.

Really, all she'd wanted was some change. Change was always good. Change brought excitement. Although, of course, that's exactly what she'd thought when she restarted school, and when she got to quit being her mother's assistant, and when Emmett and Robot became new members of their little Pepper "family." Actually, that last part was still really nice.

After the Fair, when President Arthur offered to grant Cassandra any favor as a reward for helping save half of New York, Molly expected her mother to ask for a spacious new lab or maybe a stockpile of the latest research equipment. Instead, Cassandra passed her "wish" on to Emmett, who used it on two very specific requests.

The first was for all the proper documentation he needed to stay in the country without immigration police or Jägermen harassing him—and Molly was secretly giddy about how unhappy that must have made President Arthur. It was Arthur, after all, who had signed the Chinese Exclusion Act, a law that barred Chinese immigrants from entering the country. Although Emmett had been in America legally since infancy, he was an orphan, and had no adult guardian to get his paperwork in order when the laws changed. The prospect of being shipped off to a country whose language, customs, and people were unknown to him terrified Emmett. But, reluctantly or not, Arthur held to his promise, and Emmett officially moved in with the Peppers.

Emmett's second request was to attend school. But not the isolated uptown school that most immigrants were forced to attend, which would have meant a grueling two-hour walk each way every day. Emmett wanted to go to the same nearby school as Molly, even if some teachers or white students might not be happy about it. Molly had wondered if this might have been an even more troubling prospect for the president, but he made it happen, nonetheless.

President Arthur had nothing to do with Robot becoming the fourth resident of the pickle shop, however. In fact, he could never know about it. No one could. Because the Peppers could never risk anybody learning that Robot—a singing clockwork automaton—had inexplicably developed a mind of his own after a piece of Rector's strange meteorite was implanted into his chest.

19

Robot was no longer just a machine; he could talk and think. He could *fly*. He had magnet powers. And probably a bunch of abilities the Peppers didn't even know about yet. He was also quite devoted to Molly. Robot was the only good thing to ever come from Ambrosium.

Which was why Molly hated the need to keep his existence secret. But Robot's creator, Alexander Graham Bell, would undoubtedly want him back if he learned about his newfound abilities. Bell would probably want to experiment on Robot, or worse, experiment on the chunk of Ambrosium that gave him life. And Molly could never let that happen.

So, after years of it being just her and her mother eking out a life on their own, Molly suddenly had what felt like a real family. Ironically, this new "family" structure meant she saw far less of everybody. She and Emmett were made to sit on opposite sides of the classroom at school, and once they were home, Emmett went straight to work with Cassandra.

Molly had no problem with Emmett taking her place as her mother's assistant; it was a job she'd never really wanted and one for which Emmett—a born tinkerer—was far more suited. But Molly hadn't considered that the time spent aiding her mother had also been time spent talking, joking around, and having fun. There was no fun behind the pickle counter.

Very soon, though, the Peppers would be able to put the pickle business behind them. As a Guild member,

Cassandra would have all the assistants she needed, meaning Molly and Emmett could get back to important kid business, like tic-tac-toe, and jumping in puddles, and devising a plan to bring their living automaton out of hiding. *That* was what Molly decided to focus on for the remainder of the school day—not mysterious strangers, or loneliness, or whatever her teacher was saying about John Quincy Adams.

The children returned that afternoon to find Cassandra already extinguishing lamps and pulling down shades. "Hello, children," she said brightly. "How was school?"

"Great," said Emmett.

"Boring," said Molly. "I only got in trouble twice."

"Excellent," Cassandra replied. "Drop your things and let's go!"

Molly tossed her bag over the privacy screen. It landed with a clatter. "Falling bags!" Robot said from somewhere in back.

"That was just me, Robot!" Molly called out.

"That was not you," said Robot. "That was a bag. I saw it."

"I threw the bag," Molly explained. "Sorry we can't take you with us, Robot. But we'll celebrate when we get back!"

"Huzzah!" Cassandra threw the door open and marched outside.

Emmett began to follow, looking strangely somber.

"You okay?" Molly asked gently. "My mother's about to achieve her biggest dream—I thought you'd be more excited."

"Oh, sorry! No, I'm thrilled for her," he replied, shaking the glum from his face. "I was just thinking about my father. And what happened when he achieved *his* dream."

"Ah," Molly said, wincing from the pang of guilt she felt any time Emmett mentioned his father—which he did frequently. She hoped today wouldn't be the day she'd be forced to reveal her secret about Captain Lee. "But this is completely different," she said. "My mother's not going anywhere."

"No, I'm not," Cassandra said, popping back inside. "Because no one is following me. Let's go, go, go!" And she ducked out again.

"I'll be fine, Molly," Emmett laughed. "Your mother, however, might explode if we don't get her to the Guild Hall fast."

Molly smiled. She took Emmett's hand and bounded down the street after her mother, so full of joyous anticipation that she didn't think twice about the man in the long coat, huddled behind the ice wagon across the street.

Emmett crinkled his nose as they approached Madison Square Park. "The city really has given up on street cleaning, haven't they?" he said, hopping over a fly-swarmed pile of horse manure.

"Without tourists, who do they have to impress?" Molly said, swatting a bug from her nose. "Us folks who actually live here?"

The streets of Manhattan were practically empty compared to the way they had been in May, before the World's Fair That Wasn't, when the sidewalks had been so packed with visitors that Molly couldn't travel from corner to corner without tripping over a gentleman's cane or getting bumped by a fancy lady's bustled skirt. But then came the front-page articles about the chemical leak in Central Park that sickened thousands, triggered mass hallucinations, and forced the cancellation of the Fair. Tourism slowed to a trickle after that.

That "official account" of the incident was, of course, utter nonsense, a complete fabrication concocted by government authorities to avoid a public panic. It had been decided by the men who decide such things that the public must never know about Ambrose Rector and his Mind-Melter—the true cause of the disaster. Nor could anyone ever learn that Rector was only stopped by the intervention of the Peppers and a courageous group of women called the Mothers of Invention. And nothing rankled Molly more than that she was forbidden to utter a word about her heroic actions that day. Perhaps, she thought, once her mother was a member of the prestigious Guild, they'd be able to finagle a way out of the strict secrecy agreements the government had forced them to sign.

The Peppers crossed the street to the most majestic building in all of Manhattan, the palatial Inventors' Guild Hall. No matter how many times they came here, they still craned their heads up to take in the grandeur—marble pillars like petrified redwoods, dreamlike stained-glass portraits, statues so lifelike one might think that Medusa had run amok. Molly got goose bumps at the thought of spending her afternoons in this modern-day acropolis rather than her cramped, vinegar-scented home.

She gave a pleasant wave to the security guards as she strode inside. The smattering of visitors in the grand entry chamber were all focused on the marvelous clockwork ceiling, watching its mechanical figurines chop silvery trees, slide down copper pipes, and ride tin-plated dragons. No one paid her mother any attention now, Molly thought, but the next time Cassandra Pepper walked through that entrance, people were going to swoon and wave their autograph books the way they did for Thomas Edison or Nikola Tesla.

Molly was disappointed to see that the clerk at the Welcome Desk was the same toucan-snouted, weasel-eyed man who had thrown them out a few months earlier.

"You," the man sneered.

"Me," Cassandra replied, her chin held high. "And

you'd better get used to it, because you're going to be seeing a lot of me. Well, not a lot of me. You'll only be seeing as much of me as you see right now. What I mean to say is—"

"Why are you here?" the clerk snapped. "Do I have to call the police again?"

"No, you do not," Cassandra said calmly. "And you didn't have to last time, either. I see your nose has recovered nicely, by the way. Good job on that. But, no, today I really am expected. Please tell Alexander Graham Bell that we are here to see him."

The clerk glared. "Mr. Bell is not in the building." He placed his hand on the telephone mounted next to his desk.

"Well, that can't be right," Cassandra said. "Bell *needed* to be here for the vote this morning."

"*Obviously*, Mr. Bell was present for the quarterly meeting and charter vote, but he left shortly aft—" The clerk narrowed his eyes. "How do you know about that meeting?"

"Call Edison, then," Cassandra said, keeping her composure quite admirably, in Molly's opinion. "We'll go up and see Thomas Edison."

"You will not," the clerk said. "You will leave." He stretched his neck to look past the Peppers, to the guards.

Molly was not going to let this annoying little man ruin their plans yet again. "Distract him," she whispered to Emmett before ducking away.

"What?" Emmett sputtered. "Molly, I—" Emmett stepped to Cassandra's side. "Um, hello, Mr. Pianosmith. I don't know if you remember me, but I used to *work* for Mr. Bell."

The clerk crossed his arms. "You're difficult to forget. You're the one who'd been illegally playing house upstairs after hours."

"So, you know about that, huh?" Emmett muttered. "Well, um, I guess I shouldn't be surprised. Mr. Bell always said you were the most astute of all the clerks."

"He did?" Pianosmith's voice suddenly softened. "Mr. Bell knows me by name?"

"Absolutely," said Emmett. "He was always saying things like, 'You know who keeps this whole place running? Mr. Pianosmith, that's who.'"

The clerk leaned across his desk. "He complimented my tie clip one time," the man said proudly. "But I never realized—"

"Get me Thomas Edison, right away!" Molly had snuck around the desk and was screaming into the telephone. She didn't care about getting caught—she was finally using a telephone! She shuddered with excitement at the sound of the operator's "Please hold."

"Hey!" Pianosmith barked.

But Thomas Edison's familiar voice had already come on the line: "Hello?"

"Eddy, it's Molly Pepper! We're coming up!" she blurted into the phone.

"Um, what?" Edison replied.

"He said he can't wait to see us," Molly reported, hanging up the phone before Pianosmith could yank it away. "Let's go."

The clerk buried his face in his hands as Molly, Emmett, and Cassandra marched up the gold-railed staircase in their own little victory parade.

Thomas Edison sat in a plush velvet chair, tinkering with an apple-sized gadget on his sleekly varnished desk. He gave his visitors a quick nod as they entered.

"To what do I owe the . . ." Edison trailed off, hunching down to tighten a loose wire on his device.

"I believe the word you're looking for is 'pleasure,'" Cassandra said.

"Is it, now?" Edison asked, raising one thick eyebrow. He put down his pliers and folded his hands. "Seriously, why are you here? The more we're seen together, the more people might start asking questions about you-know-who and the you-know-what, you know?"

"Yeah, but now we have a perfectly good reason to be here," Molly said, spinning the gears of a model on a nearby shelf.

"Which is what?" asked Edison. "And please don't touch that."

"Where's my office?" Cassandra asked.

Edison stared. "I don't know—somewhere down in Pickle Town. You actually forgot your own address?"

"Where is my office *here at the Guild Hall*?" Cassandra rephrased. "Will you be building me a new one, or am I taking over someone else's? I assume you've kicked out that awful Hoity-Toity Boy by now."

She and the children smiled at him.

"Okay, three things," Edison said. "First . . . No, actually, there's just one thing: What are you talking about?"

"We're talking about my mother's Guild membership," Molly said firmly. She pressed her palms flat against Edison's desk. "You know, the membership you and Bell promised to sponsor her for as soon as the Guild began letting in women?"

"Ah, I should have realized." Edison sat back and loosened his bow tie. "I will absolutely hold to that promise . . . whenever the Guild eventually changes its charter to allow female members."

Cassandra blinked. "But that vote was today."

Edison grimaced. "Um . . . yes. We voted this morning. But our proposal didn't pass."

"Didn't pass?" Cassandra repeated. "But you . . . And Bell . . ."

"We said we'd bring it up for a vote, and we did," Edison said. "Alec and I may run the Guild, but it's a democracy; all changes to the charter must be approved by a majority of the membership, and the majority voted against the motion. So . . ." He got up and crossed to the window. "Is it stuffy in here? It feels stuffy in here."

"How could you let this happen?" Emmett asked.

"Who voted against it?" Molly asked, her cheeks warming. "I want names. Tell me who they are. You call for another vote while I head straight to their offices and convince them they made the wrong choice."

"Are you talking about violence?" Edison asked. He turned to Cassandra. "Is she talking about violence? Because the girl has trashed my stuff before."

But based on the simmering look in Cassandra's eyes, the woman might have been contemplating some trashing of her own.

"I demand a recount!" Molly hollered.

"There's not going to be a recount," Edison replied. "Or another vote." He stood behind his desk chair, as if he wanted the security of some hefty wooden furniture between him and Molly. "I'm sorry, but it wasn't even close. Ninety-seven to three."

"What?" Molly shrieked.

"Don't yell at me! I was one of the three." Edison gripped the back of his chair.

"You're also the co-chairman of the Guild," Emmett said, still sounding stunned. "You weren't able to convince *any* of the others that changing the charter would be a good thing?"

"He didn't even try," Cassandra said coldly. "Because it was an unpopular idea. And he is a coward."

"Now, hold on there," Edison started.

"Are you going to pretend you actually put any effort toward getting this measure passed?" Cassandra said. "No. You may have held to the letter of your word, but your inaction beyond that reveals how little those words of yours meant."

Molly couldn't believe it was happening again. The Peppers had been strung along, only to be cut loose and told they had no place in a world run by men with golden nameplates on their doors. This was the way it was always going to be, wasn't it? People with power—whether because they were men, because they had fat bank accounts, or because they held positions that were only available to men with fat bank accounts—would tell everybody else what they could and couldn't do. Molly's mother had genius-level engineering skills, but *they* said she couldn't use them. Molly had information about the biggest, most important story of the century, but *they* said she couldn't tell anyone. It was time for Molly to have her say. But she obviously wasn't getting anywhere with Thomas Edison.

"Where's Bell?" she asked.

"Why?" asked Edison. "Do you want to trash *his* stuff again? Have at it. His office is across the hall; I'm sure you remember." He took off his brown checkered coat and dabbed his forehead.

"We know he left after the vote this morning. Probably to hide from us. Tell us where he went."

"He's . . ." Edison hesitated. "He's off-site, working on some secret project."

"Where?" Molly stared directly into Edison's eyes.

"You think Bell tells *me* where his secret labs are?"

"As if you guys don't spy on each other constantly," Molly scoffed. She picked up the gadget Edison had been working on when they entered and began tossing it from hand to hand. "Hey, Eddy, what's this?"

"Put that down!" Edison snapped. "That's my—it doesn't concern you. Just don't futz around with it."

"So, don't do . . . *this*?" Molly tossed the gizmo over her head and caught it behind her back. Edison almost keeled over. "Ooh, look how goosey you are! This thing *must* be important. What's it do?"

"That *thing*, young lady, might be the next *big* thing, bigger than the light bulb." Edison cautiously inched around the desk toward her. Emmett and Cassandra both stepped in his way. "I haven't finished diagramming it yet, though," Edison continued. "So if that prototype breaks, I might not remember exactly how to . . . Please, just . . ."

Molly held the gadget out through the open second-story window. "Where's Bell?" she asked.

Edison gritted his teeth. "Fine! He's at the seaport.

South Street and Pine. In one of those covered wharf houses. Now, will you *please* give back that machine?"

"You heard the man," Molly said, pulling the device back inside and out of harm's way. "Let's get to the seaport before the sun goes down."

"I would say 'good day,'" Cassandra said as she exited, "but as it turns out, I don't want you to have one."

Emmett followed, shaking his head. "And to think, I once *stopped* Molly from beating on you."

Molly paused in the doorway and tossed the small contraption to Edison. "Catch!" It went high over his head and cracked apart on the floor behind him.

Edison dropped to his knees to gather the scattered pieces. "You did that on purpose," he grumbled.

"Not my fault you can't catch," Molly said.

Edison tried fruitlessly to force some of the broken bits back together and sighed. "Will you at least do me the favor of wrecking Bell's fancy new boat too?"

"Oh, I might do that," Molly said as she tromped out into the hall. "But it won't be for you."

The Secret Ship

EVEN IF SHE hadn't seen the tall-masted ships tucked between long wooden piers, the powerful reek of fresh (and not-so-fresh) fish would have told Molly they'd reached the seaport. Dockworkers sprayed salty water and saltier language as they tossed netfuls of striped bass into the backs of horse-drawn wagons. Dozens of faded gray wharf houses sat along the piers, gates open to the river like nautical barns waiting for flocks of ships to sail in for the night. But some had their doors closed to outside eyes. It was in one of these long, tall buildings that Alexander Graham Bell was constructing his "fancy new boat." But which one?

"Something tells me it's the one with the men in black suits guarding the back door," Emmett said. Molly wiped her smudgy glasses with her sleeve and took a look. There was something eerily familiar about the long black coats and bowler hats on the men Emmett pointed to.

"Righty-oh," Cassandra said, in the fiercest, most determined way one could say "Righty-oh." She marched across the dirt road to the rear entrance of the wharf house.

"Wait, what's the plan?" Emmett tried to ask. But Cassandra was already reaching for the knob. The watchmen jumped to block her.

"Where do you think you're going?" one sputtered.

"In there. To see Mr. Bell," said Cassandra.

"Mr. Who? There's no—"

"We know Bell is in there," Molly said as she and Emmett ran to her mother's side. "Edison ratted him out."

"I don't care," the guard said. "This is a restricted area. Leave."

No one left. The guard waved to a third man in the same coat-and-bowler uniform across the street. "Morton, who are these people? Are they yours?"

"Shh, don't—oh, jeez . . ." He waited for a cart to pass and ran anxiously to join them. "I'm *undercover*," he whispered.

"*That* was hiding?" the first guard scoffed. "You were just standing there."

His partner shook his head. "Completely visible."

"Hey, *they* didn't see me," said Morton. "And they're the ones I'm—"

"Wait! I *did* see you!" Molly interjected. She suddenly recognized the big owlish eyes and little leprechaun nose of the man named Morton. "You were outside our shop this morning."

"No, that wasn't me." Morton coughed and pulled down the brim of his hat.

The door guards rolled their eyes.

"Who are you people and why have you been spying on us?" Cassandra snapped.

"*Nobody* is spying on you," Morton said. He glanced around for eavesdroppers. "Just watching—*protecting*. We're federal agents."

"Federal, as in the government?" Emmett took a step back.

"And who, might I ask, are you protecting us from?" Cassandra asked, with unmasked skepticism.

"Did they lie to us about Rector leaving?" Molly asked, looking around herself.

"*Shhh!*" Agent Morton hissed. "No, you-know-who is long gone. But he didn't work alone, right? You should be happy I'm looking out for you."

Molly and Emmett exchanged glances. If any food shop in Manhattan could use the services of a body-guard, it was Pepper's Pickles. But something didn't ring true about Agent Morton's explanation.

"Why not just tell us we were under guard?" Emmett asked. "Why all the secrecy?"

"Um, we're *secret* agents," Morton said. The other two nodded.

"No, it's because they're not *just* guarding us," Molly said. "They're also spying on us to make sure we don't talk about the World's—"

"*Shhhhh!*" Agent Morton did another frantic check for eavesdroppers.

"There's no need to worry, Mr. Secret Agent," Cassandra said. "We know what will happen if we break the government's Discretion Agreement. Believe me, if anyone's going to slip up, it's going to be that blibbety-blabbety Edison. You'll get no trouble from us."

And with that, Molly ducked between the agents, yanked open the door, and dashed inside the wharf house.

"Stop that girl!"

Molly didn't know what she expected to find behind the guarded door, but it wasn't the massive metallic marvel floating on the water between a colossal cut-out section of floorboards. The ship was like something ripped straight from the pages of a Jules Verne novel. It was long and wide enough to hold five Pepper's Pickles (five shops, not five pickles), and as sleek and shiny as an unused spoon. No sails, so it obviously had an engine of some kind. And its spiral-ridged, conical bow resembled a drill. But most fascinating were its legs. The boat had six multijointed steel beams—three protruding from each side and arcing down into the water like crab legs.

Molly was too busy goggling at the ship to notice the fourth federal agent until he grabbed her by the wrist. "What have we here?" he said.

Molly was about to try biting the man's hand when, from up on the deck of the futuristic ship, she heard, "Is that Molly Pepper?"

Alexander Graham Bell appeared at the ship's rail. "What in heaven's name? Forrest! Agent Forrest, unhand that girl, please. And you fellows by the door, let those others in too. I . . . I know them."

While Morton and the door guards reluctantly stepped back outside, Bell disembarked, his footsteps clanging upon the wrought-iron gangplank. "Miss Pepper," the famed inventor said in his lilting Scottish accent. "I almost didn't recognize you in those spectacles."

"Well, when I finish saying what I've got to say to you," Molly said, "you may wish you hadn't."

Bell flinched. And then flinched again as Cassandra and Emmett, both steely-eyed, joined the group. He patted Agent Forrest on the shoulder. "It's all right, Forrest. You can go finish up with the crew."

Agent Forrest cocked an eyebrow. "I'll stick around," he said. The only hatless agent they'd seen, Forrest had lustrous black hair waxed into rolling waves, and a pencil-thin mustache that he must have spent hours grooming to ensure the uniform length of each and every

37

whisker. It was Molly's turn to flinch when she saw the man wink at her mother. "Most ladies don't mind when I stick around."

Cassandra remained focused solely on Bell. "Mr. Bell," she said. "We await your explanation."

"My, um . . . I must say, I'm at a bit of a loss," Bell stammered. "This is a covert project at an undisclosed location. However did you find me?"

"Edison," Molly said bluntly.

"That figures," Bell grumbled. Then he winced. "Oh, but that also means you've been to the Guild. Which means . . . you know."

"Yes, we know you lied to us," Cassandra said, poking him in the chest. Agent Forrest moved to step in, but Bell waved him off. "We know the vote was an empty gesture that you never tried to gain support for," Cassandra continued. "We know that you only told me you'd sponsor my membership because you knew you'd never have to do it."

Emmett shook his head. "I am so disappointed in you, Mr. Bell."

Molly sucked in a breath. Coming from Emmett, that was *harsh*.

"I'm sorry," Bell said, bowing his head. "I truly am. But please understand it was never our intention—well, who knows with Edison—but it was never *my* intention for things to turn out this way." He looked Cassandra in the eye. "When Thomas and I put the vote on the schedule back in July, I fully planned to campaign for the change. But then Rector fled for the Antarctic, and I've been preoccupied ever since."

"Ix-nay on the Ector-ray," Agent Forrest interjected, raising a finger to his lips.

"It's fine, Archibald," said Bell. "These people know about Rector." The agent's eyes widened. Molly wasn't sure if the man was amused or impressed by the thought that this random woman and a couple of children were in on the big government secret.

"What we don't know about is *this*," Molly said. "What is this crazy ship and why's it so important that it made you forget the pledge you made to the people who *saved your life*?"

"Sorry, young miss, but *that* is something we are not at liberty to speak about," said Agent Forrest.

"This is the *AquaZephyr*," said Bell. "An entirely new type of water transport I've invented."

Forrest glared at him. "Did anyone explain the concept of 'top secret' to you?"

"I feel bad," Bell whined. "I muffed things up for them. Besides, if anybody deserves to know that I'm about to take care of Ambrose Rector, it's these folks."

"You're taking care of Rector? How?" Cassandra asked.

"Watch what you say, Bell," Forrest warned.

"Relax, Agent Hair-Jelly," Molly said. Her interest was piqued. "We already signed the secrecy thingy—we'll just add this *AquaZipper* to it. Now, Bell, tell us: How is this super-boat of yours gonna stop Rector? Are you chasing after him? 'Cause he left two months ago."

"Yes, Rector has a head start," Bell said. "But my *AquaZephyr* truly is, as you put it, a super-boat." His pride in his creation removed all mopiness from his voice. "Those legs? They connect to what I call hydrofoils—angled metallic sheets below the ship. Once the craft gets moving, the foils lift the hull out of the sea. Without the normal friction of boat against water, the *AquaZephyr* can travel nearly thrice as fast as the *Frost Cleaver*. Which means that even though Rector left months ago, I *can* catch him."

"Only if you leave real soon," Emmett said, sounding unconvinced.

"Indeed," Bell said. "We leave in an hour. So don't worry, Ambrose Rector will never bother you again."

"But Rector's heading back to Antarctica to get more of his space rock, right?" Molly asked. "What about the president's new rule that forbids any more South Pole expeditions?"

"Technically, we're not going there to look for the Pole," Bell said. "We're chasing Rector. So we have special government permission."

"*Secret* permission," emphasized Agent Forrest. He

40

sighed. "You people should not be hearing *any* of this."

Molly's mental cogs cranked fast. "So you're not even gonna *look* for the Pole at all while you're down there? Like all those other explorers have been clamoring to do? Like *you* tried to do once before?"

Bell blew a drop of sweat from the tip of his nose, and Molly knew she had him where she wanted him.

"Well," he said, "bringing Rector to justice is the *primary* purpose of this mission, but if we manage to make landfall on Antarctica, it would be a waste to go home without at least *trying* to locate the Pole. Think of it as killing two birds with one stone. Or two penguins with one snowball!" He grinned awkwardly, but nobody else did. "Sorry. Humor is not my forte."

"Neither is secrecy," said Agent Forrest.

Emmett gestured toward the massive drill on the nose of the ship. "That's for breaking through the ice, isn't it? Did the ship you sent my father on have one of those?"

Bell coughed into his hand. "I'm sorry, Emmett," he said. "I should have realized how this might affect you."

"I just want to make sure you're not sending more men to their deaths," Emmett said. Molly had never seen him so bitter.

"There isn't a day that goes by, Emmett, that I don't regret what happened to your father and his crew," Bell said. "But that was Rector's doing, not mine. To answer your question, the *Frost Cleaver* did indeed have an ice

41

drill. They wouldn't have reached the Antarctic shore without it. The tragic irony of your father's death is that his expedition was a success. He just . . . never made it back. Because of Rector."

"And this time, I—an official representative of the US government—have conducted thorough background checks on the entire crew," said Agent Forrest. "So, you can rest assured there'll be no criminals."

"Rector wasn't a criminal when he set out on that trip," said Emmett.

"I will also be on this mission myself," said Bell. "The *Frost Cleaver*'s troubles began when the crew mutinied against Rector and threw him off the ship. I'd like to think that my presence would have prevented such a thing."

Emmett blinked. "You mean to say that if you hadn't opted to stay home in your cushy office, my father would still be alive?"

"That's not—um, no, just—" Bell sucked in a big breath. "Emmett, by finding the South Pole that your father set out to find and apprehending the man who killed him, I hope to make amends for what happened to him."

Emmett teared up and Cassandra wrapped a comforting arm around him. Molly's gut felt hot and bubbly. She was still furious with Bell for misleading them about her mother's Guild membership—and now she was even angrier at him for ruining what was supposed to be their righteous revenge rant against him. They'd barely gotten to yell at Bell before the entire conversation changed tracks to Antarctica. Now Emmett was sad, her mother was frustrated, and Bell—the man who caused both of those things—was about to go off and become even more famous and powerful than he already was. By achieving something that should have been achieved by someone else! If anyone should get the chance to explore Antarctica, it should be—

The plotting center of Molly's brain lit up. She knew how the Peppers were going to make history. For so long, she'd been putting all her screws in one toolbox, banking on her mother's inventing career to lift them out of obscurity and poverty. But maybe there was another way to make a name for themselves. And make Emmett happy in the process.

"If you really want to make up for this," Molly said firmly, "Emmett should be the one to finish what his father set out to do."

"Um, what?" said Emmett.

"Take us with you, Bell!" Molly said.

"*That* is a solid no," Forrest said, stepping in front of Bell. "As much as I wouldn't mind having a pretty face on board"—he winked at Cassandra, who rolled her eyes—"this will be far too dangerous for women and children. Plus, in case you didn't catch it the first, oh, eighty times it's been mentioned, this is a *secret* mission. The man we're hunting isn't even supposed to exist. Even if Bell was loony enough to want you on board, I'd have to begin weeks-long background checks and—"

"Forrest, don't worry." Bell tapped the man. "I agree wholeheartedly. They cannot come along."

Emmett looked relieved. "Um, I appreciate what you're saying, Molly," he said. "But I'm not my father. For one thing, I get seasick. Curled-up, can't-walk, re-tasting-yesterday's-breakfast type of seasick."

"Yeah, but—" Molly stopped. But *what*? What was she going to say? That since it probably took Emmett's father a few days to die his slow, painful death, he might have, just possibly, tried to leave a final message for his son before he passed? And that she only knew about the man's slow, painful death because Rector had told her about it months ago and she'd been keeping it secret ever since? Was she really going to say all that? Would he ever forgive her if she did?

"It's not just about you, Emmett," she finally said. "Bell took away my mother's chance to become famous as an inventor. The least he can do is give us the chance to become famous as explorers."

"We're not sailing to Antarctica, Molls," Cassandra said. She rested her hand on Molly's shoulder. "We came here to give Bell a piece of our minds, and we have. Now we focus on putting our lives back together."

"But . . ."

A gruff-looking man with a wiry beard appeared on the deck of the *AquaZephyr*. "Engine is primed and packs are stowed," he yelled. "We're ready to set sail!"

"Looks like we're ahead of schedule," said Bell.

"But, wait," Molly sputtered. "What about us? What about the Guild? What about—?"

"I apologize for the way things turned out," said Bell. "I really do. But remember that this is not just about exploring the South Pole. It's about stopping Ambrose Rector. If he's allowed to get his hands on more Ambrosium, the tragedy at the World's Fair will end up having simply been a dress rehearsal for a much larger catastrophe. I wish you well in . . . whatever you do next." The inventor gave a quick bow and headed up the gangplank onto his ship. "See them out, Forrest, would you?"

Molly was fuming as the agent ushered them to the door. "And remember," Forrest said, "if you tell anyone about this, you'll be in violation of your secrecy contracts—and whatever you received in exchange for signing them goes bye-bye. Oh, and . . ." He handed Cassandra a business card from his coat pocket. "Look me up in about six months." He winked and strutted back to the ship.

Agent Morton awaited them outside. "Can I, uh, walk you home?" he asked, avoiding eye contact.

The sun had dipped behind Manhattan's tall buildings and dim stars began to dot the sky as the Peppers plodded silently to the end of the pier. They arrived in time to see the big aluminum gate at the end of the wharf house rattle, rise, and release Bell's hydrofoil into the East River. The engine rumbled as the strange ship puttered slowly at first, but then with a sudden roar, the entire vessel lifted out of the water, save for the thin chevrons of metal just below the surface. The *Aqua-Zephyr* sped off like a rocket, spraying massive clouds of salty mist.

Cassandra's face was flat, expressionless. But Molly's was red and scowling. "Enjoy your stupid spider boat!" she yelled. "I hope it never comes back!"

Emmett choked back a sob next to her, and she immediately regretted her words.

Someone to Watch Over Them

NOT A WORD was spoken on the long walk home until Agent Morton's "Good night" as Molly shut the door in his face. Emmett lit an oil lamp on the counter, and Cassandra, standing in its flickering light, sighed. Molly feared her mother was going to her Sad Place. Cassandra was never this quiet for this long unless she was struggling to hold back feelings she didn't want the kids to see.

"Celebrate!" Robot stepped out of the shadows, tossing balloons and confetti at them. They all screamed.

Emmett immediately cracked the door open and poked his head out to see Agent Morton standing in confusion. "Um, all okay in here," Emmett said a bit too loudly. "Just a mouse. We're all terrified of mice."

A passing couple grimaced at him.

"No, not a mouse. We're a very clean store," Emmett quickly added. "We *thought* it was a mouse. But it was a . . . meatball. Anyway, we're all good, Agent—I mean, person on the street! You can go back to hiding—*standing* behind your truck over there. Thanks!" He slammed the door again. "I am *not* good at the quick lying thing."

"Robot, what are you doing?" Molly asked once she'd caught her breath.

"I was trying to anticipate your needs," Robot replied. "You had indicated a desire to celebrate when you returned."

Cassandra watched a sinking red balloon bounce off her boot and began weeping.

"My balloons have not elicited the anticipated reaction," said Robot. "I shall destroy the balloons." Robot started stomping its clunky metal feet onto the balloons and loudly popping them.

"*Shhhhh!!!*"

Emmett opened the door again. "No worries! That popping noise was just a . . . a mousetrap. We're trying to catch the . . . meatball. Good night!" He slammed the door and locked it.

"Robot, it's not the balloons!" Molly whisper-shouted. "And you need to get back behind the screen. *Now.*" She ushered the automaton into the hidden living area. "Things didn't turn out like we expected," she explained. "Sorry, but there's nothing to celebrate."

"No, there is," said Cassandra. She grabbed a broom and began sweeping up the multicolored tidbits of paper littering the floor. "Tonight we celebrate a new direction for the Pepper family." She scooped up the confetti and dumped it into a wastebasket. "It's for the best, really," she continued as she grabbed a wet rag from the sink and began wiping down the counter. "When I think about all the time I've wasted trying to get into the Guild . . . *whew!* At least now we know for certain it's never going to happen. Now I can devote my time to more important matters." She filled her arms with gizmos from the floor and began squeezing them into empty spaces on the shelves. "Like family. My family is more important. As is this shop. And being a responsible parent." She collected their dirty breakfast plates from the table, wiped them off on her dress, and dropped them into the sink. "It will be a more . . . *proper* way of living. And it all starts right now. I should thank Bell and Edison, really."

Emmett nudged Molly and whispered, "I don't think I've ever seen her clean like this."

"I don't think you've seen her *clean*—period," Molly replied. "She's going back to the Sad Place. Like after my father died. This is not good." She cleared her throat. "Mother, what's going on? This isn't like you."

"It is now," Cassandra said brightly as she tucked in the sheets on her bed. "This is the new me, the more responsible me. No more chasing silly dreams, eh?"

She scooped an armful of tools from the worktable and dumped them into the trash.

Emmett gasped.

"Mother, stop this right now!" Molly said.

Cassandra paused. "I'm sorry, you're right." She retrieved the hammers, wrenches, and chisels from the garbage. "Just because *I* need to quit inventing doesn't mean Emmett has to. Emmett, the tools are yours now. Feel free to use them until you too learn that ambition is pointless and dreaming only leads to disappointment. I think there's some egg on the pliers—you might want to wash those first."

"Mother, what is wrong with you?" Molly climbed onto a bench to get eye to eye with Cassandra. "We've had more setbacks than I can count, but you've never talked like this. So stop it and get serious. We all know you're not gonna quit inventing."

"But I am," Cassandra said. "I have. Past tense. It's done. No more devising devices or contrapting contraptions for me."

If not for the rotten-egg smell from the coffee machine, Molly would have thought she was having a nightmare. "But . . . Peppers never give up."

Cassandra sighed. "I tried to take classes at the university; they wouldn't let me register," she said. "I tried to sell my work to the department stores; they wouldn't listen to my pitches. I literally saved the lives of the

Inventors' Guild and they won't let me into their club. There's only so much a person can take."

"I don't understand," Molly said. Her throat ached in the way it did whenever she tried to hold back tears. "We've been through so much."

"That's exactly it, Molls," Cassandra said softly. "So much." She climbed, fully dressed, under the covers of the bed she'd just made. "Blow out the lamp, will you?"

Emmett doused the lamp and took Molly around the folding screen to the front of the store. Robot shuffled after them. "Are you certain it was not the balloons?" the automaton asked.

"It was not the balloons," Emmett reassured him. "Although I am curious as to how you managed to inflate them."

Robot was about to reply when Molly erupted with frustration. "This isn't right!" she said in as quiet a voice as she was capable of in that moment. "The Guild is ruining our lives again! I'm so sick of those guys. We've got to do something."

"Agreed. So, let's talk it through," Emmett said. He hopped up to sit on the counter.

"No, let's *do* something. You always want to talk things through."

"Because that's how I *figure out* what to do," Emmett said.

"It's also how you stall, which you do all the time

because you never want to make any decisions."

"Hey, that's not why I like to talk things through," Emmett said. "Or maybe it is. There are probably multiple factors involved. Let's talk this through . . ."

"Talking is how I learn things," Robot added. "And reading. And observing. For instance, I observed that when I tilt my head like this, you tell me it's lovely."

"That's lovely, Robot, but not relevant," Molly said. She began pacing back and forth along the counter. "You know the most frustrating thing about this situation?"

"The balloons?" Robot asked.

"No," Molly said. "It's that if the world only knew about what we did at the Fair, we'd be famous already. Probably rich *and* famous. Mother's inventions would be the talk of the town. We wouldn't even *need* the Guild. *Aargh!* Who cares about those stupid papers we signed? Let's just tell everybody!"

"I wish we could," said Emmett. "It would be kinda fun to see my name in the paper as something other than a murder suspect. But if we break our contracts, they'll revoke my papers and I'll end up back in the hands of the Jägermen. Ugh, I feel so trapped."

"I see nothing containing you," said Robot.

"Metaphorically, Robot," Molly said. "He was speaking metaphorically."

"As was I," said the automaton. "I think. It is possible I do not yet grasp the art of metaphor."

Molly looked into his shiny aluminum face. With his silly handlebar mustache, clunky jaw, and big round eyes that looked perpetually shocked, Molly found it hard to believe she was once afraid of him. "You're right, Robot."

"I did the metaphor correctly?" Robot asked.

"No, you still need work on that," Molly said. "But you were right about nothing containing us. My mother might have temporarily forgotten it, but Peppers never give up. There's always something we can do. I just wish I knew what."

"I can do *this*," Robot said. He levitated a few feet off the floor, spun his head in circles, and juggled some pickles. "But I do not think it will help."

Molly wanted so badly to laugh. But all she could think about was that it was her father who'd coined their "Peppers never give up" motto. And where was he now?

5

Scientists and Muckrakers

MOLLY PEPPER WAS simply not cut out for a "normal" life. She moped through an uncreative (and mostly inedible) breakfast that her mother insisted on cooking with only the proper pans and utensils. She grumbled through the never-ending afternoon, too restless even to read a book while Emmett solemnly hammered by himself at the workbench and her mother monitored the pickle counter alone. The only joy she had left was getting in trouble at school, which she did as frequently as possible. First, it was for chewing licorice gum in class, then for telling the teacher she was wrong about what country Nikola Tesla came from. Then it was for insisting that Thomas Edison had a canister of rhinoceros hair at his lab in Menlo Park (which was one hundred percent true), and then for "admitting" that she hadn't seen it with her own eyes (even though she had), and then for "lying" (even though the only part of what she said that was a lie was the part where she said she'd lied). And that was just Thursday.

On Friday, she got scolded for asking why Emmett had to sit in the back of the room instead of next to her. And then for punching the nose of the boy who answered that question with a hateful comment about Emmett. But Emmett was punished for that one as well, and Molly suddenly wasn't so eager to get in trouble at school anymore.

All of this is why Molly was so excited to come home that afternoon to a visit from her second-favorite woman in the world: Hertha Marks, the unofficial leader of the Mothers of Invention.

And Hertha had brought along a friend.

"Emmett, Molly, so good to see you," Hertha said as they exchanged air kisses. And Molly was reminded how much she missed the cool tone of that crisp British accent. Hertha used to drop by at least once a week, often with a few of the other Mothers in tow, and always with an open invitation for Cassandra to join their group. But Cassandra turned them down every time. She always insisted that she didn't need to join the MOI, because she would eventually invite all those women to join the Guild with her. But Molly suspected that her mother might still be jealous of Hertha, whose money and status gave her access to better educational opportunities and far more advanced equipment than the Peppers had ever seen. Over time, Hertha seemed to tire of rejection, and her visits began tapering off. At this point, it had been nearly a month since she'd been by.

She was as fancy as ever, though: elegant lavender dress, frilly collar, hair wound into a sophisticatedly flouncy bun with pheasant feathers sticking out of it. Her mystery companion, on the other hand, was clad in a tweed dress that looked to have been constructed from the skins of old suitcases, and her hair was pulled back into a haphazard topknot that made her mother's hair look like Marie Antoinette's in comparison. This younger woman barely glanced at the children while they said hello to Hertha; she was too busy peering into corners and checking behind pickle barrels, jotting notes onto a pad all the while.

"Who's your friend?" Molly asked. "And why's she being so nosy?"

"My apologies," said Hertha. "This is—"

"Henrietta O'Mulligan Haversham," the younger woman said, standing up stiffly. "*Inspector* O'Mulligan Haversham to you. I'm with the New York Public Health Office. Can you tell me, please, how long this barrel of cucumbers has been sitting here, unbrined and exposed to the air?"

Molly jumped. "*Those* cucumbers? Um, not long, I'm sure. Right, Emmett?"

Emmett shot her a "why are you involving me?" look. "Long? No. They were delivered . . . Sunday? Or is that too far back? Wednesday, maybe? What are you hoping to hear?"

"Nellie, please, don't torment the children," Hertha scolded. "Molly, Emmett, I'd like you to meet my friend Nellie Bly."

"Hertha," grumbled the woman who was apparently *not* named Henrietta O'Mulligan Haversham. "How am I going to perfect the art of going undercover if you keep revealing my fake identities?"

"It was for your own good, Nellie," Hertha said. "You haven't met Molly Pepper. You're safest if she does not consider you a threat."

Molly grinned.

"So . . . she's *not* a health inspector?" Cassandra asked, trying to surreptitiously hide a moldy cucumber in her boot.

Molly cleaned her glasses and took a closer look at Nellie. "No, she's just a kid," she scoffed. "Hey, Hertha, I thought *we* were your only kid friends," Molly said. "Now I don't feel so special anymore."

Miss Bly raised her eyebrows. "I'm nineteen, I'll have you know."

"Well, it's . . . nice to meet you, Miss Bly," Emmett said, shaking her hand. "Thank you for . . . terrifying us."

"Nellie is a journalist," said Hertha.

"*Investigative* journalist," Nellie clarified. "I get the

deep stories. By going undercover if need be."

Molly perked up. "I love journalism. Maybe I've read some of your articles. Do you publish in the *Sun*?"

"No," said Nellie.

"The *Herald*, then?"

"No."

"The *World*? The *Times*? The *Bugle*?"

"No . . . not yet."

Molly narrowed her eyes. "So you're not *really* a reporter."

"Is your mother *really* an inventor?" Nellie asked wryly. "How many patents does she have?"

Molly felt her cheeks grow warm and hoped she wasn't blushing to an embarrassing degree. "Okay, point taken," she said. "But my mother's status as an inventor is a bit of an iffy subject this week."

"Whatever do you mean?" Hertha asked. She turned to Cassandra, who was standing behind the counter, polishing a tiny cocktail fork and pretending not to hear the conversation.

"She says she's quit inventing!" Molly said.

"Impossible," Hertha declared. "Cass, tell me this is one of the girl's oh-so-hilarious jokes."

"No, it's true," Cassandra said. "Would you like some tea?"

"Cass, you're one of the most brilliant minds I know," Hertha scolded. "You can't deprive the world of your genius."

"*The world* has deprived the world of my genius," Cassandra replied. She told them about Bell's betrayal and the failed Guild vote. Molly was impressed by how carefully her mother avoided any mentions of Rector, Antarctica, or the World's Fair. Hertha already knew everything—and was beholden to the same government agreements as the Peppers—so the secrecy was just for Nellie Bly's sake.

"I certainly understand why you want to give up on the Guild," Hertha said. "But that doesn't mean you should quit altogether. There's—*ahem*—always the Mothers of Invention."

"Thank you, but no," Cassandra said. "I'm all about parenting now. And homemaking. And business ownership. I've put a new foot forward. The left one. Because I typically start with the right."

"I'm sorry you feel that way," Hertha said, brushing a droopy feather from her face. "But I'm also quite certain you'll eventually come to your senses. In the meantime, perhaps Nellie and I can help."

Nellie, who had been taking notes the entire time, closed her pad and pulled a fresh one from the canvas satchel slung over her shoulder. "That's why Hertha brought me. You've been having financial troubles here at the store? Perhaps an article about the best pickle shop in New York would help."

"How is that going to help?" Cassandra asked. "It would only draw more business away from us!"

Emmett cleared his throat. "I think Pepper's Pickles would be the shop in the article."

"Oh!" Cassandra's eyes widened. "Well, we'd better improve, then." She leaned over to Nellie and whispered, "We're not very good."

"But we used to be," Molly said, intrigued by the idea of a news story about them. "Back when Father was around. He used to tell jokes and stories while he was pickling and packaging; the customers loved him. I don't think the quality of the pickles even mattered all that much. *He* was the main draw." Molly's throat clenched as she envisioned her father behind that counter.

"So, maybe the pickles aren't the story," Nellie said. She pointed to the privacy screen with her pencil. "Unless Hertha has been exaggerating your skills, Cassandra, there must be *something* back there interesting enough to captivate customers."

"Perhaps if Emmett comes up with something brilliant on his own," Cassandra said. "But my inventions are off the table. Literally. I put them all in a big box and stashed it away. I don't want to be reminded of my former life."

"Your former life?" Molly said. "It was two days ago." If only they could have Robot run the shop, she thought. They'd have people from around the world popping in to see the famous mechanical pickle seller. Of course, one of those people would be Alexander Graham Bell, demanding the return of his automaton. Unless he really didn't make it back from Antarctica . . .

"And I'm sorry, Miss Bly," Emmett added. "But I haven't created anything good enough to show off yet. Or anything, actually."

"You haven't?" Molly was incredulous. "What were you hammering away at yesterday, while I was counting ceiling tiles out of boredom?"

"One very dented tin can," he replied gloomily. "I don't know. I was fine as an assistant, but now that I have to come up with ideas on my own . . . I'm blank. Maybe I wasn't meant to be an inventor either. I should be a sailor, like my dead father would have wanted."

"You get seasick!" Molly blurted. "You're an inventor, Emmett! You have to be a—*aargh!* You people!" She ran her hands down her face.

"Well," said Nellie Bly. "I suppose I could always write a sob story about the quashed dreams of the poor Pepper family and hope it gets people to shop here out of pity."

"Spin it however you will, Nellie," Hertha said. "Just be sure to make it sound as if a visit to Pepper's Pickles is an experience no New Yorker would dare miss out on. Once something appears in the paper, people have a hard time *not* believing it."

"Like all those stories about 'evil' Alexander Graham Bell last spring," Nellie said. "Even though it was later proven that the real kidnapper was a masked impersonator, half the people I speak to still think Bell is a criminal. It'll probably take him years to shake those rumors. Unless he can manage to rewrite his own story, that is, and do something front-page-worthy. Invent something even better than the telephone."

"Or discover the South Pole," Molly grumbled.

"Ha! Sure, or maybe Atlantis!" Nellie laughed. "That would do it!"

Molly turned away to avoid her mother's chiding look.

"So, Hertha . . ." Emmett jumped in to change the subject. "How did you meet Miss Bly?"

"I sought her out," said Hertha. "I was reading through the archives of a student newspaper from a small secondary school in Pennsylvania—"

"A completely normal thing to do," Emmett said.

"—and I was thoroughly impressed by some of the exposés I found," Hertha continued. "Nellie, show them."

Nellie pulled several clippings from her bag. Molly and Emmett scanned the headlines.

English Teacher Spelled Own Name Wrong on Application

Evidence: School Bully Owen Snerd Afraid of Moths

Principal Vickers Suspended for Taking Bribe

"Whoa," Molly said. "How did you find out about this bribery business?"

"I disguised myself as a courier and took the dirty money from him myself," Nellie said proudly. "Honestly, the bribery sting was barely a challenge. Trapping Owen Snerd in a room full of moths? Now *that* was tough. And more fun."

Molly's face lit up. "Mother, I know what I'm going to be when I grow up."

"Which one, a briber or a moth?" Cassandra asked.

"An investigative journalist!" Molly cooed. Her head was spinning with possibilities. "Speaking truth to power, uncovering hidden secrets, bringing enlightenment to the masses."

"That does sound like you," said Emmett.

"So, how about it, Nellie?" Molly asked. "Need an apprentice?"

"I work alone," Nellie said. "You'd only slow me down."

Molly's estimation of Nellie Bly plummeted.

"Like I said," Nellie continued, "I go for the deep stories—the *really* deep ones. Stories buried under mysteries, buried under lies, buried under confusion, buried under even more stories, buried under dirt. But I still find them. I sniff them out."

"Like a bloodhound," said Emmett.

"No," said Nellie. "Like a bear! Bloodhounds may have the keenest nose of any dog breed, but a black bear's sense of smell is seven times stronger. I'm a news bear."

Molly laughed and popped a piece of licorice gum into her mouth. "News bear with a stuffy head cold, maybe," she scoffed. "Two feet away from the story of the century and she doesn't even get a whiff."

Nellie's head snapped to Molly. "I knew it! I've been sensing all along that there was a better story here than a puff piece about pickle pushers. You're hiding something behind that screen, aren't you?"

"No, no," Hertha said dismissively. "Molly's just—"

"Lying," Cassandra said, far too loudly to sound casual. "My daughter's lying. She's a liar. Well—a storyteller. She tells stories. That are lies."

Molly was aghast. At her mother and herself. Why had she almost revealed the one thing they were legally forbidden to speak of? Was she *that* angered by this junior journalist's ego?

Emmett cleared his throat. "Um, I think what Mrs. Pepper is trying to say—"

"I think what she's trying to say is that her daughter slipped up and said something she shouldn't have in front of an investigative reporter," Nellie said with a sly smile. She leaned over to get eye to eye with Molly. "I think you do have a story you want to tell me, Molly. What's your story?"

Molly cracked the gum in her mouth as she contemplated her response. Emmett, Cassandra, and Hertha tried to look like they weren't holding their breaths.

"Licorice gum," Molly said, flashing a black-toothed smile.

Nellie's enthusiastic grin flattened. "Your story of the century is about chewing gum?"

"Not just any gum. Licorice gum. It turns your tongue

all gross and black." She stuck out her tongue to prove her point. "So, when you want to pretend you're sick and skip school, licorice gum'll make you look like you've got the plague or something. It could revolutionize the art of truancy."

"Oh." Nellie put her pad away. "That's . . . kind of clever, actually. But far from newsworthy. I shouldn't have expected much, though. You're young."

Hertha stood up. "Well, that was fun. Thanks for the chat, Cass, but we really must be going. Miss Bly?" Nellie organized the papers in her bag and shook everyone's hand before following Hertha out the door.

As soon as the visitors were gone, Cassandra snapped at Molly. "What were you thinking?"

"I wasn't thinking!" Molly said. "She just got me all fired up with her I'm-so-perfect-and-amazing-and-I-look-good-in-tweed-and-I-can-do-anything-and-you-can't-because-you're-a-baby-and—"

"Molly, I trust you understand why that lady is the last person in the world we can allow to learn our secrets," said Cassandra. "Frankly, I'm unhappy with Hertha for even bringing her here. As it is, I had to throw a sheet over Robot the moment she started getting snoopy."

"Can I come out now?" Robot asked.

"Mother, I wasn't going to tell. You know me better than that." Molly tried to sound offended. "Although, if I had, I still don't know how the government would be able to punish us once the public knew we were heroes. I mean, that would look really bad on them, wouldn't it?"

"Is that a risk you want to take?" Cassandra asked.

"Well, I'm not the one you should be upset with right now, anyway," Molly said, deflecting the question. "You should be upset with Emmett for saying he wants to quit inventing too." She turned to her friend. "You're not really quitting, are you? You created all those neat booby traps back at your bookmobile."

"I know, but I'm just not feeling the spark anymore," he replied. "Ever since you told Mr. Bell that I should achieve my father's dream for him, I've been wondering if maybe you were right. Not about going to Antarctica— that would be crazy—but about me doing what my papa would have wanted."

"But I didn't *mean* that!" Molly insisted. "You heard my mother—I say false things all the time! What about your seasickness?"

"My father used to say I would get over it. He used to say that we Lees had salt water in our veins. That our destiny lay across the waves. Stuff like that. He never really seemed to notice that I hated the ocean. Also, I'm afraid of eels. Have I ever mentioned that?"

"Do you realize how ridiculous you sound?" Molly said. "You're going to give up something you love for something you hate?"

"I'd be doing it for *him*," Emmett said. "I used to resent Papa for always being gone, always being off on a boat somewhere instead of playing games with me or cooking interesting meals for me or making sure I was set up in a real school—all the things *you've* done for me, Mrs. Pepper. But sometimes I wonder if I've been too hard on him. Maybe he had his reasons for all that stuff. I hear you talk about the good times you had with your father, Molly, and I think, 'My father must have known what he was missing out on when he was out at sea. He must have known what he was sacrificing.' And yet he still did it."

"Yes," said Molly, still exasperated. "He sacrificed for you; he wouldn't want you to sacrifice for him."

"We don't know that," said Emmett. "We'll never know what he would have wanted."

"Mother, please tell Emmett he's not allowed to give up inventing."

"We make our own decisions in this house," Cassandra said. "Besides, I'd be a hypocrite to tell Emmett he couldn't quit something that I've already quit myself."

Molly slumped until Emmett put his hand on her shoulder. "I appreciate you saying all of that," he said, surprising Molly with how un-upset he seemed. "And for what it's worth, I was never worried that you'd actually spill our secrets. I trust you."

Molly gave him a thankful smile, even though her insides were roiling. She didn't feel very deserving of his trust. Not when she'd been hiding the truth from him about how his father really died. And not when she was holding tightly to the shred of paper that Nellie Bly had slipped into her palm during their parting handshake, a note that read, *329 Mott Street—When you're ready to tell your real story.*

Newsworthy News

THE WINDOWS OF the brick row house at 329 Mott Street had been left open, despite the gray sky and thick-air feeling of impending rain. The crisp bacon aroma emanating from within reminded Molly that she hadn't eaten breakfast. She popped a stick of licorice gum into her mouth and looked around for any signs of trench coats or bowler hats before pulling the doorbell cord. A white-haired woman in a gravy-smeared apron answered.

Molly double-checked the address on her paper. "Is Nellie here?" she asked.

The woman peered over the eyeglasses on the tip of her nose. "Who?"

"Never mind," Molly sighed. But before she could turn away, Nellie Bly rushed up. "I've got this, Mrs. Plotski! You can return to your omeleting duties." Nellie wore the same green tweed outfit as the day before, though it now looked thoroughly wrinkled and slept in. "I see you got my note, Molly. Come in."

Mrs. Plotski gave her a cross stare. "I told you no guests, Miss Blurbingham."

"She's not a guest," Nellie said. "I'm not even certain I like her. Molly, come."

Molly took one more glance over her shoulder before following Nellie down the hall to a small bedroom. Nellie shut the door.

"Aha! The news bear strikes again," she said. "I knew I'd sniffed something good yester—"

"Who's the old lady?" Molly asked.

"She runs this boardinghouse. Ignore her."

"Why'd she call you Blurbingham?" Molly hoped she hadn't made a huge mistake in coming here. "Do you use fake names with everybody?"

"Everybody I need to. Why'd you look so goosey outside?" Nellie asked. She pulled closed the window sash. "Were you followed?"

"No," Molly scoffed. She was confident she'd gotten away from Pepper's Pickles without Agent Morton seeing her—the federal agent had been snoring loudly, slumped against a lamppost, when she left. She was far more concerned with Emmett or her mother waking up and noticing she was gone, which was why she left Robot playing the role of Sleeping Molly Under the Covers. "I know how to get around without being tailed, thank you very much. I'm not a child."

Nellie crossed her arms. "You're ten."

"I'm twelve."

"If that was supposed to support your claim that you are not a child, you need to brush up on your arguing skills." Nellie moved a stack of notepads and sat Molly down in the tiny room's only chair. "Now stop wasting time and spit it out."

Molly shrugged and spat her gum into Nellie's palm.

"*Eww*. I meant your story." Nellie dropped the slimy wad into a wastebasket. "Spit it out."

Molly blushed. She was not making the impression she'd hoped. "Okay, but before I say anything, can you promise me one thing? You can never tell anyone you heard this from me."

"You have the word of Nellie Bly."

"Is that even your real name?"

"Define 'real.'"

Molly took a deep breath. If she wanted to save her family's future, she knew what she had to do. Even if Emmett and her mother wouldn't like it. But that's only because they were too glummed out to listen to reason. And if Molly's plan worked, she could stop them both from sinking any further into the gloom. "You'd better sit down for this," she said to Nellie. "You remember the World's Fair That Never Happened? Well, it did."

The Truth Is Out There!

"WELL, *THAT* IS quite a tale." Nellie tapped her pencil. "*If* it's true. Government conspiracies, flying machines, mind-controlling meteorites, the supposedly dead son of the Inventors' Guild president coming back as a maniacal villain—"

"I promise you, it all happened!"

"But I can't ask your mother or your friend to back up your accounting of events?"

Molly shook her head. "They'd deny it all. So would Hertha or any of the other Mothers of Invention. I haven't been able to convince any of them that ignoring our government secrecy contracts is a good idea." She hadn't entirely convinced herself yet, either.

"Well, breaking those agreements would be the only way for this story to ever get out," said Nellie. "And this is a story the people deserve to hear."

"You believe me?" Molly said, hope in her voice.

"One thing that's making me *lean* toward believing you is the part about your mother at Blackwell's Asylum. Hertha mentioned that place to me—told me I should investigate it, because it was corrupt and horrible. But she refused to tell me how she'd come to that conclusion."

Molly stood up. "So you believe me!"

"Possibly. But it's not just me who has to believe. No newspaper editor is going to print a story like this without a secondary source to corroborate your allegations. Was there *anyone* at the Fair who wasn't forced into signing a secrecy agreement?"

Molly racked her brain. Most of the fairgoers who had their minds addled by Rector's ray were convinced by the government that they'd been victims of a gas leak. Certainly none of the cops or soldiers from that day were going to blab. Neither would any of the Guildsmen. Who else did that leave but—?

"The Green Onion Boys!"

"The gangsters? Who Rector hired as his henchmen army?" Nellie asked. "The ones who kidnapped you and hunted you through the city?"

"Yep. A handful of them got away that day. They wouldn't be able to confirm everything, but—"

Nellie stood and tossed her bag over her shoulder.

"Grab your things. We're going to Bandit's Roost."

"What things?" said Molly. "This is *your* room."

It was not easy for Molly to look as casual and nonchalant as her older companion while they strolled past the dilapidated tenements and reeking trash piles that lined the path to Bandit's Roost. She wouldn't have thought it was possible for this neighborhood to be creepier during daytime, but at least at night the darkness helped hide the eyes glaring from cracked windows and the greasy rats in bullet-riddled doorways, gnawing on what she hoped were chicken bones.

"There it is," Molly finally said, pointing down the block.

"You didn't tell me it was all rubble," Nellie said, frustrated.

"Not that one," Molly said. "That's the building that collapsed on me and Emmett. Bandit's Roost is the one across the street."

"Ah, yes," Nellie said, stepping over a puddle of something that had probably once been inside a person. Molly stuck close, avoiding the broken glass among the cobblestones. Just as they squeezed past the lopsided gate, the door of the gangland outpost opened up and three men stepped out.

The tallest had a scar across his left eye, the second a hairy mole on the tip of his nose, and the shortest—but

74

strongest-looking—had a wide gap where several teeth should have been. These were pretty distinct-looking guys, yet Molly wasn't positive if she'd seen them before. If only she'd had her glasses back then.

"What have we here?" Mole-Nose said threateningly.

Molly stopped in her tracks, but Nellie walked right up to the men and pulled out her notepad. "Good afternoon, gentlemen. Wilhelmina Klingstoffer, Department of Destruction and Dilapidation. Might any of you have been present for the collapse of the building across the street?"

"Nice try," Scar-Eye sneered. He stepped frighteningly close to Nellie. "You ain't with no Department of—"

"I most certainly am," Nellie said. "And I'm conducting an official city investigation, so—"

"Oh yeah?" Gap-Tooth scoffed. "What's a city pencil-pusher doin' in the company of a troublemaker like Penelope von Venturesworth?"

Nellie's head whipped back to Molly.

Molly shrugged. "You're not the only one who can use fake names." Then it dawned on her these gangsters recognizing her might not be a good thing.

Scar-Eye pushed past Nellie and grabbed Molly by the collar. "You caused us a whole lotta grief, girl." He lifted her off the ground, her feet kicking uselessly. "You know how I got this zigzag on my face? You and your little buddy Emmett brought that building down on our heads."

"That's how I lost my chompers too," sneered Gap-Tooth.

"And how I got this mole," said Mole-Nose.

Mole-Nose's partners eyed him strangely.

"Point is, we'd still be pretty if not for you and Little Emmett," Scar-Eye barked. "You shoulda stayed chained up where Oogie and Edison wanted you."

"Does that count as corroboration?" Molly grunted to Nellie, while trying to twist out of the gangster's grip.

"It's a start," Nellie said, writing furiously in her pad. "Keep them talking!"

"That wasn't really Thomas Edison," Molly said.

"Sure it was," said Mole-Nose. "That's why he had us kidnap Alexander Gumball."

"Graham Bell," said Gap-Tooth.

"Grahambell's not even a word," scoffed Mole-Nose.

"No, the Edison you worked for was an imposter!" Molly continued to struggle. "He was really a guy named Ambrose Rector. He's the one who hired you all to guard the World's Fair and then backstabbed you all by zapping you with his Mind-Melter. How in the dark were you guys? And, um, Nellie, I could use a little help any time now."

"You're doing great," Nellie said, still writing. "You've got this."

"All I know," Scar-Eye sneered at Molly, "is that everything started going south for the Onions the day you showed up at Bandit's Roost." He lifted her higher.

"Nellie?" Molly squeaked.

"Unhand that girl!" shouted a man in a dark coat as he hurdled the fence. "Federal agents! You're under arrest!"

Scar-Eye dropped Molly and she scrambled to Nellie's side as the reporter secured her notebook in her satchel. "I was just about to step in," Nellie whispered to her.

Two more agents appeared, grabbing Mole-Nose and Gap-Tooth before they could run. One of the officers had a familiar sad-dog frown.

"Agent Morton?" Molly sputtered. "How did you manage to follow me?"

"I, um—" Morton dropped the handcuffs he was fumbling to pull from his belt.

"He didn't. I did," said a different agent, who now had Scar-Eye in cuffs. "After Morton's pitiful performance at the wharf, the agency didn't trust him to do his job alone. I'm the one who spotted you slipping out of your shop this morning." The man lifted the brim of his bowler to reveal a pair of cold blue eyes.

"I remember you," Molly said with a sudden fury. This was the same man who had apprehended her mother on the Brooklyn Bridge months ago, the man who sent Cassandra to suffer for weeks in a mental asylum. "You're Agent . . . Clark, right? You arrested my mother!"

"And based on the crimes I just overheard here, arresting Peppers might end up becoming something of a career for me," Clark said as he shoved Scar-Eye against the wall. "So if you two girls would kindly stay put while I finish trussing up these hooligans. I trust you'll cooperate, since I'm sure you don't want to make things any worse. Right, ladies? Ladies?"

Molly and Nellie could barely hear him. They were already darting around the nearest corner and out of sight.

Trust No One

MOLLY BURST THROUGH the door of Pepper's Pickles and straight into the rear living area, almost knocking over the privacy screen in the process.

"Molly! Where have you been?" Cassandra and Emmett were just finishing getting dressed. Next to them, Robot sat on Molly's bed with the blanket pulled up to his scuffed metal chin.

"I told them I was you, Molly," said Robot. "But they did not believe me."

"Explain yourself," Cassandra ordered. "And you'd better make it good."

"Oh, it's good," Molly said, rubbing her cramping side. "Well, not a hundred percent good . . ."

Emmett filled her a glass of cloudy water from the sink. "What percentage good is it?" he asked.

79

Molly downed the water. "Twenty? Twenty-two, maybe?"

"Molly, what did you do?" Cassandra glared sternly.

Molly took a deep breath. "Okay, but don't get angry until I explain the good part," she said. "Because you're not gonna like the beginning part."

"Molly!"

"I told Nellie Bly!"

"Told her what?" Emmett asked with trepidation.

"Everything."

Emmett threw his hands over his face and Cassandra twisted a dishrag anxiously.

"But listen!" Molly continued. "Nellie agrees—if we become famous, we're golden! Fame is—fame is like immunity! Famous people don't get in trouble! This story was gonna get out eventually, and the men in power would've spun things their way, so that we were either left out or somehow ended up the bad guys. But if we control the story, if we tell it the way we want, we can finally beat them at their own game!"

"But—" Emmett began.

"I know—the contracts," Molly said. "That's why I made Nellie promise she won't attribute the story to me. I would be an 'anonymous source.'"

"Oh, Molly," Cassandra sighed, shaking her head.

Emmett scratched behind his ear. "Well, if it's

impossible to tie Molly to the leak, there's a chance this could actually work."

"Exactly!" said Molly. "That's why that was the plan!"

"Was?"

"Well, plans don't always work out like you expect. Which is why I still haven't bought into your 'thinking things over,' Emmett."

"Just get to it, Molly! What happened?" Cassandra asked.

"The Feds kind of overheard, and now they're after me, so we should probably leave." She grabbed her carpetbag and began shoving random piles of clothing into it.

"Okay, wait—what?" Emmett sputtered. "Wait, wait— what? I mean, wait—what?"

"Your ears didn't malfunction, Emmett." Molly tossed him his own bag. "Federal agents are coming for us; we shouldn't be here when they arrive."

"I can't believe you did this, Molly," Cassandra said as she began packing as well. "Is this how I raised you to behave? Actually, yes. It probably is. *But* . . . I have become a responsible parent over the last three days— haven't you learned anything from that?"

"We're going to prison, Molly!" Emmett burst. "Because you ran off half-cocked again!"

"It wasn't a half-cocked plan! It was whole-cocked! You just said it would have worked!"

"Maybe if you hadn't let Agent Morton follow you!"

Emmett snapped. "Agent Morton! The man who we watched trying to get a lollipop unstuck from his sleeve for twenty minutes!"

"Okay, in my defense, Morton wasn't alone," Molly said. "He was with Agent Clark."

"That fellow who arrested me on the bridge?" Cassandra asked as she tossed an open tin of coffee beans into her bag. "Oh, I don't care for him at all."

"But listen," said Molly, "before everybody panics—"

"I think you're a little late for that," said Emmett.

"This can still work out," Molly continued as she shoveled spoons, books, screwdrivers, and cotton balls into her bag. "Because Nellie is still gonna publish her article. We only have to hide out until then—a few days maybe. Once the story hits newsstands—we're good! Emmett, you're not packing."

"I'm folding!" he snapped. "I'm not going to pack like a caveman just because our freedom is at stake."

"You're sure about this, Molls?" Cassandra snapped her bag closed. "The Bly woman's article can save us?"

"Yes," said Molly. "Except she can't get the story published without corroboration. So I need you two to talk to her and back me up."

"So we can *all* break the law?" said Emmett.

"I'd never ask if the law hadn't already been broken," said Molly.

"By you!" Emmett sputtered.

"Okay, we'll do it," Cassandra said. "We don't have much choice at this point, do we?"

Emmett sighed. "So, is that where we're going? To Nellie Bly's place?"

"No, the Feds saw her with me," Molly said. "It's not safe for her to go home. You can come in now, Nellie!"

Nellie Bly popped around the screen. "Hello! I want to thank you both for agreeing to go on the record about the World's Fair incident. But I don't think we should start until— What the heck is that?"

Robot put the blanket over his head.

"And I guess Nellie knows about Robot now too," Molly said sheepishly.

Emmett's face was in his hands again.

"Okay, Nellie, remember Bell's automatons that my mother rewired to help us defeat Rector?" Molly said. "This one came to life when we put a piece of Rector's meteorite in his chest. More on that later—right now, help us pack."

"I knew it!" Nellie crowed. "I knew you had something exciting back here. News bear!"

"Robot, get out of bed," Emmett said.

Robot complied. "I do not sleep anyway."

"Wherever we're going, we have to bring Robot with us," Emmett said.

"Where *are* we going to go?" Cassandra asked.

"We can't go back to the bookmobile," Emmett said,

laying his neatly stacked shirts into his bag. "It was cramped enough with two people."

"Who can we trust?" Cassandra asked as she laced her boots.

"The MOI!" Emmett dug through a box of contraptions and found the handheld Morse code transmitter that the Peppers had used to keep in touch with the Mothers of Invention in the past. He powered up its battery and speedily tapped out a message.

A reply quickly came blipping back. "It says, 'Meet by Washington Square fountain.'"

"And we're off," said Cassandra. "Molls, throw a few more spoons and a cowbell into that bag, then let's leave before—"

The shop door opened. Everyone held their breath. Except Robot, who had no breath to hold.

"Howdy-do, Peppers! I do not like to think of myself as the kind of person who would tell someone how to run their business, but there is a man in your store who would desperately like to purchase a pickle and yet there are no pickle sellers present. I am that man, by the way. I would like a pickle."

"Jasper!" Molly and her mother ran out to greet him. "We are *so* glad to see you!"

"Many people are," Jasper replied. "Except Balthazar Birdhouse. Unless it's a Tuesday, in which case—"

"Jasper Bloom, today is your lucky day," Cassandra

interrupted. "You're hired!" Cassandra tried to shake his hand, but couldn't because he was clasping his heart.

"Really and truly?" Jasper gasped. "When do I start?"

"Immediately," Cassandra said. "We have to disappear for a few days, so you're in charge of the shop until we get back. The keys are over there, the pickles are over there, and the recipe for making more pickles is . . . somewhere. Make us proud!"

"You know I will," said Jasper.

"Oh," added Molly. "And if any federal agents come by asking questions, tell them we went to . . . Altoona . . . to visit our . . . grand-uncle . . . at the zoo."

"Come out, everybody," Cassandra called to the back.

"Everybody?" Emmett asked.

"Everybody."

Emmett came around the screen, followed by Nellie, and then, with timid, clanky steps, Robot.

"Hello, Mr. Bloom," Robot said. "Congratulations on your new position."

Jasper gaped at the metal man. "Is that one of Bell's singy-dancey machines? Why is he talking to me?"

"He's alive," said Molly. She pointed a stern finger at Jasper. "And you will lose your new job if you utter one word about him to *anyone*."

"One word about what?" Jasper said. "Certainly not about a walking, talking sardine-can man, because I have never seen one of those."

"You catch on well, Mr. Bloom," said Cassandra. "But speaking of Robot's anonymity—he needs a disguise." She slipped her husband's old overcoat onto the automaton. Molly added a scarf and large-brimmed hat, while Emmett tied a blanket around his waist. Not much could be said for Robot's fashion sense, but at least his metal was mostly hidden.

"I am wearing clothes," Robot said. "Normally, I am naked."

"You can go, Peppers," Jasper said from behind the counter, where he was already wearing an apron and looking quite pleased with himself. "Your shop will be in good hands. Have fun doing whatever sneaky mystery stuff you're doing."

Emmett, Molly, Cassandra, Nellie, and the disguised Robot stepped outside.

Nellie looked up to the elephant-gray sky. "Your metal friend's not going to last if it rains."

"Robot will be fine," Cassandra said. "Aluminum doesn't rust."

"I do not rust," Robot agreed.

"What about the electric circuits and such inside him?" Nellie asked.

"He doesn't have any electric circuits inside him," Cassandra replied. "He's got . . . space rock circuits."

"Does water short out space rock circuits like it does electric circuits?"

Cassandra thought for a moment, then went back inside to fetch an umbrella.

Twenty achingly tense minutes later, the quintet huddled by the large fountain at the center of Washington Square Park. They scanned the area for friendly—or not-so-friendly—faces, and finally heard a *"Psst!"*

Sarah Goode, the youngest (and most enthusiastic) member of the Mothers of Invention, stood in the shadows behind a small brick storehouse. Molly had hoped it would be Sarah. The woman had a contagious positivity that never failed to buoy Molly's spirits. Whenever Sarah insisted she would eventually win a patent for her inventions, despite the fact that the US Patent Office had never yet awarded one to a black woman, Molly believed her. The Peppers and company ran to Sarah, and Molly wrapped her in a big hug.

"I miss you too, darling," Sarah said quietly. "But your message sounded urgent. What's the— Oh, Nellie Bly. I didn't realize— *Ahh!*" She flinched at the sight of Robot. "Now, *you* I do not know."

Robot looked to Molly. "Am I allowed to say who I am?"

Emmett stepped in. "Sarah, this is Robot. He's one of Mr. Bell's automatons, but he's alive now because he's got a piece of Rector's meteorite in his chest. It's crazy, I know; just go with it." He looked to Molly. "We're going to have to explain this a lot, aren't we?"

"So, I'm guessing Mr. Robot has something to do with why you need a place to hide?" Sarah said.

"Oh, he's not the half of it," said Cassandra.

"And it is just 'Robot,'" said Robot. "Not 'Mr. Robot.'"

"All righty, then," said Sarah. "Let's get you all some-place safe." She pried up a manhole and climbed the ladder to the sewer below. Emmett winced at the smell, but followed. As did the women. Robot, however, stood motionless, staring down at the others.

"I do not think I was constructed with the appropriate range of motion for climbing ladders," Robot said.

"Hurry, Robot," Cassandra urged.

"Someone will see you," Emmett warned.

"I think I am afraid," Robot said.

Sarah's eyes widened. "He can feel fear?"

"Doesn't everyone?" Molly asked.

"But he's a—never mind." Sarah called upward, "You can do it, Robot! Believe in yourself!"

"Believe in myself," Robot echoed. "That is an intriguing prospect." He held his metal head high. "I do believe in myself. Also, I just remembered I can fly." Robot rose off the ground and floated gently into the hole, where he levitated above the murky water.

Sarah reached up and pulled the manhole cover back in place. "I really do miss you people," she said. "Always something interesting with you."

After a half hour of snaking through dark, malodorous tunnels, Sarah climbed another ladder and pushed open a trapdoor. Molly followed her out into a large warehouse, where she was greeted by the clanking of hammers, the warm glow of electric lights, and the smiling figure of Hertha Marks.

"Miss Pepper," said Hertha. "Welcome home."

No News Is Bad News

THE FRILLY CUFFS of Hertha's velvety dress tickled Molly's wrist as they shook hands. "Lovely to see you again so soon," the British scientist said. "I do hope the dire tone of your message was just some of that classic Pepper hyperbole."

"Emmett sent the message," Molly said.

"Oh dear."

Mary Walton, a sweet-faced older woman, placed a gentle hand on Molly's shoulder. "I figured it was only a matter of time before we got caught up in the swirl of another Pepper adventure," she said, though not in a chiding way. Mary was the environmentalist of the group, always concerned with how new inventions might affect the earth, air, and water. On her head sat the flower-patterned knit cap that she clung to like a good-luck charm. "So," she said, reaching down to help Emmett up out of the tunnel, "what mayhem have you three gotten yourselves into now?"

"It's complicated," Emmett said with a nod of gratitude.

"We like complicated," said a third woman. Margaret Knight's voice came from beneath an engine the size of a pony. Margaret barely stopped working to eat, let alone to greet a visitor, so Molly took no offense. That was how Miss Knight had managed to invent about a thousand things, including the flat-bottomed brown paper bags that the Peppers used with pride in their shop.

That left one member of the MOI whom Molly had yet to see. "Where's Josephine?" she asked, while Hertha and Mary helped Cassandra up.

"Right here, child." Josephine Cochrane was the quintessential "fancy lady"—the kind of person who chided people for saying "drat" and drank tea with her pinkie extended—which was why Molly was shocked to see her slide out from beneath the big engine in a pair of stained coveralls. Josephine put down her wrench, wiped her greasy fingers on a lace handkerchief, and offered a straight-out-of-an-etiquette-book handshake. "The pleasure, as always, is mine," she said.

Molly's jaw dropped. "You're—you're dirty!"

Emmett snickered.

"I'm working, child. Did you expect me to risk a stain

on my dinner attire?" She glanced at a clock on the wall. "Oh, look at that—work time is over. If you'll excuse me, I need to go change for teatime and leisure reading."

While Mary helped Nellie from the hatch, Hertha greeted Cassandra. "Whatever the problem," Hertha said, "you did the right thing contacting us."

Cassandra looked around. "Lovely place you've got here," she said. Molly could tell how hard she was trying not to sound envious. "I love the lovely tools, all lined up so lovely-ly on the walls. And the lovely light bulbs with their . . . lovely electric light."

"My bulbs," Hertha said. "Not Edison's."

"This isn't the same warehouse you were working in before," Emmett said.

Molly looked around. He was right. This place had a pool. No, not a pool—a waterway cut into the floor, which led to a sliding steel door, just like the wharf house Bell had built his hydrofoil in.

"We're working on a new version of our Marvelous Moto-Mover," Sarah said as she climbed into the room. "You know, since the first one sank?"

"Yeah," Molly said uneasily. "Sorry about that."

"Oh, don't worry," Sarah assured her. "This one's going to be even better. And since it's going to transform from coach to boat like the first one, we moved our worksite to the riverfront."

"Actually," Hertha said to Cassandra, "we're hoping

92

this new Moto-Mover will traverse land, sea, *and air*."

Nellie pulled out her notepad. "Is this on the record?"

Molly grabbed her mother's hands. "You could do it, Mother! You could add the propellers and flying bizwits from your Icarus Chariot! You'll make the Marvelous Moto-Mover the ultimate vehicle!"

"Sorry, ladies," Cassandra said, pulling away. "I'm not inventing anymore. That's all in the past. I didn't come here to join your little club, anyway. We came for help because—"

"What in the name of Grandpa's long johns!" Mary Walton jumped as Robot floated out through the trap-door and settled next to Molly.

"Why did you bring one of Bell's automatons with you?" Hertha blurted, her crisp and calm demeanor out the window. "*How* did you bring it with you? And why is it dressed like my old chemistry professor?"

"Here we go again." Molly took a breath. "Okay, long, complicated story, but—"

"I am alive!" Robot announced.

Josephine Cochrane, who had just stepped back into the room wearing a blue brocade dress and carrying a cup of tea, proceeded to spill that cup of tea all over that blue brocade dress. She turned and left again.

"Oh, I see the confusion," Robot said. "I am Robot. I also happen to be alive. When I said I was alive, you thought Alive was my name. That would be a silly name. Unlike Robot. This explains the expressions on your faces. I apologize. I am still learning."

"How are you making it do that?" Margaret asked, sliding from under the engine for a closer look.

"We're not," Emmett said. "He's . . . alive."

"I can also do this," said Robot. He hopped on one foot, clapped his hands together, and yelled, "Whee!"

"I like him already," said Sarah.

"You said Rector's meteorite did this to him," Nellie said, jotting down notes. "But you never explained how."

"We can't really give any more of an explanation than that," Emmett said. "Robot is what Robot is."

"And his existence, Miss Bly, is *off* the record," said Cassandra.

Nellie nodded, but kept writing.

Margaret lifted her goggles and sniffed Robot's chest plate. "You ever try—"

"*Nobody's* cracking him open," Molly warned.

"Understood," Margaret said with a firm nod.

"So you stole him from Bell," Hertha said. "That's why you're on the run."

"No," said Molly. "Well, yes, but . . . wow, we have a lot to fill you in on."

"Start filling," said Hertha.

Josephine Cochrane strolled back in wearing a green brocade dress and carrying a fresh cup of tea. "Yes, tell them everything," she said as she continued to an armchair by a bookshelf in the corner. "And then repeat it to me in an hour when I'm done reading. Ta-ta!"

Over the next few hours, Nellie Bly interviewed everyone, including the Mothers of Invention. The women agreed that since they were already harboring fugitives, they might as well give Nellie all the corroboration she could possibly ask for. Nellie also interviewed Robot, though she promised not to mention him in her article. Then, with a stack of overfilled notebooks under her arm and a disguise-worthy wig on her head, the investigative journalist left. "Two days," she told the others as she took off. "Check the *New York World* on Monday. If this story isn't on the front page, I'll eat my wig."

Molly expected the next forty-eight hours to be torture, but they ended up being the most fun she'd had in months. She talked books with Sarah and Emmett—and occasionally Josephine (although Mrs. Cochrane had very different taste in books; less *Twenty Thousand Leagues Under the Sea* and more *The Sorrows of Young Werther*). She got to test several of Margaret's latest creations, including a mechanized piggy bank that puked up a penny when she pulled its curly tail. Hertha let her sample twenty different types of tea, three of which actually tasted better than a pile of dried leaves from the curb. And she played some hilarious pranks on Josephine, her favorite of which was the chewing gum in the hairbrush gag, for which Josephine vowed revenge with a spanking machine built specifically for Molly.

Molly was also delighted to have so many sympathetic ears to which she could vent her frustrations about Alexander Graham Bell's betrayal and his sneaky, possibly illegal polar expedition. She described every detail she could remember about Bell's super-secret boat.

Molly was also elated to see the Mothers of Invention pull Emmett out of his funk. Margaret allowed him to consult on seventeen of her personal projects and Sarah invited him to contribute to the design of the new Moto-Mover. Emmett beamed from the drafting desk as he sketched out his plans for 360-degree rotating side-view mirrors.

Even Robot got in on the act, volunteering to fetch a wrench, to steady a board, or to buoy spirits with a round of "Polly Wolly Doodle."

Cassandra, however, politely turned down every invitation to participate and instead assigned herself the role of mothering the Mothers. This mostly included sweeping, laundering coveralls, and cooking breakfast, lunch, and dinner for everyone. The problem with that last bit was that Cassandra only knew three recipes. And two of those involved pickles.

Nonetheless, Molly's days in the wharf house were good ones—almost good enough for her to forget they were hiding from government agents.

*   *   *

Monday morning, Cassandra hummed a tune that switched randomly between "Yankee Doodle Dandy" and "Mary Had a Little Lamb" as she laid plates on the breakfast table. The diners thanked her graciously, until they peeked under the bread and saw the warty green logs.

"No offense, Cass," Hertha said, "but if I eat one more pickle sandwich, I think I'm going to start sweating vinegar."

"I figured as much," Cassandra said proudly. "That's why I made sausages."

There was a sudden flurry of people pushing their plates away and explaining how they weren't really very hungry after all.

"Note: people do not like balloons or sausages," said Robot.

"Fine, don't eat," Cassandra grumped. "More for me." She chomped into a sandwich and turned as green as the sausages. "My apologies." She promptly began clearing the table.

"Don't take it too hard, Cass," Hertha said. "Some people take naturally to cooking and some don't. Fortunately, you *do* have other gifts . . ."

"Yes, and I'll practice them behind the counter of my pickle shop," Cassandra said as she returned to the kitchen. "With luck, I'll be back there later today."

As if on cue, the street-side door opened and Sarah rushed in with an armful of newspapers. "Here they are, ladies," she announced, handing a paper to everyone in the room. "I didn't see it on the cover of the *World*, so I grabbed all the papers." With all the page flipping, the wharf house filled with the sound of rustling newsprint.

Molly got to the last page of the *New York World* and said, "Definitely not in here." She curled her toes in an attempt to bury the swimmy feeling welling up inside her.

"Not in the *Sun* either," said Mary, shaking her head sympathetically.

"Nor the *Times*," said Hertha.

"I am impressed," said Robot, "by how quickly you can all read newspapers."

Josephine Cochrane turned to the last page of the *New York Herald* and gasped.

"Did you find it?" Sarah asked.

Josephine looked up. "Hmm? Oh, no. But there's a fabulous review of the new Anne Elliot novel. A must-read, they say."

Emmett closed his edition of the *Star*. "Maybe tomorrow?" he said, trying to sound optimistic.

Hertha sighed. "You can stay as long as you need, of course."

"We'll have to order more pickles," said Cassandra.

"Though I doubt you want to spend the rest of your lives in a warehouse," Hertha quickly added. "Perhaps it's time to consider alternatives."

Without warning, the trapdoor in the floor popped

open. Nellie Bly hoisted herself into the room and released the breath she'd been holding. "That is a tough stench to get used to!"

"Where's your story?" Molly demanded.

"I gave it to my editor at the *World*," Nellie said, anger rumbling in her voice. "He loved it, called it the story of the century, said it would grace the front page this morning! Then, nothing! As I'm sure you've seen. So I marched back to his office to find out what was what and I learn the guy notified the government about my article. They told him to kill the story, and he did!"

Molly was aghast. Another powerful man stealing opportunities out from under her!

"Can you take it to another paper?" Mary asked Nellie.

"Believe me, I'd be at another editor's desk right now if Mr. Washburn at the *World* hadn't told me to wait in his office for some government agents who wanted to ask me some questions," Nellie went on. "You don't need to be a news bear to smell something fishy in that scenario! I ran for the nearest manhole."

The atmosphere in the room felt suddenly stifling.

"I suppose we're all fugitives now," Mary said somberly.

"That won't play well at all in the society columns," said Josephine.

"I really liked school," Emmett said, plopping onto a

chair. "My father never sent me to a real school. But I'd finally gotten to experience the joy of history essays, and algebra quizzes, and sweet, sweet penmanship drills. I hoped I'd make it for at least a full semester. But I suppose it's better to have learned and lost than never to have learned at all." He laid his face flat on the table.

"I'm sorry," Cassandra said, stroking his hair. "If it helps, I can give you some math problems to do while we run . . ."

Molly hadn't felt this dizzy since that building collapsed on her head. She'd ruined everything again. She was the one with the bright idea to break the secrecy agreements. And now she'd put ten lives at risk. Her mother could get thrown in jail again. Robot could be dismantled. She and Emmett could be separated forever. Before she even got to tell him the truth about his father's death. She really should have told him the truth about his father's death.

All she wanted was credit for the incredible things she'd accomplished! It wasn't fair. She deserved that credit. So did her mother. And Emmett. And the Mothers of Invention. Even Nellie Bly. They deserved to tell their own stories their own way and not let history be dictated by a few stingy men who refused to give up—or even share—the power they so desperately clung to.

"No more running and no more hiding," Molly said firmly. "It's time we take our fate into our own hands." If the powers that be wouldn't let them take credit for their feats at the World's Fair, they'd just have to accomplish a new amazing feat to take credit for. And what would be more amazing than discovering the South Pole? If they could overtake Bell while he was busy chasing Rector, they'd truly beat the man at his own game. Plus, while they were in Antarctica, as an added bonus, maybe they'd find some kind of note or message left by Captain Lee—and Molly could just act surprised about it and Emmett would never have to know she'd kept such a big secret from him. She climbed onto the table. "Ladies, I have a challenge for you."

Hertha perked up. "You know we never back down from a challenge."

"Unless it's teatime," said Josephine. "In which case, I promise nothing."

"What's the challenge, kid?" asked Margaret.

"Can you build a ship faster than Bell's?" Molly asked.

The women of the MOI looked to one another and nodded. "Yes."

Molly grinned. She was about to solve all of her family's problems with one brilliant idea. "Then let's beat that man to the South Pole!" she said. "We do that, and they'll be building monuments to us, not putting us behind bars! Plus, we can avoid arrest if we're out of the country for a while."

The Mothers conferred briefly. "Molly Pepper,"

Hertha said, "we accept your challenge."

"Well, *they* might, but not us," Cassandra said, leading her daughter down from the table and deflating all her joy.

"Mother, we *have* to go too!" Molly kicked herself for not expecting this. "We have to be part of the group that makes the discovery! That's how we get our names in the history books!"

"Molly, you don't even know how to swim," Cassandra said.

"Good thing they're building *a boat* then! Tell her, Emmett: fame and glory are the best ways to save our reputations and the South Pole is the best path to fame and glory!"

"Okay, let's talk this through," Emmett said. He ran his fingers through his hair. "I believe the Mothers could possibly succeed in this. They are far more equipped for such things than we are. So let's say they do it on their own. When they come back as heroes, maybe they can use their newfound fame and status to help us out."

"Why take that risk when we can just be there from the start and get famous ourselves?"

"You think staying here is the risk?" Emmett said. "You're talking about sailing the world's most treacherous seas to an icy, uncharted continent!"

"I was counting on you to be my ally, Emmett."

"I am your ally! That's why I want you to think things

through before you run off and do something . . ." He glanced at the women watching them and averted his eyes, embarrassed.

"Something what?" said Molly. "Crazy? Stupid? What were you gonna say?"

"Inadvisable."

Molly set her jaw. "What would your father have advised? He'd tell you to go, wouldn't he? He wanted you to be a seafarer, right? You've got the sea in your blood!"

"You just spent days urging me to forget all that!"

"I know!" Molly took a breath in an attempt to calm herself. "But I've been thinking and, well, one of the reasons the loss of your father weighs on you so much is because there was so much left unsaid between you two. But what if he had more to say, what if he—I don't know—left you some kind of note or message before he died? And it's been down there in some snowbank waiting for you all these years? Wouldn't you want to know your father's final words?"

"If such a thing existed, of course I'd want to know," Emmett said. "If there was even a *chance* of such a thing, I'd want to know. But there isn't, so why bring it up? You really think Rector gave my father a moment to write a letter before murdering him? Come on, Molly. It's cruel to make me even think about it."

Cassandra was at his side, comforting him again. Molly tried to swallow, but her mouth was dry. This conversation was going nowhere good. But there was only one place she could take it.

"Emmett, Mother, come with me: family meeting." She took their hands and led them into the kitchen for privacy. It smelled of pickle juice and reminded her fondly of home.

"What's going on, Molls?" Cassandra asked.

"Yeah, please fill us in," said Emmett. "Because I get stomachachy whenever you get mysterious."

"Well," she said. "You know how sometimes there's something you really should tell someone right away, but for one reason or another, you don't tell them, and then later on you're thinking you really should still tell them, but you're feeling kinda bad because you really should have told them earlier, and so you *still* don't tell them, and you put it off even more, but the longer you wait, the worse you know you'll feel when you eventually tell them, so you just keep not telling them?"

"No," said Emmett. "Not familiar with that."

Cassandra shook her head. "Is that a thing?"

Molly closed her eyes. It was now or never. "Emmett, Rector didn't kill your father," she said. "Not directly. He told me your father was the only person on the *Frost Cleaver* who'd been nice to him, so he couldn't bring himself to murder him outright. Instead, he just marooned him on the ice and left him to die. Which, well, I don't know why he thought that was better. It actually sounds—oh, please don't cry. See, this is why I haven't told you. But listen, from what I know of your father, I have to believe that, if he survived even a few days, he would have tried to leave a message for you. A goodbye note, a keepsake—*something*. So maybe there really is a message down there that says, 'Emmett, I was wrong— you have my blessing to do whatever you want with your life.' If you could find something like that, it could . . . it could help you move on."

The room was painfully quiet. Molly prayed that she hadn't made another catastrophic mistake. Why was Emmett saying nothing? Why was her mother just standing there, watching the torture?

Finally, Emmett wiped his face on his sleeve and spoke. "I don't know how I'm going to trust anything you—"

"You tried to tell me, didn't you, Molls?" Cassandra interrupted. "After the Fair? When we were sitting out-side the China Pavilion watching the army clean up? You had something important to tell me, but we got distracted by those awful men from the Guild and you never got to say what it was. It was this, wasn't it?"

Molly nodded.

"If you had told me," Cassandra continued, "I would have advised against sharing it with Emmett. I would have said, 'Captain Lee is gone. And as far as Emmett knows, it was quick and painless. Learning otherwise would only upset him more. After what we've all just been through, let's focus on the positive—that Emmett has people who love and care about him once more.'"

Molly and Cassandra both turned to Emmett for a reaction.

"Do you think he really might have left a message?" he asked, his eyes misty.

"It's a long shot," Cassandra said. "But I've seen far less likely things come to pass."

Emmett looked Molly in the eye. "I understand why you did what you did, but . . . I'm sorry, I think my trust in you might be broken."

Molly blinked back tears of her own. "Can we fix it?"

"Maybe," he said. "But we have to build a boat first."

He walked back into the main room. "Okay, everybody! We're going to Antarctica!"

Onward!

THE ENERGY IN the wharf house was electric (and not just because of all the electric lights, motors, and generators). Hertha clapped her hands. "All right, people! Bell already has several days on us, and Rector several weeks. So let's get to work!"

"The Moto-Mover's half-built," said Sarah, gesturing toward the oblong frame that housed the big engine in the center of the room. "And it's already meant to travel on water. We can save days of work by reconfiguring it to a full seacraft."

"Spot on," Hertha agreed.

"Our motor here is pretty darn speedy," said Margaret, digging through her toolboxes. "But if we're going to overtake the boys, we're gonna need even more power."

"Why not borrow from Bell's idea?" Josephine suggested. "We all get the gist of those 'hydrofoils' Molly described. Let's make our own version. But better, naturally."

"Steal someone else's idea and tweak it?" Hertha smirked. "How very Edison of you, dear."

"And we should be able to make do with materials we've got in the warehouse," Mary said, scanning the room. "Reuse and repurpose! That piping from the radiator ducts should work for the legs of the hydrofoil. And we can take the side panels off of the incinerator to create the chevron plates."

Within seconds the women were hard at work, while Nellie Bly paced the perimeter of the big room, documenting everything. Molly watched with, well, a little bit of pride, but mostly relief. An hour ago, she feared she'd doomed them all. But now, she and her family were going to become famous, their legal troubles would become a thing of the past, Cassandra would find a new life beyond inventing, the MOI would get the recognition they deserved, and Emmett . . .

Molly tapped him on the shoulder. "You should help too."

"I don't need you to tell me that," Emmett said. "If this ship's sailing off in search of my father's legacy, you're darn right I'm gonna help build it."

"Language," Josephine chided from across the room.

Molly looked Emmett in the eye. "You sound upset. Are you upset?"

"About what? The fact that my father died a lonely,

excruciating death? Or that you kept it secret from me?"

"Either?" she said. "Both?"

"Of course I'm upset. Those are upsetting things. It would be weird for me to *not* be upset. But you knew that already. That's why you didn't tell me."

Molly gave a sheepish nod. "I guess what I really want to ask is if you think you'll get over it."

"My father's death, no. Your secret?" He shrugged. "Eventually."

She flashed a weak smile. "Eventually's not never. I'll take what I can get."

"Great," said Emmett. "I'm going to get to work now."

Molly ran to get a task assigned. As did Robot, who used his magnetic powers to twist and shape metal plates into the forms the women needed. The only person not working feverishly was Cassandra, who still sat silently at the dirty breakfast table. The sight angered Molly.

"Mother!" she yelled from the vehicle's control panel, where she was screwing a sheet of metal in place. "You're not working!"

"Oh, yes," Cassandra said, snapping out of a daze. She gathered the remaining plates and wiped the table with a rag.

"Mother!" Molly snapped again. She hopped down from the vehicle and marched to the table. "What are you doing? You are possibly the most skilled craftsperson in here. Drop the dishes."

"But they'll break," Cassandra said.

Molly put her hands on her hips. "Mother."

"I know what you're trying, Molls," Cassandra said seriously. "But I am no longer an inventor. I have been quite clear about my wishes and I would like you to respect them."

"What about me?" Molly said, her throat tight. "Do I deserve any respect? How about for the way I cooked and cleaned and shopped for years so that you wouldn't have to give up inventing? Hmm? And now you're telling me you suddenly *want* to do all the exhausting, boring stuff that I used to do for you? No, you don't get to do that. You don't get to tell me I made those sacrifices for nothing."

The entire warehouse had gone quiet. Blinking back tears, Molly returned, red-faced, to work. She held the aluminum sheet in place with one hand and attempted to turn a screwdriver with the other. But she kept losing her grip, and the panel kept sliding out of place. Until her mother appeared at her side and held the plate still.

"I'm not taking up inventing again," Cassandra said. "But you're right: Every set of hands helps. And I'm going to do my part."

Molly sniffled and screwed down the metal panel. "I'll take what I can get."

By the following dawn they had something resembling an ocean vessel. It was dull gray, twenty feet long, and vaguely banana-shaped, with three triple-jointed green-speckled pipes emerging from either side like crab legs. The inventors moved the ship into the exposed river water for a buoyancy test, and were happy to see that it passed.

"So, is this thing seaworthy yet?" Molly asked. Her head teemed with visions of herself sailing the open ocean, trekking across frozen wastes, and carving her name into the South Pole.

"Technically, yes," Margaret answered as she lubed the leg joints with a spray-pump oilcan. "But overall, we're only halfway done with her. We have to water-proof a lot of areas yet, stabilize the hull, test the rudder, calibrate the steering column, reinforce—"

"So, 'technically, yes' means 'actually, no.'" Molly massaged a shoulder sore from hours of hammering.

Sarah wiped her brow. "We also have to think of a name for this beautiful machine."

"Oh, well, Miss Pepper should have that honor," Hertha said. "After all, it was she who dubbed our Marvelous Moto-Mover. So, what say you, O Bestower of Names?"

Molly scrunched her brow in thought. Their vehicle was barely a quarter the size of Bell's *AquaZephyr*, but that was going to enable it to move much faster. As would the mini-rockets attached to its legs. This ship was small, but packed a wallop. Just like her. "I've got it," she said. *"The Whizz-tastic Wave-Pummeling Poseidon Puncher."*

"Or perhaps something that might fit on the side of the ship?" Hertha suggested.

"Write small," Molly replied. "'Cause that's the name: *Whizz-tastic Wave-Pummeling Poseidon Puncher.*"

Cassandra shrugged. "I like it. It will look good in the papers when they write about our historic discovery."

"I hope you don't expect those articles to mention you, dear," said Josephine. "Because there'll be no room left once they print the name of the boat."

"Maybe we can just call it the *Poseidon*," Sarah tried. "Or the *Wave Pummeler*?"

"*Whizz-tastic Wave-Pummeling Poseidon Puncher,*" Molly stated firmly. "And that's 'whizz-tastic' with a hyphen. You got that, Nellie?" There was no reply. "Hey, is Nellie hiding from the work? Afraid she'll get a blister on her delicate writing fingers?"

"Oh, Miss Bly left," Sarah said. "It occurred to her that government agents might show up on her parents' doorstep asking questions, so she wanted to head back to Pittsburgh to warn them."

"That's quite a trek," Emmett said. "I hope she can stay hidden."

"Considering how nimbly she made it here through the sewers, I'm not concerned," said Hertha.

Margaret shrugged. "Eh, she wasn't doing much anyway. So what's next? Attaching the backup motor? Piping in the auto-bail system?"

"How about breakfast?" said Mary. "We've been woring all night. We need a break."

"I do not need a break," Robot said. "I do not tire and
I do not sleep. I can, however, pretend to sleep if anyone
finds my silent, open-eyed staring eerie in the middle of
the night."

"I'm fine to keep working over here as well," Josephine
called from the corner where she sat, feeding heavy fabric through a rumbling, motorized sewing machine.

"That's because you're doing the *easy* work," Molly
taunted.

Josephine sniffed haughtily. "Would you prefer I
abandon these insulated parkas so you can shiver your
sassy little jaw off at the South Pole?"

"I want the coats!" Emmett called. "Please continue
making the coats!"

The others wiped their hands and headed for the
table. "What say I give my mother a much-needed break
and make some scrambled eggs?" Molly offered.

Emmett raised his hand. "I want the eggs! Please
make the eggs!" The others agreed.

"Hey, while I'm busy in the kitchen, Robot should
entertain you," Molly said. "We've been trying to figure out what Robot should do with himself once it's safe
for people to know about him, and I'm strongly leaning
toward a career in the performing arts. He was *built* to
entertain, after all."

"I like singing," Robot said, clomping down the gang-plank.

"Can I make an anti-request?" Margaret said. "Can we not hear 'Polly Wolly Doodle' again?"

"Ooh, I know," Molly said excitedly. "Robot, show them your juggling trick! You know, the one you did with those pickles!"

"I can do that." Robot marched straight to the front of the warehouse, opened the door, and stepped outside.

Everyone jumped up. "No!" "Don't!" "Stop!"

Robot stopped, but he was already standing out in the open on the docks. Molly ran outside to get him and the others screamed again, this time to her. "No!" "Don't!" "Stop!"

Molly dragged Robot back inside and slammed the door. "What were you doing?" she yelled at him, her heart racing.

"I was going to get the pickles," Robot replied.

"We have pickles in the kitchen here!"

"You said 'those pickles.' I thought it needed to be those specific pickles." Robot stared. "I feel you are upset with me."

"Yeah, 'cause no one's supposed to see you!" Molly cried. "What were you thinking?"

"Robot wasn't thinking," Hertha said sternly. "He's a machine. But you should have been. What's *your* excuse?"

"I'm sorry, I just—I had to protect Robot."

114

"Maybe someone *else* should have gone out after him," said Emmett. "You know, one of the people who *aren't* yet being hunted by federal agents."

"Did anybody see you?" Sarah asked.

"I don't think so," Molly replied. "I mean, there were some people. But they didn't see me."

"Well, that's quite convenient," said Hertha. "That everybody strolling the seaport this morning managed to overlook both you *and* the six-foot-tall aluminum chap you were with."

"They didn't, all right?" Molly yelled. "No one's breaking the door down to get us, are they?"

"Not yet."

Cassandra took her daughter's hand. Molly had forgotten how warm and safe that could make her feel. "Molly had a . . . lapse in judgment," she said. "But who among us hasn't when the safety of someone we care about was on the line?"

Hertha crossed her arms. "Point taken, Mrs. Pepper." She looked directly at Molly. "But it would behoove you, young lady, to take some cues from Emmett and experiment with a little thing called Thinking Before You Act."

Molly bit her lip to hold back an angry retort. Thinking too much was what made her keep her big secret from Emmett for so long—and look at all the good *that* did!

Nobody seemed to be hungry anymore. Hertha and Margaret went to the rear of the ship to fortify the rudder, while Sarah and Mary moved to the opposite corner he warehouse to begin work on a canvas "sun shield" the boat's piloting chair.

"For what it's worth," Emmett said to Molly, "if I'd een the one closest to the door, I think I'd have run after im too. The others just don't think of Robot the way ve do."

"Thanks," Molly returned. "Does this mean you forgive me?"

"For running outside? Yes."

"But the other stuff?"

"It's unrelated."

Molly nodded somberly.

Cassandra tapped her daughter's shoulder. "Molls, can you give me a hand with the stuck power pedal?" she asked. "I think I know how to loosen it, but I need an assistant."

"Emmett might do a better job," Molly replied.

"That's okay, you go," Emmett said, pulling a wrench from his back pocket. "I've got a lot of nuts to tighten on the hydrofoil rigging."

Following her mother up onto the ship, and away from everybody else, Molly passed Robot, standing in a corner with his face to the wall.

"You want to help too, Robot?" she called to him.

"No, thank you," said Robot. "I am too busy being disappointed in myself."

She'd have to give her metal friend a pep talk later,

though. As confident as she was that no one had seen her outside, she couldn't shake the nagging fear that their time was limited. And there was still a lot of work to do. She knelt down by the captain's chair and followed her mother's instructions for oiling the pedal shaft. Work continued like this for some time, somber and silent save for the sounds of pounding mallets and cranking gears. No more chatting or joking or trying to squirt Josephine with engine grease. The silence made it all the more jarring when the front door burst off its hinges and Agent Clark led a dozen men in long coats and bowler hats into the wharf house. "Federal agents! Nobody move!"

Emmett dropped his wrench into the river with a splash.

From the floor, Hertha called up to Cassandra, "You keep those children on that boat, you hear me? And if it comes to it—do what you must!"

"I will!" Cassandra shouted back. "Wait—do *what*? What did you mean?"

But Hertha was already approaching Agent Clark, demanding to see whatever documentation had given him permission to intrude upon their private property. Agent Clark did not seem in the mood for conversation, however. He spun Hertha around and cuffed her hands behind her back. "You're all under arrest for harboring fugitives," he said. "Men, apprehend everyone in the building."

The agents marched toward the women, but didn't get far. Margaret grabbed her high-powered oilcan and sprayed a sweeping arc of slippery black grease across the warehouse floor. Feet went sliding and bowler hats went flying. At the same time, the two men who approached Mary and Sarah quickly found themselves wrapped in a canvas sun shield. But still more agents came.

"There are too many of them," Cassandra said. "Molls, what did Hertha mean, 'do what you must'?"

"Never mind that—Emmett's running *into* the fight!" Molly leaned over the ship's rail. "Emmett! Where are you going?"

Emmett darted behind the Mothers of Invention, who were fending off federal agents with wind-up bolt clampers and automated wire coilers.

"Get on this boat this instant!" Cassandra shouted at him.

But Emmett continued toward Mrs. Cochrane and her sewing machine. Josephine saw him coming and tossed him a big sack stuffed with cold weather gear. Emmett caught the bag—a move that seemed to surprise even him—and turned back toward the boat, just as Josephine was grabbed by a burly agent.

Molly helped Emmett up the gangplank with the sack of clothes. "Oh no," she muttered. "Here they come." A trio of agents had squeezed past the women, but Molly smacked the button to retract the gangplank before they could reach it. "Ha!" she crowed as the three men skidded to the edge of the dock.

"Molly, look!" Emmett said.

Agents now had all the women in handcuffs except Mary Walton, who was crouched behind the motorized air purifier she'd been using to keep their work environment clear of sawdust. She gave the Peppers a wave and then cranked up the purifier on reverse. Thick dusty clouds spewed from the machine enveloping everyone on the floor and cutting down visibility.

"Mother, we have to help them," Molly cried.

"No," Cassandra called from the pilot's chair. "I figured out what Hertha wanted me to do."

She turned the ignition switch. The vessel's motor roared to life and the *Whizz-tastic Wave-Pummeling Poseidon Puncher* jolted forward. Molly and Emmett lost their balance and flopped onto the deck.

"Mrs. Pepper—the gate!" Emmett cried. The big sliding door between them and the river outside was closed. But a silvery figure flew to the gate lever and pulled it.

"Robot!" Molly screamed, grabbing the rail and struggling to stand on the trembling vehicle. "Robot! I'm sorry! I'm not mad at you! Robot!"

The gate rose just in time and the boat blasted out onto the East River. Robot followed, bursting through the dirt-gray clouds that billowed from the wharf house. He zoomed through the salty air and settled on the deck of the *Whizz-tastic Wave-Pummeling Poseidon Puncher,* where he promptly fell over. "It is very bumpy," he said. Molly threw her arms around his metal chest.

"What about the MOI?" Emmett asked, his face already a sickly green.

"The Feds are going to throw them in jail," Molly said with horror. "For helping us. We have to go back for them."

"We will as soon as we can. But right now, the only safe place for us is at sea," Cassandra replied as the boat hit a large wave and bounced high into the air. Everybody *oof*ed as it thudded back down. "Hertha knew it. In those first seconds after the agents burst in, she'd assessed the situation and realized they'd never all make it onto this boat. That's why she told us to do what we need to— which was escape."

"They all knew," Emmett said, nodding somberly. "That's why they fought so hard to keep those Feds away from the ship, even though resisting would only make things worse for them."

Molly knew they were right, but she couldn't just tamp down the urge to rush back and fight for their friends *now*. "But they'll be thrown in jail. Or worse, the asylum!"

"Where do you think we'll end up if we're caught?" Cassandra said. "I'm worried to death about them, Molls. But what option do we have at the moment?"

Despite looking like he'd come down with a very sudden flu, Emmett slid over to Molly and put his arm around her. "I know you're probably feeling like this is your fault," he said. "And it mostly is."

Molly shot him a sideways glare.

"But you're also the one who came up with this plan to get famous and use that status to help us fix things," he continued quickly. "And—I can't believe I'm saying this—that's our best shot right now. If we beat Bell—and Rector—to the South Pole, and come back with our names cleared, that's when we'll have our opportunity to help Sarah and Hertha and the others. We won't let their sacrifice be in vain."

The passengers sailed on in silence for several minutes, until there was a sudden thump beneath Molly's bottom. "What was that?"

Thump! Thump, thump!

"It's a shark!" yelped Molly.

"It better not be eels!" yelled Emmett.

"It's a news bear!" The hatch Molly had been sitting on popped open and the disheveled head of Nellie Bly popped out. "Whew!" she said, sucking in big gulps of ocean air. "I thought that was where the passengers were supposed to sleep, but it's not. It's just a storage area. Not much air down there."

The Peppers gaped at her.

"Why are you here?" Molly asked.

"Where else would I be?" Nellie said. "This is where the story is." She pulled out her notepad. "So, what did I miss? It's pretty soundproof down there. Is the tin man supposed to be with us? Where's everybody else? Does Cassandra even know how to drive this thing?"

"I'll figure it out as we go along," Cassandra said, scanning the control panel. "We should be going faster than this, shouldn't we? I need to power on those hydro-thingies. Ah, there you are, you sneaky little flickety switch. This should do the—*waaa-hooo!*"

Rockets ignited and the entire hull of the vessel lifted upward, above the waves. *The Whizz-tastic Wave-Pummeling Poseidon Puncher* whizzed forth, pummeling every wave in its path. The sensation reminded Molly more of flying in the Icarus Chariot than it did sailing on a boat. Within seconds, Manhattan Island was a mere dot on the horizon.

Emmett ducked a startled seagull. He looked greener than anything Pepper's Pickles had ever served. "I can't believe we're going to Antarctica."

PART II

Imperfect Storm

BUMPY START NOTWITHSTANDING, it took no time at all for Cassandra to look completely comfortable at the helm of a half-built, experimental vehicle that was whipping across the ocean at breakneck speeds. Hertha had preset all the coordinates into the vehicle's clockwork navigation system, so Cassandra never had to guess at which direction to steer. Still, the operation of such a complicated piece of machinery seemed an incredibly daunting challenge to Molly. And it thrilled her to see her mother tackling it head-on, instead of moping and trying to convince people that she had no business doing anything but cleaning up after them.

Despite the constant spray of seawater speckling her glasses, Molly spent as much time as she could up on the deck. She found the cresting waves and rushing winds exhilarating. Plus, Nellie Bly was always down in the cramped cabin, endlessly writing. Molly still resented the reporter's uninvited presence on the trip, but was grateful that Nellie had been smart enough to pack loads of stowing-away snacks, like apples, crackers, and some very tasty beef jerky. She figured that earned the woman at least a few days of goodwill.

Emmett preferred being up on deck too (the stale air of the cabin made his nausea worse). As did Robot. And Molly was relieved to see that her mother's theory about the automaton's rustproof-ness appeared to be correct (though she didn't want to test what would happen if Robot took a full-on dip in the ocean).

As they zoomed along America's east coast, Molly kept her eyes open for signs of the *AquaZephyr*. She had no idea how far along Bell's ship was at that point, but knowing that Hertha had set them on the most direct possible path, she assumed Bell would have chosen the same course. Once they were far enough from New York, though, they didn't see *anyone*. Molly realized she'd never truly grasped the vastness of the Atlantic.

By the fourth day of their journey, the *Whizz-Tastic Wave-Pummeling Poseidon Puncher* was cutting through the rich blue waters of the Caribbean Sea. Molly had thought water was only this color in paintings.

"It's almost too blue," Emmett said, staring over the rear rail. "Like the sea and the sky just blend together.

Maybe my father was onto something when he talked about the ocean being a magical place."

"Hey, you're speaking!" Molly said. "I've missed you these past few days. And you've only been four feet away from me. You look better too."

Emmett's pea-soup complexion had begun to fade. "Yeah," he said, uncurling from his fetal position. "Maybe my father was right about that too."

Molly joined him at the aft rail. "Makes you realize how big the world really is," she said, glancing toward the tiny island silhouettes in the distance.

"Back home, we can feel so important in our little neighborhoods, even in a city as vast as New York," Emmett said. "But, really, we're just ants."

"That is untrue," said Robot. "You are humans and I am Robot."

Molly laughed. "Maybe it's time for those metaphor lessons."

"Yes, explain metaphor," said Robot.

"Okay. It's when you describe one thing as another thing," Molly said.

Robot picked up an apple. "This is a raccoon," he said. "I made a metaphor."

"Not quite," Emmett said. "You don't just compare one thing to another randomly. There needs to be a relation-ship."

"There is a relationship," said Robot. "Raccoons eat

apples. This apple is a raccoon. Why are you laughing? Are metaphors funny?"

"Let's give an example," Emmett said.

"The sky ahead is a terrifying swirl of darkness and doom," Cassandra said from the pilot's chair.

"Ooookay. A little grim, but—" Molly turned around. "Gah! Grim and accurate! Very accurate!"

The recently calm sky had taken an ominous turn as massive, roiling storm clouds rushed in from the south.

"Where did the pretty go?" Emmett moaned. He thrust his fists at the rapidly darkening sky and shouted, "Darn you, Nature! I was finally feeling better!"

Lightning cracked overhead.

"I take it back! Sorry, Nature!" Emmett crouched and hid his head.

Fat droplets began splattering against the lenses of Molly's eyeglasses as the sun vanished entirely. "How did it get so bad, so fast?" she said, gripping the railing as the ship bobbed fiercely.

The cabin hatch opened and Nellie popped her head out. "What's going on up here? Do you know how difficult it is to write when—oh."

"I am sensing apprehension from you all," said Robot.

"Children," Cassandra said. "Go belowdecks with Nellie." The calmness of her voice terrified the children, who obeyed without question. Unfortunately, they had trouble finding the hatch. The darkness was so dark they might as well have been blindfolded. Tossed about in the blackness, Emmett and Molly smacked hard into each other. A second lightning crash finally showed them the cabin hatch, which Robot was struggling to hold open in the raging winds.

"Hurry! You're letting the water in!" Nellie yelled from inside.

Flat on her belly, Molly pulled herself to the lip of the hatch and peered inside. Rain was puddling on the cabin floor while Nellie squatted on a cot, scribbling in one of her notebooks. Working on her next exclusive, no doubt, Molly thought. *Intrepid Reporter's Firsthand Account as Sole Survivor of Shipwreck.*

"Nellie!" Molly screamed as the boat swooned and Emmett slid to her side. "We're dying up here!"

"Oh dear," Nellie blurted as if just noticing the children. "Come in!" She stood to help Emmett down.

Thunder boomed and Molly felt it in her rib cage, like the rocket explosions on the Brooklyn Bridge the day her mother had been taken from her. She turned back to the pilot's chair. "Mother, you need to get down there too!" she shouted.

"Molly, get inside," Cassandra shouted over the roar. "You can't swim!"

"But, Mother—"

"Someone needs to stay at the wheel," Cassandra said. She spat away the rainwater pouring down her face.

"It's not safe," Molly yelled back. "Come inside!"

"What if we crash into something?" Cassandra cried, shivering as she hunched over the ship's wheel.

"Molly, it's really flooding down here," Emmett called from the cabin.

An enormous wave threw the entire ship into the air. It crashed down again with a violent rattle. Molly had to grip the rail to keep from being tossed overboard.

"What is it you humans say at a time like this?" Robot asked. "Oh, yes; wheeeeeeee!"

"Robot," Molly said, as wind-whipped raindrops stung her like a thousand angry bees. "Take my mother into the hatch."

The ship began to spin turbulently as Cassandra turned to yell back at them. "You will do no such thing, Robot! Take *Molly* into the hatch! And don't let her out!"

Robot's head pivoted between the two sopping Peppers. "These actions are contradictory."

"I'm up to my knees down here," Emmett said, peeking out onto the deck.

"No more sacrificing yourself for me, Mother," Molly said. "I'll come get you myself!" She began pulling herself along the rail.

"Touch me and you're grounded!"

A bolt of lightning lit up the sky, revealing a huge, dark *something* directly in the ship's path.

"Look out!" Emmett cried.

130

But it was too late. The *Whizz-tastic Wave-Pummeling Poseidon Puncher* crashed hard into the enormous obstacle. Cassandra flew from her seat and tumbled into her daughter's arms. They both slid hard into the side rail.

"What happened?" Nellie shouted.

"We hit something," Cassandra said. "A rock. Or an island."

Their ship was moving, but differently. Something was pulling it. Lightning cracked again, illuminating long serpentine legs that arced over their heads, as if ready to ensnare their small boat.

"Sea monster!" Molly yelled.

But then the clouds broke just enough for the dim moonlight to reveal that the "monster" was, in fact, another ship—one that towered over theirs. The *Aqua-Zephyr*.

"We did it!" Cassandra cheered. "We caught up to Bell!"

"Yeah, maybe too close," Emmett said. The legs of their much tinier hydrofoil had gotten entangled with those of the larger ship and the *AquaZephyr* was dragging them along as it sped through the storm.

"Their crew probably hasn't even noticed in all this tumult," Nellie said.

"This is our chance to get ahead of him," Cassandra said, twisting the steering wheel away from the other vessel. "We'll just pry ourselves loose and—"

With a crack, three of the *Whizz-tastic Wave-Pummeling Poseidon Puncher*'s legs snapped free from its hull. The boat dipped drastically to one side, half of it plunging below the water.

"Okay, we are officially sinking," Emmett said.

"Well, Margaret did say it was only half-built," Cassandra said. "But at least the rain seems to be slowing down."

"Not sure that matters when there are three giant holes in the hull," Emmett said, climbing back onto the deck with all of their bags looped over his arms.

"What do we do?" Molly sputtered. "Where do we go?"

"To the ship that is not sinking?" Robot suggested.

"Okay, Robot," said Cassandra. "Take us up to the *AquaZephyr*."

Robot hoisted Emmett, who was closest, into his arms and began to levitate.

"Wait! Take my notebooks too!" Nellie yelled. She passed her satchel up to him, before starting to climb from the cabin.

"Oh, take the parkas too!" Cassandra called.

"Right!" Nellie ducked back for the sack of winter wear and hefted it to Emmett.

"And the jerky!" Molly shouted.

Nellie and Emmett both shot her looks of disbelief.

"It's good jerky!" Molly yelled.

With a huff, Nellie tossed the dried meat bundle to

Emmett, and Robot rose into the gradually dying winds. He set the boy down on the deck of the *AquaZephyr* and returned for Molly.

"Please don't drop me," she said as they soared twenty feet above the waves. "I can't swim." Robot set her down next to Emmett and floated away again.

There was no one in sight.

"Do you think Bell and his crew are inside?" asked Molly. "Or did they all get swept overboard? And this ship is ours now?"

Emmett raised a dubious eyebrow.

"Which would definitely be the worse option!" she added quickly. As the moonlight became brighter, she could see working machinery all up and down the deck—cranking metallic arms and spinning gears the size of wagon wheels. Molly began to feel as if she were one of the miniature figures on the ceiling of the Inventors' Guild Hall.

She looked down toward the ship's bow. Every few yards some structure or other rose from the deck, like houses in a waterborne village. She tried to guess the purpose of each, based on all the seafaring books she'd read. There was the forecastle, where the crew generally slept. And the wheelhouse, from which the captain would steer the vessel. And, well, probably some closets or something. She wasn't sure. There were a lot of them.

Robot appeared twice more, dropping off Nellie, who

immediately took back her notebooks, and finally, Cassandra.

Molly peered down over the rail to see the *Whizztastic Wave-Pummeling Poseidon Puncher* punch its final wave and disappear below the surface. She sighed. "Two boat rides, two shipwrecks."

". . . telling you, we definitely hit something!" a man's voice yelled from somewhere within the ship.

"Check it out," another voice ordered.

There was a rumbling as a hatch opened and several burly, bearded men climbed up onto the deck. The men spotted their surprise passengers and froze in place, as the voice of Alexander Graham Bell called from below. "So, what did we hit?"

"We've, uh, we've been boarded," one of the sailors shouted down to him. There was a pause, during which no one seemed to know what to say or do, then a flurry of activity from below. They could hear a frantic rustling of papers, as Bell muttered, "Pirates? In this day and age? With all I've been through, I have to deal with pirates now?"

"It's not pirates!" one sailor yelled.

Bell's commotion stopped. "Not pirates? Then who could have—?" He climbed from the hatch and his eyes landed on Molly.

"Hiya, Belly-Boy."

Bell fainted.

12

Sirens and Sea Dogs

THE FOLLOWING DAWN, as the castaways sat at a table in the *AquaZephyr*'s mess hall, Molly tried to remind herself about the positives of their new situation: beds, bathrooms, *coffee*! Plus, the larger ship cut much more smoothly through the waves and had less of an egg-beater effect on their insides. Oh, and new dry clothes! Men's clothes, yes—but *dry* men's clothes. Molly thought her mother looked charming in white sailor's pants and blue peacoat. While Molly herself was thrilled to be in trousers, she could have done without the puffy-sleeved, wide-collared shirts that she and Emmett had been given, but she hoped that their identical outfits might help them feel more like a team again.

But even with all of these improvements, it was hard for Molly to overlook one major negative. They'd officially lost their chance to beat Bell to the Pole. Yes, they were now a part of the man's polar expedition whether he liked it or not, but even if they stood by his side at the Pole, she knew their names would end up nothing more than footnotes in the story of *his* grand achievement.

But, hey, she thought, at least they weren't at the bottom of the ocean with the MOI's poor boat.

The kitchen door swung open and the aroma of grilled fish filled the room.

"Hallo, hallo!" said a smiling, red-cheeked man with a cheery Scandinavian accent. "I am Lars the navigator, and I come to say good morning to our special guests!" Lars had lumberjack shoulders and a curly golden-blond beard. He wore a red knit cap and a faded blue coat that had likely seen decades of salty ocean air. "I am also Lars the cook!" He laid down plates of fish and rice before Molly, Cassandra, and Nellie.

"Isn't there any for Emmett?" asked Cassandra.

"Oh, I have something special for the little man," Lars said. "This dish here is just for the lovely mermaids we have plucked from the sea, eh?"

Molly bristled, but wasn't going to turn down the first fresh food she'd seen in days.

"Mermaids? Hmph. Sirens, more likely," grumbled a second sailor, who slammed open the mess hall door and went to sit by himself. He could have been Lars's evil twin—just as wide and brawny, but with a deep scowl, a forehead like a cracked, neglected sidewalk, and the kind of dark, wiry beard you wouldn't be surprised to find a rat nesting in.

Lars waved him off. "Icepick, these people are guests," he said. "Be nice."

"Icepick, huh?" Emmett whispered to Molly. "Seems like a nice guy."

"Icepick is first mate, second mate, head fisherman, and chief engineer," said Lars. "He might look dangerous . . ."

"But?" Emmett asked after a few seconds.

"But what?" said Lars.

Across the room, Icepick noisily sucked the meat off of some fish bones and grumbled something under his breath. Or maybe he was trying to speak clearly and the words just couldn't make it through his beard. It was impossible to tell.

"Are there many of you on this ship?" Nellie asked.

"Oh, no, Mr. Bell has just a three-man crew," said Lars. "Four if you count my nephew, Roald, the cabin boy. He's quite the secrety one, that Bell. He doesn't want too many people knowing his business, so he takes only those of us who can perform multiple jobs. I am also Lars the dance instructor."

"Interesting," Nellie said. She covertly scribbled into the notepad on her lap as Lars returned to the kitchen.

"Hmm, people who can do more than one thing,"

Molly said in a sharp whisper. "Unlike some reporters who can't even help someone *dying in a typhoon* because they're too busy taking notes!"

"I was distracted," Nellie snipped back, glancing across the room to make sure Icepick wasn't listening. "And shush—they don't know I'm a you-know-what. Besides, I helped when you said something."

"I could have been sucked into a whirlpool by then! That's twice now you've left me hanging in a bad situation because you were—"

"Because I was getting the story," Nellie hissed. "That's what I'm here for. You've got your risky, convoluted plan and I've got mine. If I succeed in mine, it'll benefit you in the end. So maybe you should just stay out of my way and I'll stay out of yours."

"Except you'll get a much better story if we succeed in the end," Emmett added.

Nellie chewed a piece of fish and thought. "Fine. I'll lend assistance where possible, but understand that my duties as a journalist will always take priority."

"Just as my priority will always be my family," said Cassandra. She was about to add more when Lars came back from the kitchen.

He set a plate down before Emmett and the boy leaned as far from it as he could without falling from his chair. The snaky, crinkle-skinned thing curled on Emmett's plate glared up at him with sinister yellow eyes. It was like an evil wizard had turned a chain of sausages into a monster. "I'm afraid my breakfast might eat me." He tentatively touched his finger to the edge of the plate, as if the charred fish's fangs might snap at him. "Why did it have to be an eel?"

"No eel," Lars chuckled. "Just some delicious barracuda for our tough little man, eh?"

"Uh, yeah, that's me—your classic tough guy." Emmett looked like his seasickness had returned. As soon as Lars was back in the kitchen, Molly swapped plates with Emmett. The look of relief on his face made her think he might finally have forgiven her everything.

A few minutes later, with the last bite of barracuda in her mouth, Molly stood up. "Okay, let's go find Bell," she said. "Now that our two expeditions are combining, we need to be very specific about our roles in this whole foofaraw. I'd personally like to get it in writing that, as the shortest person here, I be in the front of any group photos."

"We certainly have a lot to discuss with Bell," Cassandra said as the others rose. "But I think it's best if I speak to him alone first. This might be a sensitive conversation and we wouldn't want to overwhelm the man."

"No offense, Mother, but sensitive conversations are not your strong suit."

"Nonetheless," Cassandra said. "The rest of you go explore the ship. Get the lay of the land. Lay of the sea?"

"Well, I'm coming with you," said Nellie, flashing her notebook. "For the good of the story."

"I suppose I can't stop you," Cassandra said unhappily. "You two children, though . . . go have fun. But be nice to the sea dogs." She and Nellie left the mess hall.

"I don't trust her," Molly said.

"Nellie or your mother?" Emmett asked.

"Right now, neither. I'm afraid my mother's going to make all the wrong choices now that she's being all parenty."

"You mean like putting our well-being over fame and success?" Emmett asked.

"Exactly," Molly huffed. "Whatever's best for us is never gonna be the more exciting option!"

"I don't know," said Emmett. "Sometimes I feel like it might be refreshing to go, oh, maybe more than three months without danger and mayhem. And secrets."

Molly furrowed her brow. "You're never going to let that go, are you?"

"Not yet. And sorry, but I'm going to give your mother the benefit of the doubt. It's been nice having someone look out for me again."

Molly gave him a sympathetic grin. "You've been thinking about your father a lot, haven't you?"

"Well, not during the shipwreck. During the shipwreck I was mostly wondering whether the Caribbean had any man-eating eels. But pretty much every second up to and after that, yeah. It's been hard to get him out of my head."

"So we just need more shipwrecks."

"Yeah, that's the answer."

"But seriously, we need a distraction. And since my mother's not going to let us near Bell, I guess we might as well do what she suggested. I want to check on Robot anyway." They'd instructed Robot to act like a normal, lifeless machine, lest Bell start tinkering with him.

Behind them, Icepick shattered his plate against the table. "Lars!" he yelled. "You let my plate get empty!"

"Let's explore some part of the ship where *he* is not," Emmett said. He and Molly hurried onto the deck and let the warm Caribbean sun wash over them. The feeling was glorious.

"You know, I could probably just stand here like this for a while," Emmett said.

"I've got no problem with that," she replied. They closed their eyes and leaned their heads back.

"You must be the children!" a voice shouted directly into their ears. Molly and Emmett jumped. A boy was standing between them. He looked to be a bit younger than them, with floppy blond hair, a sunburnt face, and a blousy collared shirt like theirs. "Uncle Lars said there were children. You must be them." He shook both Molly's and Emmett's hands at the same time— vigorously, as if milking a cow.

"Thank you, Mr. Distraction," Molly said, grinning at Emmett.

"No, I am Roald," the new boy said. "I am from Norway. But I am from a lot of other places too, because I am a sailor. I sail places. It is very impressive."

"Yes, um . . . very," Emmett said.

"I am going to be the first person to step foot on the South Pole," Roald said. "It is my destiny. Does that impress you? Do you appreciate a man who knows his destiny?"

"Man?" Molly said. "Who would this man be?"

"I am the man," said Roald.

"How old are you?" Molly asked.

"Eleven," said Roald. "Does that impress you? That I am eleven and I will be the first person to set foot on the South Pole? If that does not impress you, does this?" He began doing jumping jacks. After twenty, he stopped. "Now that you are impressed, what would you like to do with me?"

"I can think of a few things," Molly said. She didn't care how badly Emmett needed a distraction, she was already fantasizing about tossing Roald to the barracudas.

"Thanks, Roald," Emmett said. "But I think we're just going to give ourselves a tour of the ship."

"Oh, I can give you a better tour than you can give yourselves," Roald said. "I know a lot about ships. I have been sailing ships since I was two. How long have you been sailing ships?"

"Um, this is the third ship I've been on," Molly said.

Roald put his hands on his belly and guffawed. "Only three ships? That is adorable."

"Well, the first two sank," Molly said. "So I've survived two shipwrecks. How many have you survived?"

"Too many to count," said Roald. "I told you I have been sailing ships since I was two. Do you think a two-year-old can sail well? No. But I survived the crashes when most two-year-olds would not. That is why I am only eleven and I am on this expedition. I am a marvel of the sea."

"You sure it has nothing to do with your uncle being the navigator?" Emmett asked.

"Let us begin the tour, no?" said Roald. He pointed to the door Molly and Emmett had just exited. "That is the mess hall." He walked along the starboard deck, keeping his pointer finger very busy. "That is a railing, and on the other side of the railing is a little floaty ring to help drowning people. Those are some gears or something. Over there is a closet. And over here are a bunch of knobs."

"What do the knobs do?" Emmett asked.

"Something important, I am sure," said Roald. "Or maybe not. This ship is very different from the other ships I have been on. But please do not interrupt. Over here is a little chute that drops down to the laundry. And under our feet is the deck. That is a pipe of some kind. And that is a rope."

Forty minutes later . . . "That is a porthole. And that is another porthole. And that . . . I think that is all for this side of the ship. Let us go to the port side!"

"Actually," Molly interjected, "isn't that the wheelhouse? Is that the captain in there? Can we meet him?"

Roald paused (something Molly had thought him incapable of doing). "I do not know. Captain Stone does not like people on the bridge other than himself or Uncle Lars. Because my uncle Lars is the navigator. He navigates the ship. He also fishes and cooks. And sings. But he does not do as many things as me."

Molly struggled not to roll her eyes. She desperately needed a break from Roald's tour. Plus, she'd never met a real sea captain before and was curious to see if he was anything like Captain Nemo from *Twenty Thousand Leagues Under the Sea.* She stepped inside the wheelhouse.

The bridge of the *AquaZephyr* was loaded with far more gauges, buttons, and levers than the MOI's tiny boat. Captain Stone stood at an iron wheel with his back to them, staring out through a window almost as big as those at the pickle shop. The captain's long-tailed navy-blue coat stretched across his cinder-block shoulders nearly to the point of tearing. "Children," he said in a deep, sonorous voice. Molly couldn't tell if it was a

144

greeting or a warning. Molly sidled closer until she was able to glimpse his thick, wiry brows, hawklike nose, and well-trimmed salt-and-pepper beard.

"Ahoy, there, Cap'n! I'm Molly Pepper and this is Emmett Lee."

"Caleb Stone," the captain said.

"Pleased to meet you." Molly offered her hand, but the captain either didn't notice or didn't care. "So . . . you sail lots of boats before?"

"Yes," the captain replied.

"More than Roald?" Molly asked with a wink.

Roald was about to say something when Captain Stone answered, "Yes."

"You ever drive a fancy spider-boat like this before?"

"No."

"But you definitely know how, right?"

"Yes."

"'Cause the last ship I was on sank."

"I saw." It was hard to tell, but Captain Stone *might* have been getting annoyed.

"You know, I think the captain might be busy," Emmett interjected.

"I am," said the captain.

"Emmett would know," Molly said. "His father was a sea captain too."

"Um, we don't have to talk about that." Emmett tugged Molly's sleeve.

"Fine," said the captain.

"Hey, Roald," Emmett said. "Let's finish that tour." That told Molly how much Emmett really wanted to leave.

The three children stepped back outside.

"That is a bucket," Roald immediately said.

Molly ignored him. "Sorry, I shouldn't have brought up your father," she said to Emmett.

"It's okay," Emmett replied. "I think I just don't mix well with silent, stoic types. Although I don't really mix well with energetic, talkative types either."

Roald had continued walking and was already halfway down the port-side deck, but they could hear him trailing off in the distance. ". . . and this is a thing that gets really hot to melt ice or something. And that is some seagull poop. Over here is the lounge, and there is the brig. And that—"

"Did he say *brig*? As in a jail?" Molly said.

"For when we find Rector," Emmett guessed.

Molly's mouth formed a little O as it dawned on her that they'd forced themselves into both of Bell's missions: finding the South Pole *and* capturing Ambrose Rector. She hadn't really wanted anything to do with that second one.

They started after Roald, but before they caught up, they passed the open door to a plush lounge with far too many velvet sofas and framed portraits of Alexander Graham Bell. The man himself was inside, talking to

Cassandra and Nellie. And Robot.

"Enough!" Bell was saying. "I will not discuss your future on this ship until you explain what you've done to my automaton!"

13

Deals and Machinations

MOLLY AND EMMETT rushed into the lounge, but Cassandra raised her hand to caution them. Bell was scanning the automaton with a magnifying glass. "You say you didn't tinker with him at all?" Bell asked.

"Not mechanically," Cassandra replied. "We've taught him a few things. Robot, what's the capital of Vermont?"

"Montpelier," answered Robot.

"You told Bell?" Molly blurted, horrified. "Mother, how could you?"

"Molly, hush," Cassandra warned. "So, you see, Mr. Bell, Robot has learned from us, but we've not 'programmed' him to do anything. We dare not mess around with his inside bizwits."

"So, these actions of his? These verbalizations?" Bell asked, amazed. "They're occurring automatically?"

"I do what I want to do," Robot told him. "And also

what they tell me to do."

Bell rubbed his beard. "Will you do what *I* tell you to do?" he asked.

"If I want to," Robot replied.

"Touch your nose," Bell commanded.

"I do not want to," said Robot. Then he touched his nose. "I changed my mind."

Nellie silently recorded the exchange in her notepad.

"Fascinating," Bell said. He beamed like a child with extra dessert. "I must examine him further."

"No!" Molly thrust herself between them. "Robot is alive, he's not one of your experiments!"

"Ah, Molly!" Bell said, clearing his throat. "I understand you've become quite attached to my Robert here."

"Robot," Molly corrected him. "And he's not yours."

"I misspoke," Bell said. "He is *not* mine. He is a marvel that belongs to science. Which is why we must study him. Think of all the breakthroughs Robot could lead us to!"

Molly made a fist. "You wanna see a breakthrough?"

"Please don't punch the famous scientist, Molls," her mother said. "Do you really think I would let Mr. Bell— or anyone—crack Robot open?"

Robot blinked. "Crack me open? Like an egg?" He blinked again. "Did I just make a metaphor?"

"Technically, that was a simile," Emmett said. "But you're getting close."

"Molls," Cassandra went on. "Mr. Bell has a point. By

studying Robot, we might be able to create all sorts of new machines that can help the world. But I would never let that research harm Robot. You trust me, don't you?"

Molly *wanted* to trust her mother. But she definitely didn't trust Bell.

"Molly," said Bell. "May I please have your permission to study Robot? Interviews and observation only—nothing invasive. I give you my word." He put his hand on his heart.

You gave us your word you'd get my mother into the Guild too, Molly thought. She kept her lips pressed tight until Emmett touched her sleeve.

"Robot," Emmett said, "how would you feel about helping Mr. Bell learn more about you?"

"Knowledge is power," Robot replied. "And so is dynamite. They have some of that on this boat too."

Everyone looked at Bell.

"What?" he said. "It's for the ice, if we need it. So, um, Robot, was that a yes? You'll let me study you?"

"In the name of science," said Robot. "Yes."

Molly hoped Robot understood what he was agreeing to. "Okay," she said to her mechanical friend. "But you have permission to defend yourself if necessary."

Bell swallowed hard. "Well, I certainly hope it doesn't come to that!"

"I'd like to monitor these tests," said Nellie.

"And who, exactly, would you be again?" Bell asked.

"Katrina von Malcontent," said Nellie. "I'm with the patent office. We had some complaints from Hertha Marks and her colleagues that your *AquaZephyr* infringed upon the designs of their hydrofoil ship."

Bell cocked an eyebrow. "And so you boarded that experimental vessel with two children and an inexperienced woman and chased me all the way to the Caribbean to find out?"

"We take our job very seriously at the patent office," Nellie replied. "Which is why I insist on being present for your experimentations with this Robot character. I can foresee all sorts of issues popping up on this one."

Bell gave a haughty sniff. "I've nothing to hide anyway."

"Well, then, I'm staying too," said Molly.

"No," Bell said immediately. "One extra person is enough. This is science, not a circus."

"I wish it was a circus," said Robot. "I can juggle."

"Speaking of juggling," said Cassandra, "I think it's time we got back to discussing our place on this voyage. I know that has nothing to do with juggling, but I wanted to change the topic."

Bell opened his mouth to speak, but Molly jumped in. "Actually, Mother, maybe you and me and Emmett should talk about this privately first! Have you considered the whole capturing Rector part of Bell's mission?"

"Did I just hear someone use the no-no word in front

of unsanctioned people?" said a dapper newcomer in the doorway. Molly recognized the smug grin, the glistening waxed hair, the toothpick-thin mustache. It was the same agent they'd met at Bell's wharf house. He strode cockily into the lounge, his thumbs hooked behind black suspenders, and gave a nod to Cassandra. "I'm sure you remember me. Federal Agent Archibald Forrest. I must say, it's a pleasant surprise getting to see *you* again so soon."

Cassandra crossed her arms. "I can't say the pleasure is mutual. Although the surprise is. Why are *you* on this ship?"

"Yes, I thought this was a three-person crew," Emmett chimed in. "Four with Roald."

"Agent Forrest is not technically crew," Bell said.

"Nope," said Forrest. "I'm just here to oversee this secret mission for the good old U-S-of-A. Can't trust these scientist types, can we?"

Molly got suddenly woozy. They'd hit the high seas to flee from the Feds. Now she was on a boat with one. And a slimy one to boot.

"Um, Mr. Bell," Emmett said, apparently having the same thought. "You don't happen to have any kind of long-distance telegraph on this ship, do you?"

Forrest nodded. "Yeah, kid, I know about your little escapade back at the harbor. Kind of impressive, actually. I'd have loved to see the look on old Clark's face when you three ditched out in that boat. That guy's such a wet noodle."

Steely-eyed, Cassandra held out her wrists. "Go ahead then, Agent Forrest."

"Please, call me Archie."

"You don't let *me* call you Archie," Bell said, sounding hurt.

"Agent Forrest," Cassandra said. "Why are you toying with us? Just arrest us and be done with it."

"Well, the thing is, we're in international waters. I've got no jurisdiction here," Forrest said. "As soon as we're back home, though? Well, *then* I can become a big hero by turning you all in. Notice I said 'can.'"

"Meaning what? You might choose to let us get away?" Cassandra asked, incredulous. "You've probably already sent a telegraph back to your bosses to tell them we're on this boat."

"Nope, I'm a by-the-book kind of guy," said Forrest. "I will send no such communication until we are in American waterways. Until that time, you, me, the kids, the walking stovepipe here—we're all just passengers on this lovely cruise. A cruise that just got a little lovelier, by the way. Ain't that right, Stovepipe?" He gave Robot a friendly slap on the back.

"I am afraid I do not understand the question, Archie," Robot replied.

Forrest leapt backward, bumping the coffee table

and spilling a crystal decanter of red wine. "That thing talks?"

"And more," Molly said angrily. "Touch him again, and you'll regret it."

Bell pouted. "Even the robot gets to call you Archie?"

"Is that what it's called? A robot?" Agent Forrest smoothed his eyebrows and approached the automaton again. "What else does it do? Who knows about it?" He gave Robot a poke in the face. "*Ow!* It bit me!"

"I defended myself," said Robot.

"Can't say you weren't warned," said Emmett.

Even with his throbbing fingertip, Forrest was grinning. "So he's a fighter, eh? A mechanical soldier."

"Nothing of the sort," said Cassandra. "He sings and such. No fighting."

"I defeated Ambrose Rector and destroyed his doomsday machine," Robot added.

"Intriguing," said Forrest.

Emmett dropped his face into his hands.

"Actually, Robot is capable of far more than you'd expect," said Cassandra. "You'd be amazed at—"

"Mrs. Pepper, can we talk outside?" Emmett pulled her out onto the deck with Molly. "Um, I'd like to believe that this is all part of your grand plan, but I'm very concerned about Robot. I was worried enough that you agreed to let Bell examine him, but now you've got Forrest interested too. They're practically drooling over him in there. And Forrest is probably hoping to turn Robot into some kind of killing machine or—"

"Both of you, listen to me: I'm trying to keep us on this ship," Cassandra said. "Before you two came in, Bell was telling me how he'd instructed the captain to change course. He plans to stop at the island of Barbados so he can drop us off there. He has no intention of taking us to Antarctica with him. But I could tell he was interested in Robot, so—"

"So you're using our *friend* as a bargaining chip?" Molly snapped.

"And is it really such a bad thing for us to get off in Barbados?" Emmett added. "Even if we survive this trip, we'll still end up going back to America with Agent Forrest, and that won't lead to anything good."

"So you're saying we should let Bell dump us on some luxurious tropical island with nothing but sun and sand and coconut drinks?" Molly asked.

Emmett blinked. "Was that an argument *against* staying in Barbados? Look, Forrest is a big wild card. We have to consider what he might do with us when this is all over. Frankly, I don't trust the man not to rattle off a Morse code message about us to his friends in the US tomorrow. He could have navy ships waiting for us the moment we see Florida."

"Emmett, our times of worrying about the future are in the past," said Cassandra. "We need to focus on our present, and what it means for our future."

"Exactly," said Molly.

"You followed that?" Emmett asked.

"She's saying we worry about Forrest when he becomes a problem, and focus on making sure Bell takes us to the South Pole," Molly said. "If we make ourselves an important enough part of his team, Bell might use his heft to keep us out of jail anyway."

Emmett sucked air between his teeth. "But what if Forrest *is* a problem now? What if he sends a message back home about us?"

"He can't if we destroy the telegraph machine," Molly said.

"Somehow, I don't think vandalism is the key to making Mr. Bell want us on his ship," Emmett said drily.

"C'mon, Emmett," Molly urged. "Aren't you making this trip to honor your father's memory? If you give up on it now, you'll never stop kicking yourself."

Before he could answer, Roald came bounding back. "There you are! You missed when I pointed to the second floaty ring! It is just like the first floaty ring, but on the other side of the ship. Who is this? Is this your mother? I am Roald. I am teaching your uneducated children about ships."

"You seem delightful," said Cassandra. "Now, if you'll excuse me, I need to go give Bell a reason to keep us on this ship. And if that reason is Robot, please trust me to keep him safe."

After the way Cassandra took charge during the storm, Molly had hoped her mother was becoming her old self again. But the old Cassandra would never put Robot at risk like this. An idea sparked in Molly's mind. Maybe there was a way to keep them on the expedition, take the focus off Robot, and bring her old mother back, all at the same time. She marched into the lounge and announced, "We're not getting off this ship in Barbados."

"Molly," Emmett warned.

Bell sighed. "It's not entirely my decision," he said, adding in a low voice, "Some of the sailors consider women bad luck on a ship, so—"

"Not me," Forrest said to Cassandra. "I like having ladies around." Molly noticed that the top button of his shirt had mysteriously come undone.

"Mr. Bell, you *need* us on this ship," Molly continued. "You know what an incredible inventor my mother is."

"Molls, I—"

"Quiet, Mother. Mr. Bell, there's gotta be stuff you didn't prepare for or didn't realize you needed. My mother can help you fix those problems."

Bell checked his pocket watch. "It's only eight a.m. How am I so tired already?" He sighed. "Molly, there are no problems."

"What about breaking all that ice?" Molly said.

"Between the crank-powered axes on the hull, the heat fans on the deck, the giant drill, and the dynamite,

I think we've got it covered," Bell said.

"Well, what about the cold in Antarctica? My mother built an instant heater back home that—"

"We'll be fine with the thermo-lined parkas I've devised," Bell said.

"Molls, let it go," Cassandra said.

But Molly couldn't let it go. She needed to keep the mission alive. She needed to save Robot. And help Emmett. And remind her mother of who she really was. "What about once you're on land down there? You park the ship by the shore, and then—what?—you walk a thousand miles through the snow? You can't even get through a conversation without pooping out. So, why not build some kind of land vehicle for down there?"

"Like what?" Bell said.

Molly looked into her mother's eyes, pleading.

"Like this ship," Cassandra said. "It's already got legs. We could retrofit them with joints and pistons and turn them into real, working legs. This ship can march right up onto the shore and all the way to the middle of that blasted continent. You'd never have to leave your cabins."

"That's"—Bell paused—"an intriguing idea."

"Yes!" Molly shouted.

"*But*," Bell said quickly, "it doesn't sound remotely possible."

"I bet you thought the same thing about a flying machine," Cassandra said defiantly. "Until you rode mine."

Bell took a deep breath. "I assume we'd need supplies for this project. So I will make you a deal, Mrs. Pepper. Show me your designs for this 'snow-crawler' by the time we reach Barbados. If they seem feasible, we'll purchase the necessary materials there and you can stay with the expedition to oversee the construction. If not, you disembark and we go on without you."

Molly bit her lip with anticipation.

Cassandra offered Bell her hand. "You have a deal."

Agent Forrest waved. "Hey, anybody curious as to what the only law enforcement officer on board has to say about this?"

"Well, Archie," said Bell. "Do you have jurisdiction in Barbados?"

"First of all, it's Agent Forrest," Forrest replied. "And . . . no."

Molly jumped with excitement. "C'mon, Mother, let's get started!"

"I'm happy to help too," Emmett said eagerly. "I've already thought of a few—"

"Thank you, children, but some jobs are one-person jobs," said Cassandra. "By which I mean this job. And I am the one person."

"We get it, Mother."

"I can handle this on my own, Molls. Trust me."

Molly could tell her mother had some kind of plan, something she didn't want to say in front of Bell, so she nodded and stepped away.

"Yes, you children run off and play," said Bell. "But Miss von Malcontent should go with Mrs. Pepper."

"Who?" Cassandra asked.

"Me," Nellie said, clearing her throat. "Katrina von Malcontent? Who has been traveling with you for several days?"

"Oh, yes, *that* Miss von . . . her. But why?"

"She's with the patent office," said Bell. "She can oversee your designs to make sure you don't accidentally use anybody else's ideas."

Molly leaned over and whispered to Emmett, "He just wants to keep Nellie conveniently busy while he operates on Robot."

Nellie exchanged looks with Cassandra. "I will observe both projects," she announced.

"Excellent," said Bell, although he didn't look very happy. "Start with hers."

Cassandra scowled. "So be it. Come, Miss . . . Patent Lady. Let's find a quiet place to work."

"Yes, and now we shall leave too," Emmett declared. "Let's go for a walk, Robot."

Robot clomped over to join the children, and Molly couldn't hide her huge smile.

"But—but it was agreed that I could examine him," Bell said.

"It's a three-month voyage," Emmett said. "Plenty of time for that later."

They heard Bell grumbling and Forrest laughing as they left the lounge. Roald was waiting for them outside. "Is the man made of plumbing coming with us?" he asked.

"*You're* coming with us?" Molly asked in return.

"Of course," Roald replied. "Even though I could build the walking legs for your mother. I have been building things since I was eighteen months old. I built my own crib."

They walked to the port-side rail. "Hey, Robot, how far can you fly?" Molly asked. "Could you make it to land?"

"Where is land?" Robot asked.

"Good question," said Molly.

"I could swim to land," said Roald. "Can the shiny man swim?"

"Swim? Like *that* man?" Robot pointed out to the waves, where an emaciated man in rags clung to a dented sheet of metal bobbing in the water. "My mistake. That man is not swimming. He is drowning."

14

Man Overboard!

MOLLY HAD ALWAYS imagined it would be a giddy thrill to shout, "Man overboard!" But doing so in real life, while a real person was in distress, was disturbingly traumatic. She felt shaky as the ship slowed to a stop and Lars and Icepick pushed past her to a chrome kiosk by the rail. The sailors began pulling levers and cranking wheels.

"Robot can just fly out and get him," Emmett tried to tell them.

But a large panel had already opened on the outer hull and a two-man rowboat emerged on a metal platform. "Step aside!" Captain Stone barked, before making an agile leap over the rail, into the small dinghy.

Bell and Forrest burst from the lounge, just as Cassandra and Nellie also rushed back onto the scene.

162

Cassandra sighed with relief to see Molly and Emmett safe.

"Who's out there?" Nellie asked.

"Nobody I heaved over," Icepick grunted. He spun a wheel to mechanically lower the platform and deposit the dinghy into the water, and Captain Stone rowed out from under the ship's legs.

"What's that guy floating on?" asked Emmett.

"Something that does not sink," answered Robot.

"*Ja*, that is what I was going to say," added Roald.

"Looks metal," Cassandra said. "There's something written on it."

"There's lots of debris out there," said Bell. "Remnants of a shipwreck, I'd hazard."

"Another one?" Emmett said.

"Maybe it's the *Slush Puppy*," said Molly. "That other Antarctic expedition that sank."

"The *Slush Puppy* never existed," Agent Forrest said as he casually watched the rescue effort. "It was just a cover story so the government could cancel other expeditions and keep people from crossing paths with Rector down there."

Molly gaped at him and Nellie began writing.

"You, uh, can't tell anybody that," Forrest said. "Hey, look, the captain's made the rescue!"

For once, Molly was grateful to be wearing her glasses, because as Captain Stone lifted the shipwrecked man into the lifeboat, she was able to get a good look at what was written on the panel he'd been floating on: *Frost Cleaver.*

"It's Rector!" Molly blurted.

As the sailors worked the controls to raise the rowboat again, she grabbed the nearest weapon—a mop (which she knew about thanks to Roald's tour)—and got ready to bash the villain right back into the sea. But when the dinghy reappeared at the rail and Captain Stone helped the scrawny castaway onto the deck, she dropped her guard. The thin, weathered face was not Ambrose Rector's. But it was familiar. "Pembroke?"

The castaway's bloodshot eyes focused on hers. His skin was redder, his hair longer, and his chin covered in several weeks' worth of whiskers, but Molly still recognized the former lieutenant of the Green Onion Boys.

"Oh my goodness, it *is* him," Emmett gasped.

"You *know* this fellow?" Bell asked.

"You should too, Mr. Bell," Emmett said. "He's the Green Onion who trapped you at Bandit's Roost."

"By George, you're right!" Bell said. "Mr. Pembroke, what do you have to say for yourself?"

"Um . . ." Pembroke's eyes shifted among the eleven staring faces before him. "Thank you?"

"Anything else you'd like to tell us, sir?" Forrest said. "I'm Forrest, by the way. *Federal Agent* Archibald Forrest."

"No, um, I think 'thank you' covers it," Pembroke said tentatively. "Just happy you recovered me from the flotsam and jotsam. I been out there for weeks. Didn't think I was gonna—"

"Tell us what we want to know, Pembroke," Molly snapped. "Why were you on the *Frost Cleaver*? What happened to it? And where's Rector?"

The gangster dropped his head into his bony hands. "Why *you*? Why, of all the ventricles in the sea, did I have to be rescued by one with *you* on it? I shoulda stayed in the ocean."

"Answer the questions, Pembroke!" Molly rolled up her sleeves.

"Ease up, lass," said Lars. "The man's halfway to Hades." He attempted to offer the castaway a blanket, but Molly grabbed Pembroke by his ragged collar.

"Tell us!" she growled.

"The girl's out of her gullet!" Pembroke yelped.

Lars and Forrest grabbed Molly, which prompted Emmett to grab Lars and Cassandra to grab Forrest. Which prompted Roald to push Emmett. And Forrest to spin and dip Cassandra. Which prompted Nellie to smack Forrest with her notebook.

"Stop!" the captain hollered. Everyone froze. "You, answer the question."

"I, uh, used to be a lieutenament for the Green Onions," Pembroke said. "But there ain't no Green Onions

165

anymore. Not since the Fair." He scowled at Molly and Emmett. "For the few of us who got away that day, it was either risk jail or join up with that Rector fella and flee the country. The choice was simplicitous."

"See? He confessed!" said Emmett. "Do something, Agent Forrest!"

Forrest shrugged. "Sorry, no jurisdiction."

Molly was about to yell at him, but stopped herself. If Forrest were to telegraph his bosses about Pembroke, he'd probably mention the rest of the fugitives too.

Captain Stone pointed at the frail gangster. "Well, this is my ship and I want to know the answer. Where is Ambrose Rector?"

"Bottom of the sea," Pembroke said.

"Dead?" Emmett said.

"No, he's playing poker with starfish and octopods," Pembroke snarked.

Molly kicked him.

"Yeah, yeah, he's dead! Sleepin' with the fishes, literarily. Besides Rector, there was four of us Onions on the ship: me, Johnny Zucchini, Willie Zucchini—no relation—and Willie the Teaspoon. None of us had ever been sailing before, but Rector insisted his boat could practically sail itself."

"It was *my* boat," Bell grumbled.

"Well, then it's your fault the boat *couldn't* sail itself," Pembroke continued. "Few weeks ago, we hit

166

something—a rock, a boat, one of them big turtles, I don't know—but there was a big . . . BOOM! People flying, pieces of ship everywhere. I was the only one to make it. Johnny, Willie, Willie, *and* Rector went down with the ship."

"You *saw* Rector die?" Molly asked.

"With my own two eye sockets." Pembroke crossed his heart. "He was standing at the wheel, yelling, 'Foolish ocean, nothing can take down Ambrose Rector! Blub-blub-blub.'"

"That does *sound* like Rector," Bell admitted.

"It was," Pembroke said. "Believe me, I—"

Molly yanked hard on Pembroke's scrubby beard. He yowled, and Molly wiped her hands, satisfied. "Okay, it's not a mask," she announced.

"Remind me not to get on her bad side," Agent Forrest said with a bemused grin.

"So fascinating that you think you're not already there," said Cassandra.

"Molly had to make sure Pembroke wasn't really Rector in disguise," Emmett explained to the others. "The man was an actor—and *really* good at impressions."

"Yeah, *was*. And now he's dead," said Pembroke. He raised his hands to guard himself from Molly. "So can I please—ow! You too?"

Emmett had grabbed Pembroke's finger. "Where did you get that ring?"

"It's mine!"

"No, it isn't!" He sat on Pembroke and wrenched the ring off. It was smooth silver with a tiny green gem.

"Okay, okay, sheesh—I got it on the boat," Pembroke sputtered. "I was scrounging for snacks and found it rollin' around in a drawer."

"What is it, Emmett?" Cassandra asked.

Emmett turned it over in his fingers a few times, then looked up, as if coming out of a dream. "This is my father's ring."

Molly didn't know what to say.

"Are you certain?" asked Bell.

"I'd know this ring anywhere," Emmett said. He stared at it lovingly and slipped it onto his own too-small finger. "My father didn't have a lot of opportunities to sit me on his lap and tell me stories when I was younger, but every time he did, I'd hold his hand and spin this ring around his finger. I couldn't possibly forget it."

"Fine, keep it." Pembroke looked ready to collapse. "Can I get some food and water yet?"

Lars held a cracker to Pembroke's chapped lips, singing, "Open up, here comes the choo-choo!"

Captain Stone sighed. "Feed him in the brig."

"Good. We can hand him off to the authorities in Barbados," Bell said, as Lars led the shaky-legged gangster away. "And Mrs. Pepper, your snow-crawler plans had better be spectacular, because I can't afford to spend a moment longer than necessary in that harbor. You might think news of Rector's demise would make me breathe easier, but it has only made me more apprehensive. The man has proven himself unkillable in the past. And if he's still out there, I can't let him beat me to the South Pole."

"Excuse me, but why would Ambrose Rector go to the South Pole?" Nellie asked. "By my understanding, his sole purpose for traveling to Antarctica was to retrieve more meteorite ore."

"And by my understanding, you work for the patent office," Bell said, straightening his tie. "So I don't believe this is any of your concern." And he walked off, prompting the rest of the crew to head their separate ways as well.

"What was that all about?" Nellie asked.

"I was about to ask you the same," said Cassandra. Nellie looked at her quizzically. "You've been quite adamant about staying out of our business," Cassandra explained. "But I believe I saw that notebook of yours thrashing a certain federal agent a moment ago."

"I suppose there are some things I simply can't stand for," said Nellie. "If you'll excuse me . . ." The reporter stashed her pad in her satchel and strode off.

Cassandra headed in the opposite direction. "Take care, children," she called as she disappeared around a corner.

"Mother, wait," Molly said too late. Even if her mother didn't want help with her designs, why wouldn't she want them nearby—especially with a known criminal on board? "You get the feeling *no one* on this boat is being straight with us?"

"Hmm?" Emmett asked, looking up from the ring on his finger. "Um, sure, can we maybe do that later? I need to be alone for a bit."

"Do what?" Molly said. "I didn't even—"

But Emmett was already walking away, spinning his ring. She decided to cut him a break. That ring was the first memento of his father Emmett had encountered in years; it was probably stirring up all kinds of ideas about what else they might discover once they reached Antarctica.

If they reached Antarctica. She stared out at the sapphire sea that went on forever under a clear sky. There would be a dot of land on that horizon soon enough, though. They were forty-eight hours from Barbados.

"I guess it's just you and me until then, eh, Robot?" Molly said. "Robot?"

The mechanical man was nowhere to be seen. "Seriously? You too?" Molly began moving down the deck, peering around every cabin house and storage closet, until she was startled by a tap on the shoulder.

"I could not help but notice you are alone," said Roald. He tossed his head to swing the straw-colored hair out of his eyes. "So, what are we doing?"

Molly slumped. "*We* are not doing anything," she said.

"Yes, we are. We are talking."

"I don't wanna talk anymore."

"That is acceptable. Let us have a race around the deck, then. I will win."

Molly ran her hands down her cheeks. What had she done to deserve this? It was kicking the starving man, wasn't it?

"Actually, Roald, I could use your help," she said. "I'm looking for Robot."

"The metal man? Let us look for him! He is not by the bucket. And he is not by the mop. Hey, the mop has been moved!"

"You know, we'd cover more ground if we split up," Molly said. "I'll check the starboard deck and you scout the port side, okay?"

"I will find him before you," Roald said enthusiastically. "I am very good at finding things. Especially metal men." He ran off.

Molly continued down the deck, opening every door she saw. She came to one marked "Communications Room." It was unlocked. Inside, atop a wrought-iron countertop, sat Agent Forrest's direct line to the US government. The telegraph device, with its small arm for tapping out Morse code messages, was metal. As was the larger "signal resonator" machine it was connected to.

Metal was hard to wreck. Unless you had magnet powers like Robot. Where was Robot?

Then Molly noticed the three brightly colored cords between the two parts of the machine. Before she could talk herself out of it, she ripped the wires free, ignoring the sparks, and shoved them into her pocket. She was about to leave when she heard voices.

"... didn't expect to see you ..."

Drat! She was trapped. Someone was right outside.

"... say nothing about ..."

No, the voices weren't outside the door—they were coming from behind the room's back wall. What was on the opposite side of the Communications Room? The brig!

"... better not catch you ..."

Someone was talking to Pembroke! But who? The voice was too muffled to recognize. Molly pressed her ear against the wall.

"... follow my lead, old friend ..."

Old friend? Who knew Pembroke besides her, Emmett, and Bell?

"... be on your way home with food rockets ..."

Food rockets? Okay, that was odd. Unless the voice had said "full pockets." Yes, that made much more sense. The mystery speaker was promising Pembroke payment. But for what? Molly covered her free ear.

"... whatever happens, do not ..."

"Molly! I have not found your metal man!" Roald shouted, throwing open the door to the Communications Room. His outburst was followed by the sound of the brig door slamming and footsteps hurrying away.

"Drat!" Molly pushed past Roald and ducked around to the front of the brig, but all she could see was a speeding shadow disappearing around a corner.

"Were you eavesdropping?" Roald asked. "Because I am very good at eavesdropping. I have been eavesdropping since I was three months old. I did not understand what I was hearing, but nobody suspected I could hear them."

"Roald, go away." She pushed past him and walked off on her own. She needed to think. She began to walk toward the rear of the ship, but stopped when she saw Icepick hunched over a sack by a storage closet. He looked up and glared at her. "In a hurry?" he said, but it felt like he was daring her to come any closer. She pivoted and headed toward the bow.

Up ahead, though, Nellie was running into the lounge, out of breath. Molly turned quickly and skirted over to the starboard deck, where she saw Alexander Graham Bell check over his shoulder before stepping into the mess hall.

Molly spun away from him and bumped into Lars, who was speeding in the opposite direction. "Sorry, little lady," the ruddy-cheeked navigator said, wiping his sweaty brow with the map in his hand. "I'm just off to see the captain." He motioned toward the wheelhouse. But the wheelhouse was empty.

Molly nodded and moved on. She was beginning to sweat, herself. She hurried around the bridge to the bow of the ship, where she flinched at the sight of Agent Forrest lounging in a chair, reading *Twenty Thousand Leagues Under the Sea*. That was *her* book! It had been in her bag. Forrest gave her a nod, which she cautiously returned before hurrying on her way.

Molly had a problem. A big one.

Someone on that ship was not who they said they were.

The Investigators' Guild

MOLLY DID NOT sleep well. And not just because she was crammed into a cot with her blanket-hogging mother, while Nellie Bly tossed and turned on the bunk overhead.

When the first hint of dawn's light slipped through the room's tiny porthole, Molly carefully slid out of bed without waking Cassandra. She tiptoed to the door and cracked it open just enough to squeeze outside. That was when she noticed the top bunk was empty. When had Nellie left?

Molly hurried to Roald's cabin, which was now Roald *and* Emmett's cabin. Molly hoped Emmett was okay after a night alone with the chatty cabin boy. The look on Emmett's face when he'd heard his room assignment held no less terror than it had when Rector threatened to throw him off the Brooklyn Bridge.

She snuck inside to find Emmett curled up on the lower bunk and Roald splayed out on the upper, snoring loudly. She crouched and tapped Emmett gently. His eyes popped open with fear, but upon seeing it was Molly, he leapt from the bed, pulled her outside, and shut the door. "I'm so happy it's you," he breathed. "Do you know how many times Roald felt the need to show me that he could reach the top bunk without a step stool? 'Look, I can do it one-handed! Look, I can do it with my teeth! Look—'"

"You're happy to see me!" Molly said with a grin. "Does this mean you forgive me?"

"This is what you woke me at dawn to talk about?" Emmett sounded fatigued. "Actually, let's do it. Let's go for a walk and talk about my least-favorite subject. Anything to get away from my cellmate for a few minutes."

"No, just listen," Molly said. "I discovered something yesterday. And I've been pondering it all night. But you're a better ponderer than me." She also wanted to keep Emmett thinking about something other than his dead father, but she didn't say that part.

"Oh. I see," said Emmett. He puffed out his chest. "Well, uh . . . what did you discover?"

"We've got a traitor on board." Molly relayed everything she'd heard from the brig between Pembroke and the mystery person.

Emmett ran his fingers through his pillow-mussed

hair. "Can I *ever* go on a normal trip?"

"Normal is boring," Molly said.

"How about just non-life-threatening?"

"That's reasonable."

"So what does your mother think we should do?"

"She doesn't know," Molly said. "And I'm not going to tell her. This is important, but so is finishing her snow-crawler. If she hears about the traitor, you know she'll drop everything else."

"Yeah, she would. So, let's talk to Nellie."

Molly shook her head. "Nellie could be the traitor. What do we really know about her? I'm pretty sure Nellie Bly's not even her real name."

"But she defended your mother when Agent Forrest grabbed her."

"Unless she was just trying to get rid of the ship's law enforcement officer," Molly said. "If she'd smacked him a little harder, *floop!* Over the rail. Pretty diabolical, actually. Sorry, Emmett, I think it's gotta be just us on this."

The cabin door opened behind them. "Just us! I like it," said Roald. "I will be of much help with this. I am very good at interrogating people."

"Were you spying on us?" Molly blasted the boy with an icy stare.

"I told you I was good at eavesdropping."

Emmett whispered into Molly's ear. "Let him tag along. He'd just follow us anyway. Better to have him

177

where we can see him."

Molly nodded. "Roald, you're on the team. But you have to promise not to tell your uncle what we're up to."

Roald crossed his heart. "You will find I am very good at keeping promises."

"May I take part as well?" asked Robot, startling all three children.

"Robot, I was so worried!" Molly threw her arms around him. His metal was damp and cold. "Where have you been?"

"You asked if I could fly far enough to reach land and I did not know the answer, so I found out. The answer is yes."

"You actually reached land? From the ship?" Emmett asked, gaping. "Where did you go? Barbados? Are we that close?"

"I do not know what land it was. Do all lands have names?"

"Never mind that, Robot," said Molly. "How did you manage to sneak up on us like you just did?"

"I was hovering," answered Robot. "No footsteps."

Molly nodded. "That could come in handy." She surveyed her imperfect crew of mystery solvers. "Okay, boys—"

"I am not a boy," said Robot.

"I prefer 'man,'" said Roald.

"Maybe this isn't the best idea," said Emmett.

Molly rolled her eyes. "Okay, people—"

"I am not a person," said Robot.

"I prefer 'man,'" Roald repeated.

"I'm starting to lean toward just telling your mother," said Emmett.

Molly flared her nostrils. "Okay, *individuals* . . ." She waited for one of them to dare interrupt again. "I hereby pronounce the four of us the founding members of the Investigators' Guild."

Roald clapped his hands. "I am very good at founding things."

Molly turned and led them down the deck. This was never going to work.

"Roald, you're on lookout," Molly said as they filed into the brig. "I bet you're very good at guarding things."

"How did you know?" Roald beamed. He took position, peering out through the thin crack in the door.

Behind the bars of his cell, Pembroke sat up and rubbed his eyes. "Oh, for the love of Jiminy." He looked healthier, but still more scarecrow than human. "What do you juvenelians want with me now? And why is that giant soup can looking at me like that?"

"Congratulations, that was a good metaphor," said Robot. "Because I am not a soup can."

"Pembroke, we don't have much time," Molly said in her toughest detective voice. "Who was the 'friend' you were talking to in here yesterday?"

The prisoner snorted. "I ain't got no friends on this boat, I can tell you that."

"You just did tell us that," said Robot.

"Molly heard you talking to someone yesterday," Emmett said. "Either you can tell *us* who it was or we can let Agent Forrest interrogate you."

"Oh, you mean that sailor guy who came in here trying to intimberdate me," said Pembroke.

"Intimberdate," Robot echoed. "This is a word?"

"Pah! Brainless machine," Pembroke scoffed.

"Don't talk to Robot that way," Molly growled.

"He is not incorrect," said Robot. "I do not have a brain. I have a rock."

"So, it was a member of the crew?" Emmett asked, trying to get back on topic. "And you'd never met him before yesterday?"

Pembroke shook his head.

"Funny, I coulda sworn I heard him call you 'old friend,'" said Molly.

"Nah, he called me old Fred. That's my name. Fred Pembroke." He nodded smugly.

"You said he was a stranger. How did he know your first name?" Emmett asked. He nudged Molly with his elbow, whispering, "I feel like a detective in an Edgar Allan Poe story."

"The guy knew my name 'cause I told him," Pembroke said. "When he first comes in, I say, 'Thanks for saving old Freddy Pembroke.' Then he starts telling me to behave, and I tells him he don't have to worry about me none."

Self-doubt began rumbling in the pit of Molly's stomach. She'd only heard muffled snippets of conversation; could she have misinterpreted them? "Which crew member was it?"

"How would I know?" Pembroke said. "I been on this tub for less than a day. I don't even know all your names!"

"I am Robot."

"*Ja*, and I am Roald. Which is a better name than Robot. You should remember my name, because I am going to be the first person to step foot on the South Pole."

"Roald! Back to the door!" Molly snapped. "Pembroke, what did the person who threatened you look like?"

"He had a beard."

"They *all* have beards!" Molly felt ready to bend the bars and climb in after Pembroke.

"Someone's coming," Roald warned.

"This isn't over, Pembroke," Molly growled before dashing outside with the others. The quartet of investigators scurried to an isolated area by the stern of the ship.

"Well, Pembroke is definitely lying," Molly said.

"Possibly lying," Emmett clarified.

"That man says many things he thinks are words, but

which are not words," said Robot.

"I can go back and get more information from him," Roald offered. "I can pinch him until he talks. I have very powerful fingers. Watch me pinch this iron rail." He squeezed and grunted until his face turned red.

"No, we're good, Roald," Emmett said. "We've narrowed it down to Lars, Icepick, or Captain Stone. We just need to figure out which of them met with Pembroke yesterday."

"Were you and I in the same interrogation just now?" said Molly. "Because I haven't eliminated anyone."

Emmett frowned. "You still suspect Nellie? Pembroke said it was a man."

"Nellie's wearing men's clothes."

"He said it was a man with a beard."

"You speak as if you are someone who's never encountered a fake beard before," Molly said.

"I have worn fake beards before," Roald said. "They look very real on me."

"I have a fake mustache," said Robot. "It is part of my face."

Emmett threw his hands in the air. "Okay, let's say that Nellie was somehow a secret criminal who worked with Pembroke in the past. And that, for some reason, she only worked with him while in disguise—they were the infamous criminal duo of Captain Vocabulary and the Bearded Lady. Even if we allow for something as ludicrous as that, Nellie would have had no way of knowing Pembroke would end up on this ship with her. Why would she have packed her disguise? It doesn't make sense. You know, Molly, part of me wonders if you just want to solve this mystery to show up Nellie."

"Would that be the worst reason?" Molly asked.

"In the bottom ten," Emmett replied. "I don't think we should interrogate Nellie. Everybody else is fair game, though."

"Including Alexander Graham Bell," said Molly.

Emmett winced. "Do we really want to go down that road again, Molly? Remember how convinced you were that Bell was the mastermind behind the World's Fair plot?"

"Just because I was wrong about him once doesn't mean I can't ever be right about him," she said. "You have to admit he's been acting shady. And he definitely has a beard."

Emmett sighed. "All right, everybody," he said. "Roald, I'm sorry, but we still need to consider your uncle a suspect. Although if he turns out to have been Pembroke's visitor, maybe he really was just trying to frighten him into behaving, like Pembroke says."

"It is okay," Roald said. "I am with you guys all the way. We are the Investigators' Guild! We took an oath."

"We did?" Emmett whispered. "What o—?"

Molly elbowed him. "That's right, the Investigators'

Oath," said Molly. "None of us can say a word about this to anyone."

"Investigators!" Roald cheered. "Let us go find the killer!"

"What?" Emmett said. "No one's been killed!"

Roald threw his arms in the air. "I thought this was a mystery!"

"It is," said Molly. "Just not a murder mystery."

"There is another kind?" Roald shook his head as they went off to interrogate their first suspect. "You people do not know how to do mysteries."

Interrogation!

MOLLY FOUND AGENT Archibald Forrest just where she'd left him—reading in the slatted deck chair by the bow of the ship. She wondered if the man did any work at all. He wore his black suit pants, but no jacket or tie, and his shirtsleeves were rolled up—probably because temperatures had surpassed ninety degrees. He was also wearing spectacles with lenses so strangely dark that Molly had no idea how he could read through them.

Roald tapped her on the shoulder. "Tell me again why we are starting with the only man who does not have a beard."

"Background research," Molly said. "Forrest should know everything there is to know about the others."

"He is a mind reader?" Roald asked.

"No," said Emmett. "But let me guess—you are. And you're very good at it."

"Do not be silly," Roald scoffed. "Mind reading is not real. I was making a joke. It was a very good joke."

"Hey, Archie," Molly called out. "Enjoying my book?"

"Why, Miss Pepper, is this yours?" Forrest said. He folded the corner of a page to mark his place and Molly had to hold herself back from throttling him. "We should discuss it sometime," he continued. "That Captain Nemo is a very intriguing character—operating outside the law, but holding himself to such strict moral standards."

"I didn't realize you wore glasses," Molly said.

Forrest removed his tinted lenses and gave her a sly wink. "Oh, these are just sun-blockers. As you can see, my eyes are perfectly fine."

Molly adjusted her own spectacles, which were sliding down her sweaty nose. "You can see through those?"

"Quite clearly," said Forrest. "Alec crafted them for me. The man tries so desperately to win my approval. It's a little sad, really. Anyway, lovely chatting with you." He reopened the book, then closed it again. "Unless, Molly, your mother sent you. Does your mother need something? I offered to lend a hand with her little project, you know." He flexed his biceps.

"If she's in need of any grease, I'm sure she'll ask you to wring out your hair," Molly said.

Forrest smiled a fake nothing-can-bother-me smile and put his sun-blockers back on. "Good day, children."

"But we cannot leave yet, Mr. Archie," Roald said.

"We have not interrogated you."

Molly slapped her forehead.

Forrest peeked over the tops of his dark glasses. "Interrogated?"

"He, um, used the wrong word," Emmett said quickly.

"Interrogate means to ask questions with the intention of extracting information that a person does not want to reveal," said Robot. "Is that not what we are doing?"

Molly slapped her forehead again.

"You're going to leave a mark if you keep doing that," said Forrest. "So you kids want to interrogate me? About what, might I ask?"

"Okay, so, yeah, we want to ask you some questions," Molly said, hoping she could still smooth this out. "But not because we suspect you of anything."

"You do not even have a beard," said Roald.

Forrest raised an eyebrow.

"It's the others we're worried about, Archie," said Molly. "We don't know *anything* about the crew. And here we are, just women and children, all alone with these big, brawny strangers. We were hoping you could . . . ease our minds about them." She hated playing the frightened damsel, but Forrest seemed to be falling for it.

He took off his sun-blockers. "There's nothing to worry about," he said.

"So, when you interviewed all these men before you

left, nothing sketchy turned up?" Emmett said.

"No shady pasts?" Molly added.

"No murderers?" tried Roald. "Or werewolves?"

"Listen, kids," Forrest said. "I wouldn't have approved anybody for this mission if they didn't meet the agency's high security standards."

"So, no werewolves?" Roald sounded disappointed.

"But who *are* these guys? What can you tell us about them?" Molly asked.

Forrest cleared his throat. "Captain Caleb Stone, former US Navy. Also an explorer of some renown, having been among the first to map seventeen different Polynesian islands. Icepick Mahoney, veteran of Adolphus Greely's arctic expedition that set the current record for Farthest North. And Lars Sorenson, a thirty-year career mariner who's sailed just about every corner of the Earth—also this kid's uncle. Roald, you couldn't tell them about your uncle?"

"They did not ask me," said Roald.

Forrest sighed impatiently. "There aren't many men alive who can serve as both seamen *and* polar explorers. Trust me, these names top the list."

"Please don't take this the wrong way," said Emmett. "Because I'm sure you did an incredibly thorough job, and that those *names* belong to trustworthy men. But can you guarantee that everyone on this ship is who they say they are?"

Forrest smoothed his mustache. "No," he said. "There are four people on this ship whom I cannot vouch for: Emmett Lee, Molly Pepper, Cassandra Pepper, and the one who calls herself Katrina von Malcontent."

"Do not forget me," said Robot. "I might not really be Robot. But I am."

"Actually, I've been remiss in my duties," Forrest said. He set down the book. "I really should put you all through the same interview process as the others. Let's start now. Have you or anybody in your family ever been arrested?"

Molly and Emmett exchanged glances, but said nothing.

"Have you ever associated with known criminals?" Forrest asked.

The sun suddenly felt hotter. Sweat began pouring down their foreheads, their backs, their necks. Molly wondered if Forrest had been in the Communications Room yet today, if he'd noticed the missing wires.

"Have you or any member of your family ever been institutionalized for—"

"You know what?" said Emmett. "We can trust you. Come, let's not bother the nice man anymore."

Forrest sat back and reopened his book, and the Investigators' Guild hurried away. Before they disappeared around the corner, Molly popped back for a final word: "Use a bookmark, you animal!"

*   *   *

Crouched behind rain barrels, the children watched Icepick Mahoney stomp a foot pedal like he was trying to crush an enormous bug. Every press of the pedal helped reel in a long, heavy chain, at the end of which dangled a huge net of fish. The trollish man pulled a knob, releasing the fish to the deck, and then proceeded to pull them apart with his bare hands. He tossed flopping bodies in a bin labeled "Food" and dripping heads into one labeled "Chum." With each de-heading, he let out the triumphant grunt of a man who truly enjoyed his work. One particularly stubborn fish head seemed to be giving him trouble, so he bit it off. And didn't spit it out.

"Let's do him later," said Molly. The others nodded and they left.

Lars Sorenson hunched over a glass table in a room that was practically wallpapered with maps. His thick fingers awkwardly gripped a tiny pencil as he sketched a path onto a map of the lower Atlantic that was illuminated from beneath by electric light. When he was done, Lars pressed a button that caused the map to be rolled up by a set of mechanical arms.

"Do we really have to interrogate Uncle Lars?" Roald asked the investigators. "I know him. He is definitely Uncle Lars." For the first time since they'd met him, Roald seemed unsure and uncomfortable.

"He does have a beard, though," Molly reminded him.

"Why don't we let Roald take the lead on this one," Emmett suggested.

Molly narrowed her eyes.

"No, really. If I was in his shoes—if it was my father, say—I'd feel better asking the questions myself," Emmett said. "Besides, Roald knows Lars better than anyone."

"I will not let you down," Roald said, saluting.

"I hope you know what you're doing," Molly said to Emmett.

"Uncle Lars!" Roald bounded into the map room, beating his chest.

"Little Roald!" Lars beat his chest as well.

"I am not so little," Roald said, more soberly. "Uncle Lars, we have a mystery and we would like to make an interrogation of you."

Emmett slapped his forehead.

But Lars seemed unfazed. "Sounds fun! Go ahead," he said, chuckling.

"Uncle Lars, you know the man in the brig? Somebody had a secret meeting with him last night," Roald said.

Lars laughed. "I guess it was not so secret if you know about it, eh?"

"Okay!" Molly went to step in. "Time to—"

"Did *you* know about that meeting, Uncle Lars?" Roald asked.

Lars stopped laughing and sank in his seat. "You got me. I know all about the secret meeting."

"Holy cheese curds," Molly whispered. "Roald got a confession."

"Tell me about the secret meeting, Uncle Lars!" Roald was bouncing.

"Oh, the meeting was *so* secret," Lars said, wiggling his fingers mysteriously. "Because the people at that meeting had to cover up—"

"A murder!" Roald yelled.

"Yes!" Lars said. "A murder!"

Emmett looked to Molly. "Really?"

"And do you know who the murderer was?" Lars asked.

"A werewolf!" Roald squealed.

"That's right!" Lars roared. His face was red with laughter as he patted his nephew on the shoulder. "Oh, that was a good one, Roald. Let's do another later and maybe you can let one of your friends play detective next time. I've got to get back to the maps now, or the captain will have my hide."

Roald walked away, beaming proudly.

"What just happened?" Emmett asked Molly.

"Lars thought it was a game, didn't he?" said Molly.

"Yes," Emmett said. "But did Roald?"

"I was entertained," said Robot.

Molly could not say the same.

* * *

Peeking out from behind the privy, the kids watched as Icepick mopped a deck fouled with gloppy fish guts. The big man snarled angrily at a dark burgundy splotch, pushing the mop harder and faster until it seemed he might burrow straight through the wood. When the stain still remained, Icepick howled and broke the mop over his own head.

"There's no reason we *have* to do him next," Emmett said.

Molly shook her head.

Captain Stone sighed heavily when the children entered the wheelhouse.

"Ahoy, Cap'n," Molly said cordially. The others stayed by the door, as Molly had instructed. "Having a good day driving the boat?"

"Until now," the captain replied. He didn't bother turning around.

"So," Molly said. "That was pretty heroic of you to go out there and rescue Pembroke like that."

The captain said nothing.

"You didn't seem very happy to learn he was a criminal, though," Molly went on. "Don't like having untrustworthy people on your boat, huh?"

"No."

"I bet you'd want to make sure he behaved himself

while he was on board, right?" she tried. "I'd completely understand if you were tempted to . . . intimidate him. Know what I mean?"

"No."

"You know, pop into the brig and scare some sense into him?"

Captain Stone gave her a quick glance over his shoulder. "Not my style."

Three words! This was serious progress. "So, what *is* your style?" she asked.

"Honesty," Stone said. "So be honest with me: What are you getting at?"

Molly wasn't expecting that. Did he know something? Could he help them? Or was he hiding something? Or was she just getting the man angry? She checked back with the others. Emmett was shaking his head. Robot was nodding. Roald was following a fly around the room.

"Nothing, sir," Molly said. "Sorry to bother you." Captain Stone was too difficult to talk to. He wasn't even fun to annoy. He just made her feel cold inside. She left the wheelhouse, feeling defeated.

This time Icepick was picking under his toenails with the bill of a swordfish.

"Time to talk to Mr. Bell," said Emmett.

* * *

Alexander Graham Bell was pacing the lounge and pulling at his beard when the children entered with Robot. "Oh," he said, looking up. "Are you finally ready for me to conduct my examination of our automaton?"

The investigators turned around and left.

"Excuse me, Mr. Icepick?"

Icepick sat on an overturned bucket jamming heavy iron hooks through slick, wet fish heads. He looked up and snarled. "Why are you talking to me?" Without warning, he slammed his fist against the wall, leaving a dent in the metal exterior. "I don't like being disturbed while I'm working."

Molly cursed her legs for shaking. "We, um, we just wanted to—"

"What?" Icepick barked.

"We were hoping to . . ." Emmett couldn't get it out either. "Roald, why don't *you* ask?"

"Because he is scary," said Roald.

"Has somebody given this man a balloon?" Robot asked. "He looks very unhappy."

"Get out of here," Icepick snarled. "Or I swear I'll feed the lot of you to the piranhas."

Emmett raised his finger. "Piranhas are, um, freshwater fish, actually."

"Enough!" Icepick snapped. "Out!"

"No, no, wait! Where were you yesterday about thirty

195

minutes after Pembroke was put in the brig?" Molly rattled off the question so quickly, she barely understood her own words.

"What is this, some kind of interrogation?"

"*Ja, ja!* That is it!" Roald said, and then covered his head.

"I was here!" Droplets of angry spittle caught in his wiry beard. "Doing this!" He squeezed the fish head in his hand until pink-gray goo burst between his fingers.

The children ran, the bucket Icepick threw at them narrowly missing Molly's head. "You just *had* to correct him about the piranhas," she grumbled.

A gull squawked somewhere in the distance. Molly had read enough seafaring tales to know that meant they couldn't be too far from land. "Time is of the essence, people," she said, sitting on the deck with her back against the rail. "Did we learn *anything* today? Other than that Icepick is a maniac, the captain is grumpy, Forrest is an obnoxious pig, and Lars is a big goof? No offense, Roald."

"None taken," said Roald. "I like goofs."

"I learned that there are wet, mushy things inside fish," said Robot.

Emmett sat down next to Molly and shielded his eyes from the sun. "You gave it a shot," he said. "But not everything works out. We'll talk to your mother and—"

"No," Molly said brusquely. "She can't be distracted

from her work. If she doesn't wow Bell with those designs, he's gonna force us off at Barbados. That means we never get to Antarctica, never find the South Pole, never become famous, never get to find out if your father left you a message."

"I am very good at finding things," said Roald.

"Please stay out of this, Roald." Emmett gritted his teeth in exasperation. "I understand the stakes here, Molly. But what if Mr. Bell isn't the only one who could ruin things for us? You obviously think our mysterious traitor is a threat too. And I agree, considering the connections to Rector and the Onions."

"Exactly! The guy could be dangerous," Molly said, jumping to her feet. "That's why we have to find him ourselves. I can't risk losing my mother again."

"But you're fine risking me?" Emmett said, standing and turning his back to her. "Well, that explains a lot."

"That's not what I was saying," she replied. "My mother and I have a very special connection, but that doesn't mean—"

"Oh, that's right, I wouldn't know anything about parent-child bonds." Emmett faced her bitterly. "You know, since I never knew my mother and my father was never around like yours was, right?"

"Hey, it's not my fault what your father did or didn't do," Molly shot back.

"No, it's mine, right? I get it—you were a better child

than I was. You sacrificed everything for your mother, while I selfishly clung to my own goals and interests, instead of just pretending and becoming the person my father wanted me to be."

"You're twisting my words," Molly said.

"I don't know," said Emmett. "They're coming out pretty twisted on their own."

"You know," said Roald, "my father—"

"Stay out of it!" Emmett barked. He turned back to Molly. "Look, you do what you need to do, but I'm done here. I'm out of your little detective club."

Molly's gut clenched. "If that's what you really want—"

"It is."

"Can you—can you please still not tell my mother? Even if you won't help, can you just let me finish this?"

Emmett paused. "I won't tell her," he said. "And you can trust me on that. Because *I* would never lie about something important."

"Fine, Emmett! I lied to you!" Molly cried. "But you *know* why I did it. You said you understood. So why can't you just get over it and forgive me already?"

"Because I trusted you!" Emmett snapped back. His eyes were watery. "Do you have any idea how hard that is for me? The only person I ever really trusted was my father. My whole life revolved around him, even when he wasn't there. I trusted him to take care of me, to educate me, to feed me. I hated that he went away so much, but I trusted him to always come back. And then he didn't.

I didn't know if I'd ever be able to trust another human being again. Until you came along, Molly. And you got me to trust you. You and your mother made me feel safe again for the first time in years. So, yeah, it hurt when you broke that trust. And I don't know how I'm going to get over it."

Molly dabbed her eyes with her sleeve. "So you hate me now?"

"No!" Emmett threw his arms in the air. "Why can't you understand that a person can feel two different— Aargh! I can't do this now!"

"That is all right," said Roald. "I can do it for you. I am very good at understanding people. Molly, I think Emmett—"

"What is your problem, Roald?" Emmett snapped. "This is between me and Molly! Why are you even here?"

"To help," the cabin boy said. "I am very good at helping."

"No, you're not!" Emmett yelled. "You're not good at everything! You know what you're good at? Annoying people with your ridiculous, endless bragging! You're so desperate to make people like you, and you're so bad at it! Go play with your uncle!"

Emmett ran off.

Molly had never seen Roald so deflated. His eyes were red, his shoulders slumped. "I think some of that was really aimed at me, Roald," Molly said.

"No, Emmett was speaking to Roald," said Robot.

"Roald is the one who annoys people by bragging about himself."

"I will leave now," Roald sniffed. He walked off slowly, his head hung low. Molly considered calling out to him, but didn't. She didn't really want to speak to anybody.

"What are we investigating now?" Robot asked.

Molly huffed. "Nothing."

"Am I still an investigator?" Robot asked.

"No, Robot," she grumbled. "The Investigators' Guild is officially disbanded."

"What should I do, then?" Robot asked.

"I don't know!" she barked. "Jeez, Robot! Do whatever you want! Just—just leave me alone."

"All right." Robot soared off into the sky, and Molly immediately began kicking herself. She'd just given the most literal mind she knew the vaguest directions ever. Who knew when she would see him again?

She wandered the ship until the sun plunked below the horizon like a penny into a piggy bank, making whatever quick turns or about-faces she needed to in order to avoid other people. As dusk fell, she nestled between a pair of barrels on the aft deck and chewed some of Nellie's salvaged jerky in lieu of visiting the mess hall for dinner. She wondered if Emmett was in there dining with the others. And if Roald was, and how awkward that must be. She wondered if her mother was questioning her absence. Or even noticing it, since the woman hadn't so much as checked on her once in the past forty-eight hours. Molly sighed. She'd finally pushed her mother back into inventing; she should be ecstatic. So why was she sitting alone in the dark, feeling for all the world like a girl who just wanted her mother's arms around her. Ugh. Why couldn't a child's feelings about their parents ever be simple?

She reached into her pocket and pulled out the frayed wires she'd torn from the telegraph, her trophy from the one thing she'd done right on this voyage. *I don't deserve these*, she thought, and threw them into the sea.

Molly sighed again at the sound of approaching footsteps. Still not in the mood for conversation, she scooted as far as she could into the shadows behind the barrels. As she did, her elbow mashed into a button on the wall and a panel slid open. Molly froze and waited for the person to pass before shifting onto her knees and peering into the hidden compartment. It was too dark to see anything, so she cautiously reached a hand inside and felt around. She flinched when her hand grabbed on to something soft and hairy. *A rat!* No. The hair pile didn't move. Holding her breath, she pulled the furry thing from the hole in the wall and held it in the moonlight.

It was a fake beard.

17

"And the Culprit Is . . ."

"WHAT'S THE MEANING of this?" Alexander Graham Bell asked as he walked, bleary-eyed, into the hazy morning sun, waving the note that had been slipped under his door. The note, written in pencil, said, "Emergency Meeting on Central Deck, 0700 hours. MISS IT AND YOU WILL BE KEELHAULED!" And then it had a drawing of an angry pirate.

Lars, Icepick, Roald, and Emmett were already there, grumbling with varying levels of impatience. "I don't know anything about it," Emmett said. "We all got the same note."

Bell looked at Emmett's note. "Hmmph. Why doesn't my pirate have a parrot?"

"What's the emergency?" Cassandra and Nellie hurried to join the others on the deck.

202

"*You* don't know?" Bell asked. "I assumed you had something to do with this."

"There's going to *be* an emergency, if something doesn't happen soon," Icepick snarled.

"Okay, whose idea was this?" Agent Forrest said, stretching and yawning. "Because I explicitly told you all that my mornings don't start until nine."

"I am the only person on this ship who should be calling meetings," Captain Stone said as he approached. "And I didn't write these notes."

"I wrote them." Molly popped from her hiding spot in a crate of fishing tackle and stepped into the circle of people.

"What's this about, Molls?" her mother asked.

"Yeah," Emmett said slowly. He looked hyperalert, as if expecting a jaguar to pounce. "I hope you know what you're doing."

Captain Stone crossed his arms.

"Do you even know what keelhauling means?" Forrest asked through a yawn.

"I can show her," Icepick threatened.

"I called this meeting," Molly said, "because we have an imposter among us." She paced the circle with her hands clasped behind her back. "It all started shortly after Pembroke was brought on board. I overheard someone talking to him in the brig. I couldn't hear everything, but it definitely sounded like the two were in cahoots. We interrogated Pembroke and—"

"You what?" Cassandra asked.

"Please, let me continue."

"Are you certain you want to do this?" Nellie asked in a cautionary tone.

"I know exactly what I'm doing," Molly said. She noticed Emmett looking green, even though he hadn't been seasick in days. He really didn't trust her. She needed to change that. "Pembroke said he didn't know the person who spoke to him," Molly continued, "but that the person had a beard. Then, last night, I found . . . this!" She pulled the false beard from behind her back. People began shooting one another looks of confusion, skepticism, and suspicion. "This disguise confirmed my theory that someone on board this ship is not who they say they are," she continued. "But which one of you? Who does this fake beard belong to?"

This key piece of evidence had helped Molly narrow the culprit down to one of two people: Agent Forrest or Nellie Bly. She had her reasons for suspecting both, but only one, in her opinion, had revealed their true colors.

"Our traitor," Molly announced, "is the one man here without a real beard: Agent Archibald Forrest!" She mashed the faux facial hair against Forrest's mouth.

"Archie, is this true?" Bell asked, horrified.

"Pah!" Forrest swatted the beard away. "Of course it's not true. I would never wear such an unflattering disguise. You know girls and their wild imaginations. Also, you don't get to call me Archie."

Molly refused to let Forrest smooth-talk his way out of this. "If you're so innocent, why are you sweating?"

"Because it's a hundred and fifty degrees," Forrest said. But everybody's eyes were on him. "The rest of you aren't buying into this, are you? Cass, can you please put a leash on your daughter?"

"Don't listen to him," Molly appealed to the others. "You've gotta throw Forrest in the brig with Pembroke until we find out what he's up to! I'm telling you, Forrest is the bad guy!"

"Nice try," Nellie said.

Molly whipped around. "What?"

"Someone is up to no good on this ship," Nellie said. "But it's not Agent Forrest."

She stepped forth and took the beard from Molly. *No,* Molly thought, suddenly shaky. How could she have been so wrong? She'd trusted Emmett and his estimation of Nellie. The woman had defended her mother. But *why* if she was also—?

"You see, I've been conducting an investigation of my own," said Nellie. "And while Molly was correct about there being a traitor in our midst—she had the wrong man."

So Nellie isn't the traitor? Molly thought. *She's just trying to show me up by proving herself a better investigator?*

That might actually be worse.

"The traitor," Nellie went on, "is still wearing a false beard now. He needs multiple backup beards because he is such a messy eater that he constantly gets fish innards stuck in the whiskers. Isn't that right . . . Icepick Mahoney?" Shocking the big man, Nellie gave Icepick's whiskers a powerful yank, peeling them straight off his face. There were gasps as Icepick leapt back and threw his meaty hands to his chafed, red cheeks.

"Drat," Molly cursed.

"So, what do you have to say for yourself, Mr. Mahoney?" Nellie asked proudly.

"Heh. I say you can wipe that know-it-all smile off yer face," he snarled. "'Cause that other beard ain't even mine! The little girl was right—that one's Forrest's. He just thought he was too handsome to wear it. So, ha!"

"Idiot," Agent Forrest muttered, rolling his eyes.

Molly and Nellie exchanged looks. "I'm confused now," Molly said. "Were we both right?"

"Both right—and still, so wrong," said Captain Stone. He sighed. "You ladies really do ruin everything, don't you?" His voice had changed. "I suppose this is my fault for hiring morons. But the damage is done, nonetheless. On the bright side, I suppose we can *all* chuck our disguises now. It really is far too hot for extra fur on the face, anyway."

Captain Stone peeled away his own beard and flung

it overboard. Then he pulled off fake eyebrows, a fake nose, and a wig. Molly staggered backward upon seeing the new face of Captain Caleb Stone.

"That's right, it's me—your old pal Ambrose Rector!"

Bell spoke for everyone when he stammered, "I—I—I don't understand."

"Of course you don't, Bell," Rector said. "You never understand anything. And based on the gawking faces behind you, you're not alone in your befuddlement." He removed his coat—and with it, the padding that had made him look more broad-shouldered and muscular. "So, let me educate you," he said with excitement. "Oh man, I missed this part. The talking, I mean. Do you have any idea what torture it was to stay in the persona of that boring stick of lumber, Captain Stone? Ugh, it killed me. Figuratively. Not in the actual way that I'm going to kill you."

"Agent Forrest, what—what are you standing there for?" Bell shouted. "That's Rector! The man we're after! Arrest him!"

"Um, Mr. Bell, I'm pretty sure Forrest is working for Rector," Emmett said.

Bell frowned. "Oh, Archie. You disappoint me so."

"Agent Forrest. You call me Agent Forrest."

"Why?" Molly snapped at him. "You're not even a real federal agent!"

"Oh, but I am," Forrest said. "Just an easily corruptible one."

Rector, laughing, wiped a tear from his eye. "Looks like you so-called detectives couldn't see the Forrest for the treason. See what I did there? With the punning? Never mind. You people are the worst. Although not as bad as Forrest. He really is the worst. Which was admittedly a lucky stroke for me. I approached him months ago, as soon as I found out he would be the man responsible for approving Bell's expedition crew. I was fully prepared to blackmail or threaten him into helping me, but it turns out all the man needs to make him betray his country is a big pile of cash."

Forrest shrugged. "I'm easy."

"With Agent Forrest on my payroll, it was simple enough to fill Bell's entire crew with loyal henchmen," Rector said.

"The entire crew?" Roald asked, shocked. "Even Uncle Lars?"

Lars pulled off his beard. "*Ja*, it's true, boy. I am a criminal," he said apologetically. "But also a good uncle, eh? I am still taking you to the South Pole like you wanted, no?" He chuckled and ruffled his nephew's hair. Roald stared blankly.

"Yes, Lars here has smuggled stolen goods from seventy-three different countries," Rector said with admiration. "With his experience in lawbreaking *and* seafaring, he was perfect for my team. And kudos to you, Lars, for being the only one on this cruise to successfully hide his secret from a couple of snoopy kids. You win.

Here, this is for you." He handed Lars a small metal pin from his pocket.

"Ooh, thank you for the honor, sir," Lars said, popping the pin onto his collar. "Look, Roald, how many uncles win the Best Henchman award, eh?"

Rector leaned over and whispered to Molly, "He's an idiot too. That was a safety pin."

Molly struggled to keep her face free of emotion. She despised this man and his attempts to endear himself to her. Did Rector still think that Molly was anything like him? Could the man actually be dumb enough to still hope she would join him on his trek to Antarc—

Molly slumped. She *had* joined him on his trek to Antarctica! He'd made it happen. She'd walked right into it.

"So, Mr. Icepick over there is actually an accomplished mariner as well?" Bell asked.

"Him?" Rector said. "Heavens, no—he's just a maniac. I'm not sure he's ever seen a boat before."

"I strangled a man in a canoe once," said Icepick.

Cassandra cleared her throat. "I'm still in the dark on something. You told us *how* you managed to take control of Bell's crew, but *why* put yourself through the trouble? You already had the *Frost Cleaver*—why not just sail back that ship?"

"Excellent question, Mrs. Pepper," Rector said. "And I will give you an excellent answer: revenge, the oldest motive known to man. I'm not above admitting that in addition to global domination, I also yearn to rub my success in Bell's scruffy face like a wad of spiteful shaving cream. Why Bell, you ask?"

"Did someone ask that?" said Emmett. "I don't think anybody asked that. We all know you hate Mr. Bell."

"It's because Alec here is the one who started it all," Rector continued. He had a far-off look, as if he was seeing something no one else could. "Sure, I *could* have taken his mediocre *Frost Cleaver* down south, scooped up some Ambrosium, and zipped back to conquer the world, but that wouldn't have felt *personal* enough. I wanted to add a bit of poetic justice to my ultimate victory, by leaving Alexander Graham Bell to die on Antarctica the same way he left me."

"I wasn't even on the *Frost Cleaver!*" Bell protested. "If you're going to blame anyone, blame the crew. They're the ones who—"

"My father was on that ship," Emmett interjected. He looked Rector in the eye. "And he never did a thing to hurt you. He thought you were his friend. And you still abandoned him to a slow, painful death."

"Ooh, I see Molly has finally shared that juicy secret," Rector said. He put his hand to his mouth, feigning embarrassment. "And it only took . . . four months? Ouch. That's gotta be awkward."

Emmett seethed silently.

"But, hey, at least she eventually came clean," Rector continued. "Unlike a certain co-director of the Inventors'

Guild who *still* won't accept responsibility for what he did to me! So I'm going to *make* him take responsibility. *That*, Mrs. Pepper, is why I felt the need to guile my way onto this ship—to fight fire with fire. Or in this case, ice with ice."

Nellie looked shell-shocked. "I can't believe this was all right under my nose and I didn't see it."

Rector pouted with feigned sympathy. "Don't be so hard on yourself, Miss Bly—yes, I know who you really are—I doubt anyone could have uncovered my ingenious scheme. My favorite part was how I got the police off my back by paying Mr. Pembroke and his Green Onion buddies to publicly sail off in the *Frost Cleaver* and make everyone think I was already long gone. Classic. And everything was working so perfectly until the uninvited appearance of the Pepper Family Players and their Pet Trash Can. Wait . . . where *is* that aluminum demon?" He hunched into a defensive stance and looked around, as if expecting Robot to swoop from the sky and sock him in the jaw.

"He's gone," Molly said, a plan percolating in her mind. "As soon as I suspected foul play, I sent him ahead to Barbados to notify the authorities. By the time we get there, there'll be an army waiting." She felt both proud of this excellent lie and frustrated with herself for not having thought of it early enough to make it true.

"You're bluffing," Rector said. But he sounded tentative.

"Nope, Robot has already gotten the word out," Molly insisted. "You're going to jail the moment we dock in Barbados."

Rector cracked his knuckles anxiously. Molly held her breath.

"We could just *not* stop in Barbados," said Forrest. "We were only going there to drop this bunch off, but you're obviously not going to do that now. You know, since you've told them your entire plan. So, let's skip it. Any supplies we need, we can pick up at a port along the South American coast."

Rector grinned. "I knew there was a reason I hired you, Archie. Well, *another* reason."

"Great, that's settled," said Forrest. "So, what do we do with these folks now? Because I'm still not happy about being made to wake up this early. I need at least another ninety minutes of sleep."

"The brig," Rector ordered. "Oh, and you can let Pembroke out. No reason to keep him locked up any longer. Unless we just want to be cruel. Who wants to keep Pembroke locked up just to be cruel?"

Only Icepick raised his hand.

"Fine, let him out," Rector said, disappointed.

Forrest, Lars, and Icepick began ushering away the stunned prisoners. Icepick stopped and grabbed Roald by the hair. "What about this one?"

"Oh, yes, Moldy-Roaldy," Rector said. "Well, you

might not have been an official member of Team Rector from the start—in fact, I never wanted you on this trip to begin with; your uncle just showed up with you—"

"The boy *really* wanted to see the South Pole," Lars said. "How could I say no to his baby-seal face? Do the face, Roald."

Roald's face remained flat.

"You need to make a choice, Roald," said Rector. "Squeeze into that crowded, sweltering cell with the others, or take your place at your uncle's side and fulfill your dream of reaching the South Pole."

Molly began seriously regretting the things she and Emmett had said to him the day before.

"Who's your favorite uncle, boy?" Lars said, holding his arms open. "Who taught you how to climb a tree? And how to swear in five different languages?"

"And who taught me how to hide a knife in my sock and dance the Peloponnesian Jig?" Roald grinned with pride and ran to his uncle.

Molly dropped her head and made a solemn march to the brig. Everything she'd been hoping to accomplish had just become a whole lot harder.

Floating Prison

"WHOEVER'S ELBOW IS in my armpit, can you please remove it?" Molly grunted as she slid herself along the cold tin floor of the prison cell, trying to get herself into a position remotely resembling comfort.

"There's a free inch and a half next to me on the cot here, darling," Cassandra offered. Molly tried to climb to the bed using Emmett's back as a stepping-stone, but ended up sliding into the space between the cot and the wall.

"Ugh, why'd you make this cell so small?" Molly grumbled.

"It was only meant to hold one person!" Bell retorted from the other end of the tiny cot.

"And that person is running free around your ship," Emmett said bitterly. He sat by the bars with his knees pulled up to his chest, spinning his father's ring.

Bell dropped his head. *Wow*, Molly thought. Emmett was the one person who always stood by Bell. *Getting zinged by him must hit the old guy pretty hard.* Or maybe he was just down because it was now clear that Agent Forrest was never going to be his best friend.

"A word of advice, Mr. B.," Molly said. "From now on, whenever you meet someone, first thing you do is pull their beard."

"There's no need to throw blame around," said Bell.

"Of course not," said Cassandra. "We all know it's your fault."

"And mine," Nellie said gloomily. "I'm the news bear. I sniff out the truth. That's what I do. But I didn't."

"Hey, at least you were just as right as I was," said Molly.

"That doesn't help," Nellie replied. "I let myself down. Even now, look at me—I'm at the heart of the biggest story of our time and I'm moping here, beating myself up instead of working on it. I mean, I don't have my notebooks, but I can work in my head. Writers are always working, you know. Even if you can't see it. Half the time I'm talking to you, I'm also thinking about why you chose one specific word over another, which expressions on your face I should describe, whether or not the loose threads on your sleeve are an important detail to mention. It can be quite exhausting."

"Wow," Molly said. "Maybe the break in jail will do you good."

"Jailbreak!" Cassandra said perkily. "That's what we need to do. Come on, people. It's a little tight in here, but we should be grateful that Alec only built this vessel with one cell, otherwise Rector might have separated us. But as it stands, he's made a serious miscalculation by allowing us all this free time to make a plan together."

"Two months of it," Bell muttered. "I fear there's not much we can do until we reach Antarctica."

"You mean when Rector tosses us into the snow to die of frostbite and starvation?" Emmett said. "No thanks, I'd rather think of a plan before then."

"Rector only said he intends to maroon *me* on the ice," Bell replied. "We don't know what he has in store for the rest of you."

"True, he might just murder us outright," Emmett said. "Thanks, I feel much better now."

"Don't worry, Emmett," Cassandra said soothingly. "Peppers never give up." She tried to pat him on the shoulder but couldn't manage to get her arm close enough, so she did it with her foot.

The five prisoners sat, pressed against one another, yet staring off in different directions, as their bodies swayed with the undulations of the speeding ship. The silence was as uncomfortable as the accommodations.

"First thing we need to do is get out of this cell," Nellie eventually said.

"So, you're going to help us?" Molly asked hopefully.

"My notebooks are out there," said Nellie. "So, yes, let's figure a way out of here. Then we head straight for Forrest's telegraph and send out a distress call."

Molly cringed. "That's, um, not going to work."

"It sounds like a fine plan to me," said Bell.

"Except I sort of sabotaged the telegraph machine," Molly confessed. "Tore all the wires out."

Nellie slumped.

"Don't despair," Bell said. "Wires can be reattached. Where are they?"

"The ocean," Molly said sheepishly.

Bell sighed. "Okay, you can despair now."

"No, we're getting ahead of ourselves," Emmett said. "Let's focus on getting out of this cell first."

"Yeah," said Molly. "Most of you people are inventors; one of you must know how to fashion a lockpick out of some spit and a shoelace or something?"

Bell was unenthusiastic. "Say we do break out—what then?" he said. "Escape in a dinghy? We've turned away from Barbados, getting farther from land by the minute. Even if we had the stamina to row to port from here, we couldn't possibly outrun the *AquaZephyr*. Rector would just recapture us."

"It *would* be a lot easier to sneak off this ship if we had some land to sneak *onto*," Cassandra admitted.

"Who knows when that will happen," said Nellie.

"Somewhere along South America, Bell said. That could be weeks from now."

"Then we need to give Rector a reason to turn back to Barbados before we get too far," said Molly.

"Unlikely when he knows Robot has the police waiting for him there," Bell said.

"I'll tell him I made that up," said Molly.

"He won't believe you."

"But I did make it up," said Molly.

Emmett shook his head. "Another lie?"

"I didn't lie to you—I lied to Rector! I'm telling *you* the truth."

"Okay, that one I can forgive," Emmett said. "But where *is* Robot then?"

Molly shook her head. "I have no idea."

"How do you lose a six-foot-tall man made of metal?" Bell asked.

"Asks the man who built him and hasn't seen him for five months," Molly retorted.

"Touché," Bell mumbled.

"Mother! Your snow-crawler!" Molly said with a burst of enthusiasm. "Rector probably still wants it. If we tell him there's no danger in Barbados, maybe we can still convince him he needs to stop there to get parts for the snow-crawler. Tell him waiting until South America won't give you enough time to—"

"There is no snow-crawler," Cassandra said bluntly.

"What?"

Cassandra looked directly at Molly. "I have no viable design for turning this ship into some kind of giant spider-walking vehicle. I only said I did to buy us some time, Molls."

Molly was stricken. "Then what—what have you been doing all this time?"

"Trying to come up with some *other* idea to keep us on the expedition. Something realistic," Cassandra said. "I knew you wouldn't approve of anything that didn't involve me inventing on the spot. That's why I sent you and Emmett away."

Molly's eyes grew red and her jaw tightened. "So you lied to me? You didn't even *try* to come up with a design? And why? Because you thought I couldn't handle the truth?" She turned to Emmett. "I am so, so sorry."

"Now, now, Molly," Bell cautioned. "I never truly believed the snow-crawler concept would work. I was simply humoring you as well. You can't blame your mother for being unable to achieve the impossible."

"What are you talking about?" Emmett said. "'Achieve the Impossible' is the Inventors' Guild slogan! Maybe you should spend more time working toward that goal yourself instead of condescending to the women who believe they can. And Mrs. Pepper, we don't need lies to protect us. Molly and I know you didn't quit inventing to be a better parent; you quit because you were scared. If you can't trust people with the truth, how will they ever trust you to give them the truth?"

Cassandra sniffled in the silence that followed.

"Okay, so now that you've all made it *really* awkward in here," Nellie said, "can we get back to plotting our escape? Is there some way we could take control of the ship ourselves?"

"Commandeer the ship by force?" Bell scoffed. "Miss Bly, you have no idea how dangerous Ambrose Rector is."

"Because of his crazy super-weapons?" Nellie guessed. "What was it? The Mind-Melter? And the Magneta-Ray?"

Emmett nodded. "Those two were destroyed, but he's probably built dozens more since."

Molly felt her will seeping away like air from an old balloon. The last time they faced Rector, they had the Mothers of Invention, a whole team of automatons, and a slew of other inventions at their disposal—and even then, they barely defeated him. This time, they had nothing but their wits and their bare hands against an evil genius with machines that could probably make their heads explode at the touch of a button.

Molly jumped to her feet (and smashed her shoulder on the cot as she did).

"A bomb!" she said.

Cassandra shook her head sternly. "Molly, we are not making a bomb."

"No, listen," Molly said. "I knew there was something

off about Pembroke's story. Then it hit me . . . Boom! When Pembroke told us how the *Frost Cleaver* went down, he said there was a big, loud boom and everything went flying to pieces. Big metal pieces. That's not what happens when a ship hits a rock! That's what happens when there's a—"

"Bomb," Cassandra said. "Rector put a bomb on that ship. He never intended for it to return."

"Why would he do that?" asked Bell. "He had an ice-breaking ship powered by a magical meteorite. It was the perfect vehicle for his return to Antarctica—why destroy it?"

"What if it wasn't a special boat anymore?" Molly said.

"Oh." Cassandra's eyes widened. "Oh! Oh, that's brilliant, Molls."

"What?" Bell asked. "What's brilliant? The *Frost Cleaver* was very special. I built it. I—"

The outer door to the brig swung open and Robot floated in. The crowd in the cell fought to stifle their squeals of glee. "I have solved the mystery," Robot said. "Captain Stone is, in reality, the man you call Ambrose Rector."

"We know," Molly said, misty-eyed, reaching through the bars to grab his aluminum hand. "But how do *you* know? I thought you'd flown away forever!"

"You told me to decide something for myself," said Robot. "So I decided to continue investigating. I like investigating. Are you angry?"

"No, relieved! And impressed!" Molly's mind reeled. "I didn't realize you were able to make decisions like that for yourself."

"I don't think he *was* able," said Emmett. "Robot's becoming more . . . human."

"I am not human," said Robot.

"We know," said Cassandra. "But that rock . . ." She stared at Robot's chest plate.

"Mrs. Pepper?" Emmett asked. "Are you all right?"

Cassandra nudged Molly aside to stand at the bars. "Robot, can we peek inside you?"

Robot backed away.

"Please," Cassandra implored. "Just for a moment. No one's going to hurt you—I promise. We won't even touch you. We just need to look."

Molly's heart clenched when she realized what her mother wanted to check. "It'll be okay, Robot," she said. "We'll just look for a second."

Robot cautiously flicked the clasp on his chest plate and opened it to reveal the glowing orange stone sitting inside among a nest of gears and tubes. He kept the hatch open for exactly one second, before locking it again.

"Did it look smaller to you too, Molls?" Cassandra asked.

Molly nodded. The chunk of meteorite jammed into Robot's chest months ago had definitely diminished in size. There was still plenty there, but the difference was noticeable.

Emmett saw it too. "The Ambrosium wears down as it gets used," he said.

"That's what Molly had just figured out," Cassandra said. "It's why Rector destroyed the *Frost Cleaver*. It was out of meteor power, just a regular ship."

"And he has no new weapons either!" Molly said.

"We certainly don't know that," said Bell.

"Think, Belly-Boy," Molly said. "If Rector built a bunch of new Ambrosium-powered weapons, where are they? The guy can't resist showing off his magical super-doodads. The moment he revealed himself, he shoulda been rattling off all the creative ways he planned to kill us. But he didn't! Because he's got nothing!"

"Molly's right," said Emmett. "Rector's totally out of Ambrosium. That's why he's so desperate to go back for more. And why he needed to pull off such a convoluted plan in order to hitch a ride to get there."

"But wait, it gets better," Molly said, her excitement growing. "Remember how Rector told us he'd been eating bits of Ambrosium every day to make himself super smart? What if, without it, he's losing the intelligence he gained? What if he's turning back into the hapless twit who so annoyed you and Edison at the Guild?"

"I think you're right on that too, Molly! Look at the evidence," Emmett said. "There's Rector's tactical error in caging us all together. And remember how long it took him to even notice that Robot was missing this morning? Rector's growing vulnerable, which makes this the perfect time to strike back."

"Ha!" Molly raised her arms in victory. "Who's the news bear now, Bly?"

Nellie shook Molly's hand. "Cub," she said. "I'll give you news cub."

Cassandra remained somber. "There is one downside to the Ambrosium's rapid decay," she said. "Robot is powered by Ambrosium too."

Molly reached out and squeezed Robot's hand. "Does this mean he can . . . die?"

Emmett rested his head against the cell bars. "I'm sure that flight to Barbados and back didn't help."

Cassandra rubbed both children's shoulders. "There's plenty more space rock in Antarctica, right? Once we deal with Rector and his goons, we'll make our way down there, grab a nice new hunk of meteor, and give Robot a . . . a . . . heart transplant."

Molly nodded, but she wasn't convinced. Would that even work? Was Robot's "soul" in the rock in his chest? If they switched it out, would it change Robot? And what if he ran out of rock before they could make the switch? She couldn't bear to think about it. "You're very important to us, Robot," she said.

"Yes, I am."

"I don't suppose you know how to pick a lock?" Nellie asked the automaton.

"I do not," said Robot. "I only know how to open them with keys like this." He held up the key to their cell.

"How did you get that?" Molly asked with delight.

"Magnet powers," said Robot. He dropped the key on the floor and then made it fly back to his hand. "The key was in the pocket of the man called Lars. Now it is not." Robot cocked his head. "Was that stealing? Stealing is bad."

"It was not stealing, young man," Bell said. "Because this whole ship, including this cell and its key, belongs to me."

"I am young, but I am not a man." Robot passed the key to Bell.

"Now we can get out whenever we like!" Nellie said. "But we still need to finagle our way to Barbados. How can we force Rector to stop at the nearest possible port?"

"Boom?" Emmett tried.

"Boom," said Cassandra.

"Boom?" Bell asked, sounding nervous.

"Boom," said Molly. She gave Bell a sympathetic pat on the back. "Sorry, Belly-Boy. We've gotta wreck another one of your boats."

Tropical Getaway

NO ONE SPOKE. Which, with this group, was rather unnerving. But it had been a full thirty minutes since Robot left on his crucial mission, and tensions were too high for chitchat. The quintet of prisoners all stood in their tiny cell, listening, sweating, and waiting. It was Bell who finally broke the silence. "You do realize we've put our freedom in the hands of a machine?"

It had been decided, much to Bell's relief, that rather than resort to the dynamite, Robot would use his magnetic powers to peel back one of the steel plates on the *AquaZephyr*'s hull.

"Robot is not a normal machine, Mr. Bell," Emmett said defensively.

"No, he isn't," said Nellie. "But could that end up being a problem? If he's really growing more autonomous, what if he changes his mind and decides to . . . I don't know, put on a fake beard and join the crew?"

Cassandra snorted. "That would look so silly."

"We can trust Robot," Molly insisted. "He cares about us."

"Does he?" Bell asked.

"Well, not you, maybe," Molly replied.

"I mean to say, *can* he care about you?" Bell continued. "Even if Robot truly can 'think' for himself, 'caring' would require *emotion*. And that—"

The ship listed violently to one side and everyone tumbled into a big pile. The vessel righted itself a moment later.

"What was that?" they heard from outside. And then another muffled shout: "Did we hit *another* boat?"

The prisoners froze in their awkward positions and listened as frantic footsteps echoed around them.

"Something's wrong!" someone yelled outside.

"Lars, go belowdecks and check the engine room!" It was Rector, not far from the brig. "Forrest, head to the aft rail and—!"

"I don't do that stuff," Forrest replied.

"Icepick, head to the aft rail and take a look at the rudder," Rector ordered. "And punch Agent Forrest on your way."

"*Ow!*"

"Hull's been breached!" yelled Lars. "We're taking on water!"

"Out of my way, buffoons!"

Inside the brig, the prisoners could only guess as to what was happening amid all the hollering and commotion. Eventually, the door opened and Forrest peered in. "They're all present and accounted for!" he shouted.

Then he stepped inside and shut the door behind him. "None of you would happen to know anything about how a gaping hole was torn into our hull seemingly out of nowhere, would you?" he asked softly.

"I think you've been spending too much time in the company of hooligans and madmen, Agent Forrest," Cassandra said. "You're beginning to sound as paranoid as they do."

"I figured you'd deny it," Forrest said. "But if you did somehow have anything to do with it . . . well, I just hope no one gets any more foolish ideas. Trust me, you're better off just keeping quiet and following orders."

"Thanks," said Cassandra. "But we don't need advice from the likes of you." She crossed her arms and sat down in a manner that was clearly meant to convey how cool and unflappable she was. It might have been successful had she not sat on top of Nellie.

"Listen, Cass," Forrest said. "I could probably pull some strings to get you out of that little space. If you want."

"I would rather be folded in twelfths and squeezed through the holes of a saltshaker," Cassandra said.

"Is that a no?" asked Forrest.

"No."

"No, that's *not* a no?"

"No, it *is* a no!" Cassandra snapped. "I want *nothing* from you. Ever."

Forrest pressed his face against the bars and whispered, "Cass, there's something you should know about me . . ."

Molly wanted so badly to poke the man in his eye, but at that moment, Icepick barged into the room. "Get out here and help us plug the gap until we make harbor!"

"Relax, pal," Forrest said, putting his hands up in mock surrender. "And keep those fangs away from me. If we got shipwrecked, you'd eat half of us before the first sunset, wouldn't you?"

As the brig door closed behind them, Molly bounced with excitement. "We did it. We're going to Barbados."

Twelve excruciating hours later, Emmett sat up, snapping out of his foggy daydream state. "We've stopped moving," he said. "I think we're here."

"You sure?" asked Nellie. "I still feel like we're swooshing."

"Trust me, I am *very* sensitive to the motion of watercraft," Emmett said. "We've stopped."

"Now we just wait for Robot," said Cassandra.

One hour passed, then two. Eventually, they heard Rector outside, issuing orders: "Lars, Icepick—head down to that village and grab whatever supplies we need!" That was followed by the rumble of the lowering gangplank.

"Their two strongest are gone," said Bell. "It's now or never." He pulled the key from his pocket and unlocked the cell door.

"We can't yet," Molly protested. "We have to wait for Robot."

"Well, where is he?"

"I don't know, but he's our way off this ship."

"There is more than one way to get off a boat, dear." Bell squeezed past her and cracked the outer door of the brig. "We have a clear path to the dinghy."

"The dinghy has to be lowered down mechanically," said Nellie. "Are you volunteering to stay behind?"

Bell thought for a moment. "We'll make a dash for the gangplank, then."

"What if Rector spots us?" Emmett said. "Or Forrest or Pembroke?"

"We have to give Robot more time," said Molly. "Right, Mother?"

Cassandra gave her a pinch-lipped look and Molly's heart sank. It was the look Cassandra got whenever she was about to say something she knew Molly wouldn't like. "I'm not entirely certain we should wait," she said. "Lars and Icepick could return anytime. What if this is our only chance? Trust me, I will get you off this ship."

Molly looked away. Trust her? After she'd lied to her, "humored" her like a baby, and completely betrayed the dreams they'd pursued together for years? Molly thought of all the time she'd spent oiling gears and hammering nails for her mother, cheering her mother on with every new idea, laughing with her about the paint they'd spilled in their hair and the giant ball of twine they'd accidentally tied themselves together with. She thought about the nights after her father died, when her mother dried her tears on her nightgown and rocked her to sleep. "I trust you," she said. "Let's do it."

Cassandra turned to Nellie. "Promise me that if I don't make it, you'll get Molly and Emmett to safety."

"Mother," Molly began. But Cassandra shushed her.

"Promise me, Nellie."

"Look, Cass, I told you that my priority—"

"Nellie, I've seen you," Cassandra said. "You want everyone to believe that you're all business, but when something important is on the line—"

"Okay, I promise," Nellie said. "Now can we go?"

The five of them ducked out of the brig and Molly was caught off guard by the sight of the vast island before her, with its rolling tropical forests that seemed to stretch off into infinity. She'd never seen that much green in her life. And not the kinds of trees she was used to—swaying palms, vine-strewn fig trees, trees whose branches sagged with bright-hued fruit. Their ship was docked in a small harbor along with what seemed to be its only pier. A few dozen small houses, all painted in vibrant colors, were grouped along the edge of the treeline. And between the town and the dock, there was a beach. A real beach! With jagged black rocks and smooth white sand and scattered seashells. She was a hundred percent certain that a pirate treasure was buried out there somewhere. If they ended up having to remain fugitives forever, Barbados might not be a bad place for it after all.

A few local fishermen stood by rowboats in the surf, their forgotten nets dangling from their hands as they gawked at the drill-shaped bow and freaky spider legs of the *AquaZephyr*. Molly waved to the men, who waved back in a friendly but confused way.

"Molly!" Emmett's whisper snapped her out of her reverie and she dashed to join the group. A fat pelican rested on the gangplank, then took off with a squawk as they approached. But it hadn't been them that scared the bird. The long metal gangplank was rumbling and sliding back up into the hull of the ship. Suddenly, there was nothing before them but a thirty-foot drop to the wooden pier. Icepick laughed, his hand on the gangplank's control lever.

"You—you were supposed to leave with Lars," Bell stammered at him.

"I don't do shopping," Icepick said. "I told the big chucklehead to go by himself." He smashed a button and alarm bells began ringing throughout the ship. Rector, Forrest, and Pembroke burst onto the scene.

"Shockingly predictable," Rector said, shaking his head. "Of course you would try to escape. After all, it was you who put that hole in the hull. The moment I saw that hole in the hull, I knew it was no natural occurrence."

"Hey, I'm the one who said that," Icepick griped.

"I noticed it before you said it," Rector snapped. "But just like the woodsman who waits until the wolf has eaten both the grandmother and the little girl before he finally decides to strike, I too have waited to spring my trap."

"Spring your trap?" Molly asked. "You already had us locked up. Why would you need to—"

"Get them!" Rector barked.

The henchmen charged. Molly and the others dashed back the way they'd come and found Robot hovering out of the brig. "You were not where you were supposed to be," said Robot.

Sadly, there was no time for I-told-you-so's, so Molly just said "Take Emmett!" and kept running.

Emmett protested, but Robot scooped him up and flew over the rail.

As Molly and the others ducked around a small equipment shed, they found themselves face-to-face with Pembroke and Forrest.

"Sorry, gang," Pembroke said. "But you're not running from me a third ti—"

Cassandra broke a broomstick over his head. As he fell, Cassandra raised her splintered weapon to clobber Forrest, but the agent threw his hands up to shield himself. "Not the face!" he cried.

Cassandra jabbed him in the gut instead, causing him to double over and fall to his knees. "You do care," he wheezed as the escapees ran past.

Having a feeling that a weapon might come in handy, Molly turned back to pick up the discarded half of the broken broom. But in that moment, she lost track of the others.

"Mother?"

Forrest was beginning to rise, so Molly took off—the wrong way. *Drat!* She was back outside the brig. And Roald was waiting for her.

"You," she said.

"Yes, me," said Roald.

She'd never really thought of Roald as a friend, so she had no idea why his betrayal bothered her so much. "I can't believe you chose the bad guys," she said.

"I am good," said Roald.

Molly expected there to be more to that sentence, but Roald just stood there. So she quickly shoved him inside the brig and jammed her broken broomstick through the door handle to bar it shut. Roald yelled and banged, but couldn't get out. *I guess he's not very good at escaping things*, Molly thought.

Then she was grabbed from behind. She began to struggle, until she realized it was Robot. A second later, she was flying over crashing surf.

"Please don't drop me," she said.

"I know, you cannot swim," Robot replied. "Perhaps you should learn." He set her down on an isolated section of beach next to Emmett.

"Get my mother next," she said.

"I will get everyone," said Robot as he flew back toward the ship. "I believe in myself."

Emmett hugged Molly. "You're okay!"

"But the others . . ." She and Emmett watched from afar as Cassandra, Nellie, and Bell continued to run along the deck. First they saw Forrest grab hold of Bell and drag him away. Then they saw Icepick swinging what appeared to be a heavy metal hook on a chain.

"Yikes!" Molly shouted. "Did this guy raid a medieval castle?"

"It's an anchor," Emmett said with trepidation.

Molly bit her lip as Robot flew to her mother. But Cassandra yelled and pushed him away. *What are you doing?* Molly shouted in her head. She got an answer as Robot turned and picked up Nellie instead. *Oh, Mother.*

The moment Robot flew from the deck with Nellie, Rector got his hands on Cassandra and began tying her wrists. *Not again.*

"Look out!" Emmett cried.

Icepick was at the rail. He whirled the anchor over-head, then let go and sent the heavy iron projectile flying straight at Robot. The thick chain tangled itself around the automaton's legs and Robot was violently jerked down into the water. He splashed hard into the blue, with Nellie still in his arms, the weight of the anchor pulling both of them beneath the waves.

Molly felt planted in the sand, unable to move, as she watched the agitated water where Nellie and Robot had sunk. How long had they been under? Thirty seconds? A minute? It felt like hours. Then Nellie burst from the water, gasping for air. She immediately dove under again.

"Wh-what do we do?" Emmett stammered.

But Nellie soon reappeared, paddling desperately for shore. The children ran out, wading up to their bellies to meet her.

"Are you okay? Where's Robot?"

"I tried to help him. Really, I did." Nellie panted as she finally reached water shallow enough to stand. "But we couldn't get the chain off. And he—he kept trying to talk to me, and the water kept rushing in and filling him up. I couldn't help it—I needed air. When I went back down, he just—he wasn't moving."

"But he's not—I mean, he's not *dead*," Molly said. "I'm going to get him." She started to trudge farther out, but Emmett pulled her back.

236

"Molly, you can't swim!" he said.

"Then you go!" she screamed back.

Emmett was about to dive when the familiar rumble of the gangplank sounded behind them. Molly grabbed his arm. "We have to run." He was all she had left.

They helped Nellie back to the sand as the fishermen rushed over.

"Are you all right, young lady?" asked one man in a straw hat.

Molly looked over her shoulder. Robot had not surfaced.

"No," she said. "I am not all right."

Nellie glanced toward the ship and saw Icepick and Forrest rushing down the gangplank to join Lars, who was approaching from the road, pulling a small box cart full of building supplies. Icepick yelled and pointed in the direction of the escapees. She took the children's hands and rushed toward town. "If you'd like to help us," Nellie called to the fisherman as they went, "tell those others that you don't know where we're going!"

The man shrugged. "I *don't* know where you're going."

Molly didn't know either. All she knew was that she'd lost her mother again.

Tourists Trapped

RUNNING ON SAND was not easy. With every step, Molly's feet sank below the loose white grains and she had to pump her legs twice as hard to get any speed at all. Her only solace was in seeing that the three large men chasing her were having just as much difficulty, lifting their legs in what seemed like slow motion. It felt like forever before she, Emmett, and Nellie finally stepped onto more solid ground and were finally able to sprint down the dirt road into town, with their pursuers still a fair distance behind.

"I'm so tired already," Molly panted. Heat and hunger added to her fatigue. She hated being in such an intriguing place without the opportunity or ability to explore. On either side of each winding dirt road, small blocky houses were grouped tightly together, creating a labyrinth of narrow alleys between them—a good way to lose their pursuers. Many of these alleys were attractively lined with cheery little gardens, however. As the escapees dashed between homes, Molly made sure not to trample any long-leafed lilies or flatten any pretty pink bougainvillea.

"We need a place to stop and hide," Emmett said, ducking under the branches of a tree, from which dangled large green fruits covered in pointy spines.

Molly's stomach growled and she wondered if a food that looked so uninviting could possibly taste any good. She reached for the fruit, but a monkey swung down from a higher branch and snatched it first—a little guy with white tufted cheeks and yellow, almost greenish, fur. Molly shrieked. As did the monkey.

"They might've heard that," Nellie said, turning quickly onto the next street. "Pick a house, kids."

The houses were all virtually the same—same size, same boxy shape, same wooden construction, same high-gabled corrugated metal roofs. They all had the same double doors in the front and the same shuttered windows lining those doors in perfect symmetry. And they all seemed to rest on piled rock or brick bases. Yet no two of these homes could be mistaken for one another, as each was painted in its own set of strikingly bright colors—purples, yellows, aquas.

"What are we going to do?" Emmett asked. "Just

knock on a door? How do we know—?"

With more screeching, the terrified monkey suddenly skittered down the street past them.

"This way," they heard Icepick shout from somewhere nearby.

"Duck!" Nellie shoved the kids between two houses and pulled them to the ground behind a shrub with rubbery tennis-racket leaves.

"That was a little monkey," Lars said from somewhere nearby. "I know you don't like cute things, Icepick, but—"

"Shut it," Icepick shouted. "They're down here, I tell you."

Lying on her back, Molly couldn't see anything other than red undersides of begonia leaves and the eaves of the pink house she was squished up against.

"Check in between!" Icepick barked.

"We're looking. Relax." Agent Forrest suddenly appeared in Molly's frame of vision, stepping past the corner of the very house they were hiding behind. He was standing almost directly over her. She held her breath and tightened every muscle in her body. Forrest glanced down. Molly cringed, waiting for him to shout.

"Nothing," Forrest said, shaking his head. "Let's check the next street." And he walked off.

"I could've sworn he'd seen us," Emmett said, sitting up.

"Maybe he needs those glasses after all," Molly responded.

Emmett shook his head. "I don't understand that man."

"I don't *want* to understand him," Molly added.

"Hide now, analyze the bad guys later," said Nellie. She brushed herself off and scurried over to the front double doors of a sky-blue house flanked by orangey-red flowers shaped like tiny lobster claws. "Follow my lead," she said as she knocked. "We need to keep a low profile."

"Hello!" The door opened, revealing a smiling young Barbadian girl who appeared to be riding a rainbow-striped donkey. On second glance, it became clear that the girl was *wearing* the colorful animal—a costume, made to look as if she were riding the beast. "You're the first! Come in!" the girl said in what Molly assumed to be a Barbadian accent. "Papa, we have auditioners!"

"You have what?" Emmett asked.

"You must have seen our posting by the standpipe," the girl said, ushering her guests into a modest living room where several wooden chairs had been pushed up against the walls to clear space in the center for three men in bright blue vests with yellow lacing.

"Um, what's a standpipe?" Molly asked, trying to take it all in.

She was answered by loud, lively music as two of the men began beating away on drums and the third tootled on a pennywhistle. The girl in the donkey costume joined in, energetically dancing while tinking a steel

241

triangle. Nellie raised her hand in an unsuccessful attempt to interrupt, but the performers did not seem to notice. "Not sure this fits the definition of 'low profile,'" Emmett said nervously.

"Yeah, but they're really good," said Molly. She noticed a curtain across the room, pulled halfway closed, and two thin beds in what was obviously a sleeping area behind it. Reminded of her own home, she felt suddenly, instantly comfortable.

The band finished their song and took a bow as Molly and Emmett applauded. The young girl grabbed some other costumes from nearby chairs and held them up. "Which one do you want to try out for?"

Molly was about to reach for one that looked like a bear made of multicolored ribbons when Nellie waved the girl off. "Sorry for the confusion," Nellie said. "But we're not here to audition for your group."

"Oh, well, that's embarrassing," said a tall man with a double-headed bass drum strapped across his chest. "Let us make it up to you with a song."

The band started playing a new tune.

"No, no, please." Nellie waved her arms. "If I could just speak with you a moment!" The musicians stopped, and Nellie cleared her throat. "Thank you. I am Eugenia P. Hornswaggle, with the International Society for Drumstick Management. I am here to—"

Molly stepped in front of her. "I'm Molly. This is

Emmett and Nellie. Sorry, Nellie, not the time. Anyway, we need help. There are some really bad men looking for us. Can we hide out here?"

"Of course they can," said the young girl. She turned to the tall drummer and shot him a look that dared him to defy her. "Right, Papa?"

Her father scratched his bald head with the tip of a drumstick. "Um, yes, yes, of course. Please, tell us what we can do."

"As Molly said, we need some place we can stay out of sight for a bit," Nellie said, still blushing.

"You talk different," the girl said. "Not British, and definitely not Bajan. Where are you from?"

"Cecelia!" her father cautioned. "Let the lady speak."

"I bet they're from that weird ship in the harbor," said Cecelia.

"Cecelia!"

"We are from that ship," Nellie said.

"And New York before that," Emmett added.

"But we escaped from the ship," Nellie said.

"Because of the bad guys," Molly threw in. "They have my mother."

"And Alexander Graham Bell," said Emmett.

The musicians looked utterly perplexed.

"Well, my name's Gideon," said the bald man. "This is Clement and Ephraim. And my daughter, Cecelia, of course."

"And we are the Turtle Bluff Tuk Band!" Cecelia announced with a flourish. "Looking for some dancers to join us before we take our show on the road. We play parties, wedding, festivals—Tuk music's good for anything, really. Sure you're not interested?"

"Cecelia!" Gideon continued. "Now that we all know each other, maybe you can tell us—with a little more detail—exactly what's going on?"

There was a pounding at the door.

"Don't open it!" Molly warned in a whisper. "It's them!"

"Or it could be more auditioners," said Ephraim, the pennywhistle player.

Cecelia led Molly, Emmett, and Nellie behind the big curtain as her father opened the door to reveal Icepick. The burly henchman's face was red, his shoulders heaving. "You see a couple of—?"

"Welcome!" Gideon called out, and the band kicked into a lively marching tune with sharp, pulsing drumbeats and a speedy cascade of high notes from the flutelike whistle.

"Couple of kids!" Icepick shouted over the music. "Have you seen—" The band played louder.

"Eh, what's that?" Gideon asked, never slowing his drumming. "You need to speak up over the music."

"Stop the—*grrr!* I'm looking for—"

"Oho! Dance time!" Lars appeared next to Icepick, jiggling his hips. Icepick was about to punch him when

244

Pembroke ran up between them, panting.

"Stop . . . come . . . need you back," Pembroke said between breaths.

"Why?" Icepick snapped.

"Boss wants everybody back to fix the ship," Pembroke said. "He says the runaways ain't important enough to preoccupate yourself with."

Lars tipped his hat to the band before heading back toward shore with the others.

Gideon shut the door and his guests cautiously stepped back into the main room. "It's a shame," he said. "The ginger-haired one had decent rhythm. Now, please, tell me who those men were."

Molly began to rattle off an abridged version of the events that had led them to Barbados, but Gideon interrupted at the first mention of a certain name.

"Excuse me, but did you say *Ambrose Rector*?" he asked.

"I knew that freaky spider ship meant trouble," added Cecelia.

"You know Rector?" Molly asked, perplexed.

"Turtle Bluff is a tiny fishing village," Gideon said. "Most sizable ships go straight past us, down the west coast to Bridgetown. Your strange vessel out there now is the biggest one we've seen in these parts since about four years ago, when the *Frost Cleaver* stopped here. Twice."

Emmett leaned in.

"First time the *Frost Cleaver* stops here, it's heading south," Gideon said. "The whole crew comes into town to stretch their legs. A friendly enough bunch. It's Crop Over Festival at the time, so there's lots of food—coucou and conkies and sweet bread and nutcakes. Lots of rum, and music too, including ours, of course. So the men very much enjoy themselves. All except the one called Ambrose Rector. He keeps to himself. Doesn't even talk to his friends from the ship. Some people are quiet, though—that's okay! It doesn't strike us as strange until, about five months later, the same ship ports here again. But this time, only one man disembarks—Ambrose Rector! He says the others are all sick on the boat. Bad clams, he says. But something doesn't sit right about his story. When we ask if we could bring medicine to his ailing crewmates, he yells to keep off his ship. Then he drags ten, twelve bags down the gangplank and pawns them off to Uriah Grimsby's secondhand shop. We had no proof of wrongdoing, but it looked to us like the man was selling off his crew's belongings."

"He probably did," Emmett said bitterly. "Because those men were all dead by then. Rector killed them."

The musician's eyes went wide. "And you say Rector has your mother and—who else?—Alexander Graham Bell? The inventor?"

"Yes," said Emmett. "There's a kidnapping murderer in your harbor right now. And it's time we put an end to his reign of terror. Where is the police station?"

"The main constabulary is in Bridgetown," Gideon said. "Southwest side of the island. If you leave now, you could reach it by evening, but you would not get back here with the authorities until well past dark."

"That explains why Rector steered us straight to this particular village," said Nellie. "It was a port he was familiar with. And he knew he wouldn't run into the law here. What if we took a coach or wagon?"

Gideon shook his head. "Town's too small for coaches. You might be able to hire one back from Bridgetown, though. I'd offer you my donkey, but he's so slow, you'd get there faster on your own two feet."

"What about Grimsby?" said Clement, the other drummer. "He's been bragging about that new pony he won in a card game."

"It's possible," said Gideon, tapping his chin. "You might be able to rent that pony from Uriah Grimsby. He's an Englishman. Not the friendliest, but he's always looking to make a deal. His shop's on the edge of town, past the standpipe—" He paused, seeing the confusion on their faces. "It's a pipe. People get water from it. If you go past the standpipe to the other end of the beach, you'll see Grimsby's."

"If that animal's as fast as old Uriah says, you could

probably make Bridgetown in ninety minutes or so," said Clement.

"Ninety minutes there, ninety minutes back, plus time to talk to the police . . ." Molly tried not to despair. "Any of you know how long it takes to repair a hole in a metal hull?"

The men looked to one another and shrugged. "Few hours, maybe?" Gideon guessed. "Hard to say without seeing the damage."

"I'll go take a look," Cecelia volunteered, heading for the door.

"Cecelia! Did you hear them say 'murderer'?" her father shouted. "I don't want you anywhere near that boat."

"Okay, just a quick peek," the girl said, rushing outside in her donkey costume.

Gideon shook his head. "I hope you two are better at listening to your elders."

"We try to be," said Emmett.

"No, not really," said Molly.

"Well, it sounds like we don't have much time," Nellie said. She dug around in her trouser pocket and pulled out a drippy green bill. "Do you think this Grimsby fellow accepts damp American money?"

Ephraim laughed. "That man takes anything worth anything."

"It's decided, then. I will head to Bridgetown and get

the authorities back here before Rector fixes his ship and leaves again."

"In that case, we should—" Gideon began, but Nellie stopped him.

"No. Thank you, but I don't want to drag you and your family into this. I'd be grateful, though, if you let the children stay here while I'm gone."

"Of course," Gideon replied.

"I'll draw you a map to Bridgetown," Ephraim added, grabbing some paper. "It's too easy to get lost on those forest roads if you don't know the way."

"We can come with you, you know," Molly said to Nellie. Emmett nodded.

"I can probably travel faster on my own," Nellie replied. "And you'll be safe here." She sounded uncharacteristically emotional. "Please let me keep you safe."

Molly looked her in the eye. "Why are you helping us?"

"I made a promise to your mother," Nellie said.

"That didn't mean you were going to follow through on it," said Molly. "And we know you didn't want to get involved—"

"I am involved," Nellie said. "I have been from the start. It was foolish to pretend otherwise. I wanted to document the story, not take part in it. But sometimes you can't separate the two."

Molly wasn't expecting the tears that welled up in the

corners of her eyes. "I know you tried to save Robot," she said. "Thank you."

"I'm so sorry I couldn't," Nellie replied. "Let me make up for it now." She saluted them, took Ephraim's map, and left.

"Mr. Gideon," Emmett asked after a moment, "when the crew of the *Frost Cleaver* came ashore here, did that include the captain?"

Gideon squinted at the boy, then opened his eyes wide with understanding. "Oh! Why did I not realize sooner?" he said. "You are the boy the captain spoke of. But that means your father is . . . I'm so sorry, child. He missed you, your father. He talked of how he hoped his boy would be proud of him. In fact, you were all he talked about. When he wasn't dancing, that is. Are your moves as good as your father's?"

"My father danced?" Emmett gasped. He smiled and rubbed his father's ring.

He looked like he had a thousand follow-up questions, but a knock at the front door caused Gideon to quickly usher the children into the house's only other room. They stepped down a few inches into a cool, shady kitchen with a stove crafted from stacked stones and a table arrayed with iron pots and wooden bowls. There was a sharpening stone alongside a rack of knives and ceramic basin, in which sat a ridged wooden scrubboard. There was also a heavenly aroma that started

Molly's stomach rumbling again.

"Do you have any food?" she quickly asked.

"Help yourself to anything in the larder," he said before stepping back up to the living room and shutting the door.

The children huddled by the thin wooden partition, listening.

"Auditioner!" they heard Gideon shout. And the band jumped into another catchy tune.

"Sounds like a real one," Molly said, and shifted her focus to the larder, a large wooden food cabinet in the corner. She opened the doors, revealing jars of spices, sacks of grains, and numerous fruits with which she was completely unfamiliar. "What is *this*?" she asked in awe, holding up what appeared to her to be a giant seed—hard, greenish, and half the size of her head.

"Pretty sure that's a coconut," said Emmett.

"Wow, the guy who illustrated *Treasure Island* did not do his research," said Molly. "Well, gotta find your bright sides where you can—I'm finally gonna eat a coconut."

"How are you going to open it?" Emmett asked.

She first tried banging it on the edge of the table, which was frighteningly loud. So she poked, stabbed, and sliced at the coconut with every knife and skewer in that kitchen. Nothing made a dent. "Fine," she grumbled. "What else we got?"

Emmett examined a bumpy green fruit that was

almost as large as the coconut, but much softer. He cut into it with a knife and tried a slice of the fleshy, white inside. "Mmm," he said. "Tastes like bread."

"No fruit tastes like bread," Molly scoffed. She tried a piece.

"See? Bread," said Emmett.

Molly ate some more. "I'm not sure what it tastes like," she said. "But definitely not bread. Good, though." She downed a third slice. "This might just be the hunger talking, but this is the most delicious thing I've ever eaten."

Emmett nodded in agreement, chewed the pulpy fruit slowly. He glanced at the ring on his finger as he ate. "I can't believe he danced."

"Surprised, huh?" Molly asked. "How you feeling? About . . . everything?"

"A thousand different ways," he replied. He sat on a short wooden chair by the window. "I mean, I can't believe Robot is gone."

"I know. And just when he . . . Icepick's gonna pay for that." Molly choked back a sob. It had been bad enough to learn that her time with Robot would be limited, but she hadn't expected it to be *this* short. It hurt too much to think about, so she changed the subject. "But, hey, you sort of got a message from your father. And you didn't even have to wait till Antarctica."

"Yeah, but if he missed me so much, why did he leave

252

so often?" Emmett said. "And . . . and . . . he *danced*? Not once in my life did I see my father dance. What else about himself did he hide from me? And why?"

Bother beans, Molly thought. She'd wanted to help Emmett resolve his feelings about his father, not complicate them further.

Sticky, sweaty, and smelling of salt water, the two sat there, listening to one audition after another and eating far too many of the big bumpy mystery fruits. They went on that way for quite some time, until the window shutters suddenly opened behind them. They jumped as Cecelia hauled herself onto the sill, then watched in confusion as the girl struggled to squeeze her bulky donkey costume through the window frame. After a minute, Cecelia cleared her throat. "Maybe people don't get stuck in windows in New York, but when they do here, the others who are present usually help them."

"Oh, sorry!" Molly said. And actually, I did get stuck in a window in New York. My mother had to use a crowbar to get me out. It's how I met Emmett."

"New York sounds like an interesting place," said Cecelia as Molly and Emmett grabbed her hands and pulled her into the room.

"So, you don't use the door?" Emmett asked.

"Not when my father's gonna yell at me," she replied. "Hey, you ate all the breadfruit!"

"Ha! Breadfruit!" Emmett crowed. "See, Molly, I told

you it tasted like—Um, I mean, sorry, Cecelia. I guess we were hungrier than we thought."

"Well, I saw your ship, you know," the young girl said. "That fuzzy, angry man who was at my door is now hanging from a rope, pounding the ship with a big hammer."

Emmett began pacing. "I hope Nellie makes it back in time," he said. "Because Rector's not going to stick around a second longer than he needs to. I'm sure he assumes we've run off to tell the authorities."

"Your other friend went to Bridgetown?" Cecelia asked.

"Yes, Nellie's been gone two hours now," Molly answered for him. "But she could still make it. She was going to rent a pony from Uriah Grimsby. What's he like?"

"Old Grimsby?" Cecelia shrugged. "Cranky, British, smells like last week's okra."

Emmett suddenly perked up. "Mr. Gideon said that Rector sold the bags from the *Frost Cleaver* to this Grimsby fellow. Do you think one of them could have been my father's?"

"Absolutely," Molly replied. "We should go!"

Cecelia jumped to her feet, donkey head wobbling. "I'll take you!"

"But Nellie could be back any minute," said Emmett. "What if we miss her?"

"Even if she's got the fastest pony in the Caribbean, she'll be gone at least another half hour," Cecelia said.

"Come on, Emmett," Molly urged. "Maybe that ring was just the beginning."

The music died down and Cecelia put her ear to the kitchen door. They heard her father call for the next auditioner, and the same song quickly started up again. "They're gonna be busy for a while," she said. "Let's go!" She climbed into the window and promptly got her costume stuck. "A little help?"

Emmett crouched as he walked, trying to stay behind Cecelia's donkey costume. "This doesn't feel safe," he whispered. "I didn't realize we'd be coming this close to the dock." They walked a street parallel to the shore, but between each building, they had a clear view of the *AquaZephyr.*

"Don't worry," said Cecelia. "Grimsby's is just ahead." She pointed past the next cluster of homes to a little plaza surrounding a stone fountain. Several Barbadian women, their heads wrapped in colorful scarves, chatted and filled buckets of water from the tall iron spigot in the big stone basin.

"Yeah, but we'll have no more houses to hide us for that last fifty yards or so," Emmett said.

"Don't worry," Molly said. "There's a whole beach between us and the ship. They're not going to spot us from all the way over there."

"If you're not scared of being seen," said Emmett,

"why are you hunched over too?"

Molly lifted the bottom of her shirt to show him the big green coconut tucked under there.

"Seriously?"

"Hey, for a girl from New York, a coconut is a once-in-a-lifetime opportunity," Molly said. "I'm not missing out on it."

"New York sounds like a very strange place," said Cecelia.

"Come on, let's just go," Molly said. "We're far enough away. Look, if I take off my glasses, I can't even see Icepick hanging by the hull."

Emmett froze. "Put them back on."

"Why? What's—oh. Icepick's not hanging by the hull anymore. Where, um, where is Icepick?"

Cecelia pointed him out, climbing back onto the deck as Lars reeled in his harness.

"Did he see us?" Molly asked.

"Worse," Emmett said. "He's finished."

Molly's eyes scanned the side of the *AquaZephyr*. There was no hint there'd ever even been a hole.

"He's a surprisingly good repairman," Cecelia said.

"But Nellie's not back with the police yet," Molly said. "We can't let them leave. Not with my mother. What do we do?"

Emmett looked around, as if hoping to spot a sign with helpful instructions. "We . . . We have to delay them," he said. "Nellie could be back in as soon as twenty minutes, right? We just need to keep that ship in this harbor until then. But what can we do from down here?"

"Nothing," Molly said. "But if we get back on the ship . . . Look—the gangplank is still down. Maybe we can get into the engine room. Or the wheelhouse. I'm good at wrecking stuff."

"Too risky," Emmett said. The Caribbean sun felt hotter than ever.

"Even if we get caught, it's just until Nellie gets here with the cops," Molly said. "This is about stalling for time, not overpowering the bad guys."

"I can help you," Cecelia said, her voice somewhere between concerned and thrilled. "Wait here." She ran back to her house. Molly figured she'd gone home to change out of her donkey costume, but she returned three minutes later, still wearing it. Although she now also had two drums slung around her neck.

"I'm sorry, how does this help?" Emmett asked.

"Distraction!" Cecelia said. "Do they not use distractions to accomplish sneaky business in New York?"

"We do, and you're right," Molly said. "We won't even be able to walk up that gangplank unless the crew's attention is diverted elsewhere."

"Your father's not going to like this," said Emmett.

Cecelia shrugged. "My father doesn't like anything I do."

Emmett ran his fingers through his hair and took a deep breath. "Okay."

"I'll do it alone," Molly said. "You go on to Grimsby's. See if he has your father's stuff. That's important too."

"No, it's not," said Emmett. "Not like this. Not like us staying together."

Cecelia began beating her drums. "Tuk music to the rescue!"

From their hiding spot behind a beached rowboat, Molly and Emmett watched Cecelia put on the show of a lifetime. The girl twirled and shimmied while playing two drums at the same time. It wasn't long before some fishermen from the beach and people from the standpipe strolled over to watch her and clap along. It took a while longer, however, for the sailors on the *AquaZephyr* to take notice. Pembroke was the first to arrive at the aft rail, pointing to the spectacle below and calling to his shipmates. Agent Forrest came next, with Lars bopping by his side. And finally Icepick, who seemed more annoyed than entertained.

"C'mon, Rector, where are you?" Emmett muttered.

"We've got four out of five bad guys looking the other way," Molly whispered. "This might be the best we get."

Emmett sighed and nodded.

They ducked out from behind the boat and skittered down the shoreline to the dock where the gangplank landed. They hurried up the walkway as quickly and quietly as possible and zipped straight for the wheelhouse. But as they neared it, they froze—Rector was at the helm, preparing to set sail. He flipped a switch and they felt the motor stir to life below them.

"Other way," Molly whispered. They scurried along the starboard deck and down the hatch to the lower level. The engine room was a better place for sabotage anyway. And they knew exactly where it was, thanks to Roald and his ridiculously thorough welcome tour.

"Hello," said a somber voice behind them.

"Roald!" Molly yelled. "Drat! I forgot about you!"

Roald slumped. "Of course you did." He was sitting by himself in a dark corner. The boy looked miserable.

"Look, Roald, I'm so sorry for the things I said," Emmett said. "But please—"

"I am not going to tell the captain," Roald said.

Molly let out the breath she'd been holding. She didn't care why Roald was willing to look the other way, but—

The hatch opened above them and Icepick clomped down the steps from the deck. "What the—?" Before Molly or Emmett could even react, the sailor grabbed both children by the hair and dragged them, howling, back up to the deck.

"Of course you wouldn't stay to watch the happy fun music," Molly grunted.

Icepick called for Rector, who rushed from the

wheelhouse. He paused and blinked several times when he saw who his henchman was holding. "I'm not even going to ask why," Rector said. "Gift horses and mouths and all that. Let's just get you two reunited with your parental figures."

When the brig door was opened, Bell moaned and Cassandra leapt to her feet.

"Don't worry, Mother," Molly said. "This is not as bad as it looks."

"That's a relief," said Cassandra. "Because it looks *terrible*."

It felt pretty terrible too. But Molly reminded herself that they just had to keep Rector there until Nellie returned. And for all she knew, Nellie was riding up the street right now with a dozen Barbadian constables.

"We've got Rector right where we want him, Mrs. Pepper," Emmett said. Both children held their chins high.

"Okay, I'm intrigued," Rector said. "What is it that you think you've accomplished?"

Molly squirmed in Icepick's grip so she could look Rector in the eye. "You might as well save yourself the trouble and turn yourself in now. You're as good as caught. Notice how Nellie's not with us? That's because she rode to Bridgetown hours ago and notified the authorities. They put out an all-island alert. There are going to be ships waiting for you at every port on this island. No matter which direction you go, you will . . . why are you laughing? It's not funny, Rector. You're done."

Rector wiped a tear as his mocking guffaws died down. "Well, that's—that's a good story," he said. "There's even a small chance I might have bought it—a very small, infinitesimal chance—if not for the fact that I know it isn't true. Miss Bly never left Turtle Bluff."

Molly's gut clenched. "Yes, she did," she squeaked out. "She'll be back any second now."

"Miss Pepper," said Rector. "Have you not noticed how good I am at paying people off? Did you think I would not have people loyal to me on this island? Why do you think I told the crew to stop looking for you? Because I'd paid new people to do it for me. Who, you ask?"

"I didn't," Molly said. "But . . . I do want to know."

"I figured that if you wanted to leave this village you'd need a mount," Rector said as Icepick opened the cell and tossed the kids inside. "And pretty much the only person to rent an animal from around here is my old pal Uriah Grimsby. I doubt you'll be seeing Miss Bly again."

Molly felt the room spin around her. She reached for Emmett, but he looked just as queasy. "What did you do with Nellie?" she asked, not sure if she wanted to hear the answer.

"*I* didn't do anything with her," Rector said as he turned the key to lock them in. "If you want details on her fate, you'll have to inquire with dear old Grimsby. Not that that's going to happen. You know, it's a shame, Emmett, that you didn't get the opportunity to meet Mr. Grimsby. I gave him your father's old things years ago. Might have been nice for you to see some of Daddy's old trinkets, no? Although, now that I think about it—you'll be seeing your dear departed dad himself soon enough." He left the brig, then popped back in. "Because you'll both be dead. That was clear, right? Okay, just making sure. Toodle-oo!" And he left for real.

Emmett crumpled in the corner of the small cell.

"I hope this little stunt of yours was worth it," Cassandra said. She threw her arms around her daughter. "What's wrong with your belly?"

Molly untucked her shirt. "I brought you a coconut."

"Oh. Well, I am rather famished." Cassandra gave the fruit an unenthusiastic once-over. "How do I open it?"

Molly slumped against the bars, her back to the others. "So . . . how long till we get to Antarctica?"

PART III

Breaking the Ice

ONE WEEK OUT from Barbados, when the air had cooled slightly and the humidity was a bit less punishing, Rector released his captives from the brig.

"You suddenly trust us not to escape?" Cassandra asked, squinting in the harsh sunlight.

"I don't trust you at all," said Rector. "But escape is no longer a concern. See that tiny dot way out there? That's Brazil. If you want to swim for it, by all means. I hear they make a wonderful pork stew there. If you make it to Rio, you deserve a double portion. Treat yourself."

If their release was some kind of trap, Molly didn't care—she was finally out of that cell. For days, her hair and stomach had both been in knots. Her limbs ached from lack of use and she smelled like toe lint. Emmett, Cassandra, and Bell seemed to feel the same. (They definitely smelled the same.)

Rector put his prisoners to work. Molly—by far the best chef on board—was charged with kitchen duty, while Bell was forced to gut fish with Icepick, because it was so obviously the job he least wanted. Emmett was tasked with swabbing the deck, a chore that was only torturous in that he had to do it with Roald—and the cabin boy, overjoyed that "they were all friends again," constantly pointed out how much better he was at mopping. Cassandra was the last to be appointed a role on the ship, because Rector had special plans for her.

"Our friend Alec may refuse to acknowledge your talents," he said to her. "But I, my dear, would like to let you shine. Until I kill you, at least. I want you, Cassandra, to follow through on your plans to turn this vessel into a snow-crawler. While we were in Barbados, I had my men acquire all the tools and parts you'd listed on your design plans."

"Those plans were gibberish," she replied. "The whole thing was just a ploy to fool Bell. I scribbled down nonsense, so it would look like I was working. There's never going to be a snow-crawler, though. It's impossible."

Rector stared for a moment, then laughed. "I knew it! I obviously instantly recognized those plans as a fraud. Why else would you need a melon baller? I was testing you just now, because I wanted to see if you would try to continue your lies with me. Congratulations, you passed the test. Now to assign you a real task."

Forrest swaggered up. "I could use an assistant on my security detail, Cass."

Cassandra's face remained flat. "I'll clean the latrine."

Two weeks out from Barbados, there was no sign of land in any direction—not even a pinprick. South America was off in one direction, Africa the other, but no proof of either's existence could be seen from the *AquaZephyr*. By that time, however, the prisoners' chores had become second nature. Bell had even gotten used to the stink of fish guts under his fingernails. The prisoners went about their tasks without complaint, occasionally even enjoying the cool ocean breeze, the sight of a passing dolphin, or the off-key lilt of Lars's sea chanteys. Molly and Emmett even found times to share a covert laugh together, such as when Roald decided to list off all the things he could crush between his biceps and forearm (pistachios, small potatoes, Christmas ornaments, bars of soap, and what he referred to as "lesser grapefruits"). There were days when Molly managed to forget that this cruise was actually a kidnapping. Never when she saw Icepick, though. Every time she heard that man hawk up a wad of phlegm, got a glimpse of his dirt-caked hair, or caught a whiff of his tar-and-mildew aroma, she contemplated shoving him overboard for what he'd done to Robot.

*　　*　　*

Three weeks out from Barbados, when the air began to cool and everyone had traded their loose shirts and bare feet for jackets and boots, the four captives had become, by all measures, model members of Rector's crew—a development that the villain found endlessly intriguing.

He watched Molly clear dishes from the breakfast table one morning, after everyone else had left the mess hall. "So, no more troublemaking, eh? Don't feel like taking a stab at mutiny?"

"What for?" she replied, dropping the plates into a soapy basin. "As long as we're on this boat, we're at your whim."

Rector looked pleased, but skeptical. "Have I finally broken the indomitable will of Molly Pepper? Have you actually given up?"

Molly shook her head. "Don't get ahead of yourself, Amby. I just said it was pointless to cause trouble *on this boat*."

"So . . . What, you're just riding along with us in the vain hope of turning the tables on me once we get to the South Pole?"

"Yep." She didn't even look at him. She simply continued to scrub out filthy coffee cups.

"And you think you'll be able to do that, even though you've given me weeks to plan contingencies against anything you might attempt?" Rector tried to sound bemused, but Molly was pretty sure she heard concern in his voice.

"Yep."

He walked over and grabbed her arms, causing her to drop the pan she'd been wiping. "Aren't you afraid that telling me this will just make me throw you overboard now, before we reach the Antarctic?"

Molly swallowed and blinked a few times, hoping to hide how startled she was. "Nope," she said in the calmest voice she could muster. "Because I figure you've got some use for us once you get down there. Otherwise you'd have tossed us the moment we uncovered your identity. No, you've definitely concocted some diabolical master plan, and we're part of it. I just have to hope we can outmaneuver you when you put it into action."

Rector let go of her and walked around the table, rubbing his chin. "You're a clever one, Molly Pepper," he said. "But overconfidence will be your downfall."

Molly said nothing. But inside, she grew more and more certain that she was right about Rector losing his boosted intelligence. The man had no plan. He was making this all up as he went along.

Unfortunately, so was she.

Four weeks out from Barbados, it was parkas and gloves for everyone. Fewer and fewer fish appeared in the nets, but no one minded the smaller meals, as the contents of their bellies were constantly being tossed about by rough waves.

Five weeks out, the sea seemed to get angrier by the day, thrashing the ship around like a dog trying to dislodge a tick. But not one soul on the *AquaZephyr*, no matter how green-faced or woozy-headed, voiced a word about turning back.

Six weeks out, they reached the ice. Molly stood between Emmett and her mother, her gloved hands gripping the bow rail as she watched Bell's drill work its magic. The massive steel cone, with its spiral of jagged teeth, roared and spun, grinding colossal sheets of frozen ocean into fairy dust. For the first time in weeks, Molly's cheeks hurt not from the cold, but from smiling.

Three days later, the *AquaZephyr* made landfall.

Molly and Emmett were belowdecks when they heard Lars shout, "Ho! It is land!"

"'Ho, it is land'?" Molly grumbled. "Who says, 'Ho, it is land'? It's 'Land, ho!' Hasn't he ever read a book?"

"Molly, focus. We're here," Emmett said, raising the hood of the parka he'd taken to wearing twenty-four hours a day. "We've reached Antarctica."

"Land, ho!" Molly shouted as the two buttoned up and rushed outside to finally lay eyes on the legendary Seventh Continent. The air stung their cheeks the moment they stepped on deck, and snowflakes swirled around them (but not, Molly noted, the nice fluffy kind that tasted good on the tip of her tongue).

"Let's go, children," Cassandra called, joining them in a run to the rail.

If the tropics of the Caribbean had been an alien landscape to Molly, Antarctica was another universe entirely. The "shore," if one could call it that, was a jumble of black rocks, beyond which lay nothing but vast expanses of white, interrupted only by haze-shrouded mountains in the distance. On one flat rock, not too far from the ship, lay a large, rotund animal of some sort. It took Molly a moment to figure out, much to her delight, that it must be a seal. Emmett pointed toward an outcropping farther down the shore, where funny little black-and-white birds waddled around, bobbing from side to side.

"Penguins," Emmett said in awe.

Molly couldn't believe what she was seeing. Until, suddenly, she could no longer see it. "Argh! These stupid eyeglasses have frosted over again!" She pulled her spectacles off and wiped the lenses clear. Three seconds later, they were back to being a foggy blur. "Bother beans! How am I supposed to see anything?"

"Allow me," said Agent Forrest, grinning from within the velvet-lined hood of his monogrammed parka. He took her glasses and walked away.

"What do you think you're doing?" Molly groused. But he was already back in his cabin.

"Look what that seal is doing now, Molls!" her mother cried gleefully.

"Wow," Emmett chimed in. "Hurry, Molly, before it stops!" Molly looked out at the fuzzy gray blob on the fuzzy black smear, surrounded by lots of other fuzzy dark shapes.

"It's doing something?" She turned away and shouted, "Forrest! You are—"

Agent Forrest reappeared and placed Molly's spectacles back on her face. She turned around quickly and looked down at the seal. It was lying totally still. "What's it doing?" she asked.

"Nothing now," her mother said. "It stopped."

Molly huffed. But then realized that her glasses hadn't refrosted yet. "Did you do something to them?" she asked Forrest.

"A dab of shaving foam," he said. "It worked on the sun-blocker glasses that Alec made for me. Won't last forever, but it should get you by for a while."

Molly squinted at him—out of suspicion, not because she couldn't see clearly. "What are you playing at, traitor?"

Before he could reply, Icepick appeared. "Everyone on the main deck!" He'd grown a real beard that looked exactly like his fake one. "Captain's orders!"

The entire crew—prisoners included—met on the port-side deck by the gangplank, which had been lowered to the wave-slicked rocks below. Rector, bundled in a jet-black parka, addressed the group.

"Hereby begins the human race's first successful expedition to the Earth's southern pole," he announced, throwing his arms up in melodramatic fashion. "Let me congratulate each and every one of you, for you are all present to witness history in the making. Although, for most of you, the part you get to witness ends with seeing my back disappear over those hills out there, because you don't get to leave the boat. Lars, Icepick—get the packs. You two are coming with me. Because I don't like to carry things. The rest of you get to wait here until I return and tell you how amazing it was. Oh, except for Molly and Emmett. You two are coming as well."

The kids looked to each other in surprise.

"You know, that's okay," said Emmett. "We'll just stay on the boat, thanks."

"It was an order, not an offer." Rector's eyes went dark. "You see, I'm leaving Mrs. Pepper and Mr. Bell under the watchful eyes of Forrest and Pembroke. You children will be my insurance that your adults don't try anything sneaky while I'm gone." He reached into a bag at his feet and pulled out two metallic tubes, each of which had a red button at one end. He passed them to Forrest and Pembroke. "These are flare cannons," Rector said. "Point them at the sky, press the button, and—*ka-boom!*—a signal that's unmissable from just about anywhere out there." He directed his attention to Cassandra. "If I see a pretty explosion in the sky, I kill a kid." He turned to Emmett and Molly. "Likewise for you two. If either of you attempts to run off—which would be the height of foolishness in a frozen wasteland—I'll fire off a flare and signal to have your favorite grownups slaughtered. Everybody got it? Good."

Molly hated the idea of separating from her mother yet again, but she knew Rector was serious. Just because he was getting dumber didn't mean he was any less murderous.

"You know, all of this sounds great," said Agent Forrest. "But I'm gonna pull rank and switch places with Lars. As much as I hate to throw away a chance to spend more time with the lovely Cassandra, I'm a trained federal agent, not a prison guard. My talents will be more useful out there." He walked over and stood next to Rector.

Lars shrugged. "It's fine with me. I like it on the boat!"

Rector stood nose to nose with Forrest. "Okay, Archie. You're not a prison guard; you're a nanny. You're in charge of the wee ones."

Rector handed his pack to Forrest, and the two of them strode down the gangplank. Icepick, with two more packs slung over his shoulders, followed. Molly and Emmett gave Cassandra a quick hug. "Don't do anything reckless," Cassandra said to her daughter.

"I would never," Molly replied.

"I thought we agreed not to lie to one another anymore," Cassandra replied. "Seriously. Please, don't do anything I wouldn't do."

"But you just said nothing reckless. Make up your mind, Mother."

Cassandra gave a short, bittersweet laugh.

"We'll look out for each other," Emmett said.

Cassandra nodded. "I know you will." Then she got closer and whispered, "Watch out for Agent Forrest. If that man's choosing a laborious trek over the opportunity to hover around me like an annoying gnat, he's up to something."

The children nodded and headed to the gate. Within a few steps, both kids lost their footing on the iced-over gangplank and slid to the bottom (which, if Molly was being honest, was kind of fun). She sat at the bottom for a moment, stunned by the lonely starkness of her surroundings. She had never felt farther from civilization, farther from life. She might as well have been on the moon.

She picked herself up, and discovered that the rocks were dangerously slippery as well. Slowly and cautiously, she and Emmett made their way across the stones.

"The air hurts here," Emmett said, pulling his hood tighter. "Why does the air hurt?"

"Maybe humans aren't *supposed* to be here," Molly

replied through chattering teeth. "Maybe the earth is showing us it's mad by shattering our eyebrows."

Emmett's foot skidded, but Molly caught him before he fell onto the jagged rocks. "This place is going to kill us, isn't it?" he said.

"Not if Rector kills us first. Let's not fall too far behind."

They finally reached the pebbly shore, and found Forrest waiting.

"We don't actually need a nanny, you know," Molly said to the federal agent. "We're perfectly capable of—"

"Shut up and listen. I'm going to speak fast," Forrest said, glancing over his shoulder at Rector and Icepick, who were dozens of yards farther into the tundra. "I'm a double agent. I tried to tell your mother a few times, but she's not great at letting a guy get a word in edgewise."

"What?" Molly scoffed. Emmett's eyebrows shot up.

"I know I'm not the most trustworthy guy in the world," Forrest said. "But the one thing I will never betray is my country. I've been stringing Rector along from the moment he first approached me with a bribe. There's no telling what havoc he might wreak if he brings that meteorite back to the States. I'm letting him lead me to the rock, so I can retrieve it before he does."

Emmett blinked snow from his eyes. "So, Lars and Icepick—"

"No, those guys are criminal slime," he said. "I have

no idea where Rector found them. I've been half-expecting Icepick to snap and bite one of our ears off this whole time. But I had to sign off on them or I'd have blown my cover."

Molly peered at him through her clear, clean eyeglasses. "So . . . you being a jerk was all part of an act?"

"When was I a jerk?" Forrest asked. "Look, no one else can know about this. If Rector finds out about me before we reach the stone, this whole mission is scuttled. I'm telling you now so you don't get in my way when I make my move."

"What are you planning to do with the Ambrosium?" Emmett asked.

"Other than impress a certain lady inventor?" He gave a wink that made Molly scowl. "Take it back to the US and put it somewhere safe, of course. Somewhere it can't fall into the wrong hands. We've been talking too long. Don't wanna look suspicious." He left the kids on the shore and jogged to catch up with Rector and Icepick.

"Do you believe him?" Emmett asked.

"I think so," Molly said. She recalled that moment in the brig when Forrest had said, "Cass, there's something you should know about me . . ."

"Wow," Emmett said softly. "Forrest is a good guy."

"No, I think he's a genuine jerk," Molly said. "But he's a jerk who happens to be on our side."

"Yeah," said Emmett. "We should— Molly, look!"

277

A trio of curious penguins waddled cautiously toward them. Molly smiled, even though the wind made her teeth ache. She crouched down and held out her gloved hand, hoping the birds would come close enough to pet. "It's okay, Pengy," Molly said gently. The penguins inched closer.

"Friends! Friends!" Roald came bounding up behind them. "Friends, I'm coming!" The penguins scattered, diving into the water and swimming away in black-and-white blurs.

Molly seethed.

"Are you supposed to be here?" Emmett asked.

"No one told me I could come, if that is what you mean," he answered. "But I *am* supposed to be here. It is my destiny to be the first person to step foot on the South Pole."

"And apparently it's our destiny to suffer," Molly moaned.

They rushed to reach the adults.

"Hey, is Lars's corn-headed imp-weasel supposed to be with us?" Icepick asked.

Rector waved his hand dismissively. "Whatever. If we run into anything large and carnivorous, he'll make a good distraction while the rest of us flee."

The six explorers tromped into steadily deepening snow. Every few minutes, Molly turned to glance back at the *AquaZephyr*. She could still see the four figures standing at the rail. Over time, Bell, Pembroke, and Lars vanished from the deck. But not her mother. Molly knew that despite having warm cabins to shelter in, her mother was not going to move from that spot until they literally couldn't see each other any longer. When that moment finally came, at the bottom of a shin-deep snow-bank that blocked all views of the ocean, Molly cursed the tears frozen in her eyelashes.

22

Secret of the Cave

HOURS INTO THE march, Molly's legs were tired and sore. Each plodding step through the deep snow took three times the effort of a normal footstep. It was worse than running in sand. Her pack weighed her down immensely—and she wasn't even carrying all the rope, tools, and other equipment that the adults were. How could some jerky, blankets, and a fold-up tent be so darn heavy? There were times she had to reach behind her to make sure Roald hadn't climbed aboard for a piggyback.

And then there was the cold. With the thick boots, gloves, and hooded parka, her eyes, nose, and cheeks were the only parts of her exposed to the brutal Antarctic air, but she still felt as if the wind might crack her down the middle at any moment. She was grateful at least that the flakes falling around them had turned from harsh wet pellets to soft, feathery cloud bits. This fluffier snow made for a comfortable landing whenever she lost her balance.

She pumped her legs hard to keep up with Rector, who was always in the lead. "We're going to the space rock first, right?"

"Yes."

"'Cause you need that meteorite in order to find the Pole," she said, wondering if he would admit to his failing intellect.

Rector narrowed his eyes at her. "I do not *need* the rock to find the Pole," he said sharply. "But I will retrieve it first, nonetheless."

"Do you know where you're going?" Molly asked.

"Of course I do."

"How far is it?"

"Far."

"Hours far, or days far?"

"You'll see when we get there."

"You don't know where it is, do you?"

"I know where it is." Frustration crept into his voice.

"You sure?" Molly prodded. "'Cause everything kinda looks the same around here."

"In case you've forgotten," Rector said, "this isn't my first trip to this continent."

"Yeah, but it's not like there are a ton of landmarks," Molly said. "You really remember exactly where to go?

From almost four years ago? I don't see you looking at a map."

"I made the greatest discovery of my life here," Rector said firmly. "I could never forget."

"So how far is it?"

"You gonna talk the whole time?" Icepick grumbled.

"Yes," Molly said.

Icepick shoved two handfuls of snow into his ears.

Molly was thinking up more questions to bother Rector with when Roald called out, "I have an idea! Let us play I Spy. It is a pleasant way to pass the time, *ja*? I will go first. I spy with my little eye . . . something white!"

"Hey, Roald," Molly said. "I bet you're very good at running ahead by yourself. Why don't you show us?"

Roald lowered his head and dropped to the back of the group.

"Are we being too hard on the kid?" Emmett asked Molly.

"He sided with the enemy," Molly said bluntly. "That was his choice."

"Yeah, but he made that choice right after we were pretty mean to him," Emmett said. "And he probably felt pressured by his uncle. Roald hasn't done anything . . . evil. He's trying to make up for his betrayal."

"Yeah, by pretending it never happened."

"I don't know," Emmett said. "I get the feeling Roald's not the enemy."

"Well, he's gonna have to do a lot more than a game of I Spy to prove it."

The marchers paused to look up. In the direction they were headed, the horizon had become a swirl of shimmering colors. Ribbons of pink, yellow, and orange swam across the sky like luminous serpents.

"The so-called southern lights," Rector said. "The siren song of the Ambrosium! See? I told you I knew where I was going."

"You're aware that 'siren song' refers to something that's calling you to your doom, right?" said Emmett.

"Your space rock is casting those colors into the sky?" Forrest asked.

"Yes."

"It looks very far," said Roald.

"Like several-days far," Molly added, rubbing her cramping thighs at the thought of it.

"Doubting your ability to make it?" Rector asked smugly.

"No," Molly lied. "I'm actually glad it's that far. Gives me more time to think up a way to defeat you."

Rector laughed. "Like the hound who thought he could sniff out the leprechaun's gold only to find that the little green man was hiding amid his treasure pile, waiting to yank the dog's hairy tail, you too—"

"I didn't think it was possible," Molly said, "but your analogies are actually getting worse."

Rector grabbed both sides of her hood and yanked her closer to him. For several tense seconds, everyone watched and waited. Finally, he released Molly, grabbed his pack from Icepick, and opened it. "We camp here tonight!" He unrolled his insulated canvas tent and unfolded its tin-pipe frame.

Molly turned to Forrest. "Shouldn't we be going as far as we can while we still have daylight?" She dreaded the thought of making this trek in the dark.

"We're on the rump of the globe, kid," Forrest said, unpacking his own tent. "Sun's not going down any more than it already is. Twenty-four-hour daylight."

Molly scanned the endless white wasteland. Never-ending days. The thought was simultaneously comforting and unnerving. As the others went about setting up their shelters, Emmett trudged over to help Molly assemble theirs.

"Should you be taunting Rector like that?" he asked her.

"It's throwing him off," Molly replied softly. "He's getting flustered. You see it, right?"

"Okay, so you're keeping him mentally off-balance," Emmett said. "How do we use that?"

"I'm hoping to figure that part out before we reach the meteorite."

Emmett flopped melodramatically into the snow.

"Hey, if you've got any ideas, toss 'em my way," Molly said.

"Hold the presses," Emmett said from the ground. "Did Molly Pepper just suggest that we talk it over and come up with a plan?"

Molly kicked snow onto his face.

"I deserved that," he said, wiping the slush from his brows.

They finished assembling the tent and slipped inside. It was tight inside the one-person tent, but they still opted to share. A week in the brig had prepared them for cramped quarters, anyway. "We're in a tough position here," Emmett said. "We're the only thing standing between Ambrose Rector and the stone that will make him powerful enough to take over the world. When I think about what he did with just a tidbit of Ambrosium at the World's Fair, I get sick imagining what he could do with even more of the stuff."

"I know," said Molly. "I still really want to find the South Pole, because, you know, the whole reason we came here, but there's no point in becoming famous in a world controlled by Ambrose Rector. Stopping him is our top priority."

"Glad to hear you say it," said Emmett. "So, how do we get the Ambrosium before Rector? Should we run ahead while the others are sleeping?"

"The moment he notices we're gone, he'll fire off his flare and then . . . *kcchh!*"

"Right, we can't put your mother and Mr. Bell in danger." He let out a long, slow breath that turned into a billowy fog between them. "I guess we shouldn't rule out allying with Forrest. I despise the man personally, but if he can help . . ."

Molly nodded. "We should talk to him." She pulled open the tent flap to see Roald crouching at the opening.

"Hello, friends," said Roald.

Molly sighed. "Why are you here?"

"I told you, it is my destiny."

"Why are you *in our tent*?" she clarified.

Roald looked glum. "The grown-ups don't want me around."

"Neither do we," said Molly.

He climbed into the tent with them and sat down. "But maybe if I apologized to you," he said. "I am very good at apologies."

"That's not a great start, Roald," Emmett said gently.

"But I *am* good at them," Roald insisted. "Watch." He sat up as straight as he could, his head pushing against the canvas of the tent. "I am sorry. I have tried to be friends with you, but I have not succeeded. Because I do not know how to be friends with people. It is not easy when you know your destiny so early in life. Because you know you are going to do this very big, important, impressive thing, but nobody is going to believe you unless you are big and impressive in other ways. The only one who ever acted impressed by me was Uncle Lars. That is why I stood by him, even when I found out he was evil. Which I do not approve of, by the way. I do not approve of evil."

He cast his eyes downward. "But then, I overheard the captain saying he should throw Uncle Lars overboard for dragging that annoying boy on the trip without permission. And Uncle Lars responded that he did not have a choice, because he had promised his sister—my mother—that he would get me out of her hair for a while. He does not really think I am worthy of discovering the South Pole. He lied to me. Uncle Lars is just like everybody else."

Roald raised his head again. "You two are the only people who have been honest with me. You were not always nice, but you did not lie. It makes me realize I should be friends with people like you, instead of thieves and murderers. And that is why I am sorry. I stood by the wrong people. And now I am hoping you will give me a chance to stand by the right ones. By which I mean you. You are the right ones."

Emmett put his hand on the other boy's shoulder. "You know, Roald? That wasn't bad."

"Oh, and Molly, I thought you could use this." Roald pulled Forrest's can of shaving foam from his pocket. "I took it from Mr. Archie, because I saw your spectacles were getting frosty again."

Molly accepted the stolen gift. Maybe she could give Roald a second chance after all. "Thanks. But you still have to sleep in your own tent," she said. "There's seriously no room in here."

Roald nodded gratefully and crawled out into the snow. As he did, Molly glanced eastward toward where she knew the *AquaZephyr* lay somewhere in the distance. She was relieved to see that the only fireworks in the sky were the supernatural ones in the opposite direction.

The sky was clear and bright when they woke. "Good . . . morning?" Emmett said as they crawled from the tent. They had no idea what time it was. It could have been noon or three a.m. "Wow, this is going to be disorienting."

The three children marched together that day. The snow was no longer falling, but the terrain they passed through was overrun with deep drifts. Molly was particularly pleased, though, that the wind had died down. It was now only gut-numbingly cold as opposed to skin-disintegratingly cold.

"At least we're wearing out *different* muscles today," Molly said as they pulled themselves up a steep rock outcropping.

"Tired already?" Roald asked. When the others glanced sharply in his direction, he added, "That is okay. I will not mock you for it. Some friends tire faster than others. But they are still friends."

The group paused here and there for brief rests, and by what Molly's growling belly told her was lunchtime, they were trudging along the ridges of a forbidding mountainside, where relentless gusts of icy air began battering them once more.

"Ah, so here's where the wind was hiding," Molly shouted over the roar. The higher they climbed, the stronger the gales grew, and conversation became all but impossible. That didn't stop Emmett from crying out, though, when he saw something move along the ridge ahead of them.

"Did you see that?" he yelled. "Behind that rock up there?"

"Just another penguin," Forrest said.

"We should go after it," said Rector. "Penguins make good eating."

"We are not eating anything that adorable," Molly protested.

"So starve," said Icepick. "I'm eating it." He charged toward the rock and sent the terrified little penguin squawking into a nearby cave. The henchman followed the bird inside, greedily rubbing his hands.

Molly ran after him. But by the time she reached the cave, Icepick strolled back out, licking his fingers. "You beast!" Molly cried.

Then she noticed the metal can in his hand. He dipped his fingers in and scooped out fingerfuls of vanilla pudding. "Where'd you get that?" she asked.

"The cave," Icepick said. "Lots of stuff in there."

The others joined Icepick as he sauntered back inside. The dark hollow was deep enough that the rear half of it was shrouded in shadow. But the sunlit area by the opening was littered with boxes and tins, most of which were empty and marred with tooth marks. The rust and faded labels made it clear that this detritus had lain there for a long time, possibly years.

While the others looked around, Emmett surreptitiously scooped up the tiny penguin and set it outside to waddle to freedom.

Forrest pulled a metal tube from his pack and Molly flinched, thinking it was his flare. But when the agent flicked a switch and the soft glow of incandescent light beamed from it, she realized it was some sort of electric torch, presumably another gift from Bell. Forrest stepped deeper into the cave and shone his light on a pile of ragged blankets. "Someone was sheltering here," he said.

Rector stooped down and picked up a sardine tin. He sniffed it, made a disgusted face, and then read the label. "Ah, these are from the *Frost Cleaver*," he said. "Must be some of the food I left with Captain Lee."

"My father was here?" Emmett grabbed the can from Rector and examined it, as if he could find his father's essence somewhere in the scent of old sardines.

"I *told* you I didn't kill him," Rector said. "You know, Emmett, you and I have a lot in common."

Emmett huffed and began rooting through the old trash.

"Bah! You're just like Molly," Rector went on. "'Oh, no, I couldn't possibly be anything like that handsome super-genius Rector!' But think about it, Emmett: my father also drove me relentlessly toward a future I never wanted. 'You *must* be an inventor,' old Johann Rector would say. 'Inventing is the only truly admirable profession!' But all I ever wanted was the stage, the spotlight, the adoring fans throwing boxes of raisins at me. Why raisins, you ask?"

"Actually, yes," said Molly. "This time I'm asking: Why raisins?"

"Because I don't like chocolates. What I'm saying, Emmett, is that I know what you're feeling. And you, of all people, should understand why I need to prove myself—not just to my father, but to the world!" He rested his hand on Emmett's shoulder. "It's not too late to join me, you know. Miss Pepper didn't accept my offer, but perhaps you're the smarter of this motley duo?"

Emmett said nothing.

"Fine. Suit yourself," Rector said. "Seriously—*suit yourself.* I see some jackets and such in the corner back there. You could probably use some extra layers."

Molly glanced into the shadowy recesses. "Hey, he's

right." Forrest joined her with his torch. "Emmett, come look!" she called. "There's an extra parka and—Emmett, don't look!" She tried to block his view, but it was too late. Emmett had seen the human remains inside the old parka.

"It's a skeleton!" Roald yelled. "Your father is a skeleton!"

Molly turned on Rector. "You knew he was back here."

"I didn't say the man didn't *die*," Rector said. "I only said I didn't *kill* him."

"You did kill him, though," Emmett growled. He lurched toward Rector, but Icepick caught him and shoved him to the ground.

"Don't touch Emmett again," Molly warned, her finger right in Icepick's face, daring him to snap at it.

"Yeah, don't touch him again," Roald echoed.

"Take care, gentlemen—I believe the pubescents are rebelling," Rector drawled. "Look, Emmett, I'm sorry about your father. I know you probably don't believe me, but I *did* like the man. I simply couldn't let anybody from that crew get back to New York. It would have completely ruined my plans."

"You mean like *we* did?" Molly said.

"Yes, like you— No! Not like you did. You didn't ruin— *Urrgh!* Why are you still alive?"

"Because you need us, remember? For your diabolical secret plan."

Rector took a few deep breaths through his nose.

"Give Emmett some time alone to say goodbye," Molly said. "It's the least you can do."

"No, I could do less," Rector said. "But I'm not heartless."

"No, just brainless," Molly snarled. "Because you don't have your precious space rock to keep you smart."

Rector glared icily. "You have five minutes."

Icepick and Roald left the cave. Forrest handed the torch to Emmett and followed. "Do you want me to go too?" Molly asked as Emmett knelt beside his father's remains.

"Please stay," Emmett said. With his free hand, he reached down and ran his thumb along the embroidered patch that read "Lee." He sniffled as he began to unbutton the coat. "I feel like—like we should, um, check—" His hand was shaking.

"Let me." Molly crouched next to him and felt around inside the dead man's parka. In the chest pocket, her fingers found a folded piece of paper. *A note!* But when she unfolded it, she saw only a child's crayon drawing: father and son standing on a tiny boat. She'd never seen the drawing before, of course, but she knew Emmett had made it. She'd heard that very picture described in Captain Lee's last letter to his son. She handed the paper to Emmett. "This was the only thing in there."

Emmett nodded. "This is . . . nice, I suppose," he

continued. "I hadn't even considered that we might actually find *him*. At least I can say goodbye. And some of the other stuff I never got to say while he was alive." Molly began to back away, but he squeezed her hand. "Father, I am so sorry," he went on. "I'm sorry I'm not the son you wanted. I'm never going to be a sailor, like you. I've had a lot of experience on boats recently—it's not my thing. But you know what is? Inventing. I'm pretty good at it. And with instruction and practice, I can be great. I hope you would be proud of me for that. I made a track-based candle-lighting system. And a mechanical claw that picks books from shelves. And I threw together an ink-jet dart gun in about three minutes when we needed to escape from the Green Onions—oh, yeah, I've also done some stuff you wouldn't be too happy about. But I did it to help people. To save our country. I'd like to think you'd be proud of that too. Papa, what I'm trying to say is, I need to make my own decisions about my life. And when I choose a path that you maybe would not have chosen for me, it doesn't mean I don't love you or appreciate everything you did for me. Ironically, it was your absence that led me to find inventing. And now it's a big part of my life. And so are the Peppers. And I wish you could learn more about that part of me." He gave a short, bittersweet laugh. "You know what's funny? In a sad sort of way? I don't think this conversation would be any different if you were still alive. You were gone so much anyway. It's probably not fair of me to say that, but . . . it feels good to finally put it into words." He wiped his face on his sleeve.

"I should go," Molly said softly. "In case there's stuff that's just between you and him. Take your time."

Emmett nodded, and Molly left the cave, dabbing her eyes. She couldn't help but remember being at her own father's sickbed the moment she said goodbye to him for good.

Agent Forrest grabbed her arm, startling her. He led her around a large boulder, out of earshot of the others. "Is it true what you said in there about Rector losing his intelligence?" he whispered, glancing over his shoulder. "Or were you just ribbing him?"

"Um, both," she said. "The only reason he was ever a super-genius was because he was eating bits of space rock. But he's out of Ambrosium now and his mind is slipping."

"Hmm, the stone's effects aren't permanent, then," Forrest said, wiping the foggy lenses of his sun-blockers. "That's an important factor to consider."

"To consider in what?" Molly asked. "What is it again that your real bosses want to do with the Ambrosium?"

"Keep it away from Rector," Forrest said.

"And nothing else?"

"Forrest!" Rector was calling.

"Wait here a minute before you come back out," the

295

agent said. "Don't want it to look like we've been chatting." He ran off.

Emmett emerged from the cave a moment later. He rubbed his thumb across the ring on his finger before pulling his gloves back on.

"How are you?" Molly asked gently.

"I'm good. Really good," he said. He scraped the icicle tears from his face and wrapped her in a hug. "Let's go get that space rock."

Into the Light!

THE LANDSCAPE HAD flattened again and Molly's legs didn't feel as tired from the constant marching anymore. Perhaps all the exercise was making them stronger, she thought. It had been five days since the cave. Or at least five different periods of marching and sleeping; she could never be quite certain whether it was truly day or night. Some days, the weather was almost bearable, no worse than a rough winter day back home; others, the wind made her forget she even had a face. Making the journey all the more disorienting were the snow clouds, rolling in and out like the tide. Every time they blotted out the sun, the temporary darkness made Molly's body want to drop into a deep slumber.

This seventh "day" of the trek was of the sunnier variety, though unusually blustery. Molly was surprised she was able to hear the growling of her stomach over the howling of the wind.

"Hungry!" Icepick barked. Had it been *his* stomach she heard? She held her hand to her belly. No, she was ravenous too. All the trekkers were. Rector had been allowing fewer and fewer meal breaks.

Forrest stopped. "Come on, Rector! We're long over-due for a snack break! Icepick is going to eat one of these kids."

Rector backtracked to join the others. "I would love to stop and have a little picnic," he said. "But we're low on food."

"Because you didn't pack enough," Molly said sharply.

"No." Rector glared at Roald. "Because *someone* wasn't supposed to be with us. Someone who eats twice his body weight at every meal!"

"I am a growing boy," Roald said sheepishly.

"Don't blame him for this," Molly said.

"Well, you can blame him a little," Forrest said. "He *did* eat way more than his share."

"The point is," Molly said, "Rector didn't even pack enough for the five of *us* on a journey this long."

"What are you insinuating?" Rector asked. He stared Molly down, his hands on his hips.

"Same thing I've been saying for days," Molly replied. "You don't know where we're going."

"Molly Pepper," Rector said. His voice was a low,

simmering rumble. "You . . . You are . . ." He started breathing heavily, his muscles tensed.

Molly took a step back. Had she pushed him too far?

"Hey! Why don't we just try to *find* some food?" Emmett suggested.

"Oh, why didn't I think of that?" Rector said, dripping with sarcasm. He bent over and pretended to pluck imaginary plants from the snow. "Let's feast on this delicious invisible Antarctic produce! I have an absolutely delectable imaginary dressing to pour over it."

"I'm talking about fish," Emmett said. "Because I'm pretty sure we're standing on a lake. Or an inlet from the ocean, or something." He kicked away some snow to reveal a base of ice underneath.

"Well, look at that," Forrest snickered. "I guess all the women who've said I could walk on water were right."

Rector grumbled. "Icepick, see if you can hook us some lunch."

While the children cleared away snow, Icepick assembled a mechanical handsaw and carved a hole into the ice. The frozen surface was several inches thick, but eventually, he burst through to liquid water. Icepick licked the saw blade. "Salty," he announced, and then unfolded a collapsible fishing rod. The others—including Rector, who was suddenly in a much better mood—sat on their packs in a circle around the fishing hole and watched Icepick dunk his line.

After a long, boring while, during which the dreaded storm clouds began sailing in from behind the mountains in the west, Icepick's line finally began bobbing. With a decent amount of struggle, he reeled in what everyone assumed to be some sort of sea life thrashing on the hook. The thing was more snake than fish—three feet of angrily wriggling body that ended in a circular, sucker-like mouth full of tiny fangs.

"Flaming flapjacks! What the heck is that?" Molly blurted.

"Oh, I've encountered those before," Rector said nonchalantly. "I call that a hagfish. Remember, I spent weeks here by myself. I've probably seen—and eaten—every animal Antarctica has to offer."

"Eels," Emmett muttered. "Why did it have to be eels?"

"Not eel—hagfish," Rector reiterated.

Icepick ripped the whiplike creature from the hook. But as soon as he had his hands on it, the thing squirted copious amounts of milky gray slime onto the man's hand. The hagfish slipped from his grasp and dropped to the ice, where Icepick stomped his hefty, booted foot onto the animal to pin it down. More slime oozed from its hide and Icepick slipped backward into the snow.

"Well, there's your lunch," Rector said. "Try some, it's delicious. I'm going to have some of our remaining canned fruit over here, but the rest of you, by all means, eat the hagfish."

"If it doesn't eat us first," said Emmett.

Icepick jammed a knife into the eel and it finally stopped thrashing.

"Monster!" Roald shouted.

"Because he killed the hagfish?" Molly asked, feeling that Roald was being a bit melodramatic.

"No, by the hole! A monster!" Roald pointed at the hole in the ice, from which another bizarre creature was crawling. Its bumpy red torso was at least a foot long, and its eight multijointed legs were each even longer. A pincerlike beak snapped open and shut below beady black eyes as the thing skittered up into the quickly accumulating snow.

"Oh, that's just a . . . sea spider," Rector said dismissively. "Very common around here."

"I'm pretty certain it's some species of crab," Forrest said.

"That would explain the claws," Molly said, backing away.

Icepick snatched the animal up in one hand, plucked one of the long, kicking legs straight off the thing's body, and proceeded to suck the meat out of it. "Yeah, it's crab," he said.

"Well, obviously," Rector said. "But I call it a sea spider."

"It's not a spider, though," Molly said.

"What was I supposed to call it? A sea crab? That would be redundant!"

As thicker snowflakes began swirling, a second sea spider emerged from the ice hole and darted for Molly. She got ready to give the nasty thing a boot to its bug-eyed face, but Agent Forrest jumped in and did it first. As the creature scurried back into the water, Forrest grabbed the edge of his hood and made a motion as if tipping his hat. "Be sure to tell your lovely mother I've been looking out for you."

Molly huffed. She didn't care whose side Forrest was on; she was tired of his demeaning nonsense. "My mother. Does. Not. Like. You!" she said in her loudest, clearest voice. "I know it's hard for obvious thoughts to make it through that oil-slick head of yours, but she wants nothing to do with you!"

Icepick laughed and Roald hid his face. Forrest grabbed Molly by the arm and pulled her several yards away. "Watch yourself, girl," he whispered through clenched teeth. "Remember whose side I'm on!"

"Not my mother's," Molly snapped back.

Emmett skidded through the snow to Molly's side. "Just because we share a common enemy doesn't mean Mrs. Pepper owes you anything."

The agent's frost-brittled mustache trembled with rage. "She doesn't deserve me, anyway," he grumbled. "It's not like she's out here with us trying to stop this madman."

"You have no idea what she's sacrificed," Molly hissed.

"Sacrifice? You want to talk sacrifice?" Forrest pulled

down his hood. "Look what this parka has done to my hair! Listen, I'm going to need your help when I make my move on Rector, which is going to be soon. We're getting close to the source of those lights. I need to know I can count on you two to distract Rector while I grab the rock. Watch for my signal." He plodded angrily back to the fishing hole, where Icepick had built a fire and begun roasting the sea creatures he'd caught.

Molly hugged herself, rubbing her arms. She longed to get near that fire, but she held back to talk to Emmett. "I bet you anything Forrest wants the Ambrosium so the government can make its own superweapons," she said, her numb lips making it difficult to speak.

"Well, we're in a 'lesser of two evils' situation," Emmett said. "Either Forrest gets the rock, or Rector does."

"Unless *we* do," Molly said.

"Yoo-hoo, babies!" Rector called out. Icepick and Forrest were putting out the fire and repacking their things. The snow had gotten so heavy suddenly that Molly and Emmett felt like they were viewing the others through a gauzy curtain. "We are moving on. Fall behind at your own risk. We need to find shelter before this storm gets so bad we can't see what's in front of our own faces."

Two hours later, they could not see what was in front of their own faces. One minute, Molly was marching with her focus on a pair of hills in the distance; the next minute, all she could see was whiteness. Every step became a leap of faith. She couldn't even see her own feet.

"Stay next to me," Molly yelled to Emmett over the thundering gales. No reply. "Emmett?" Nothing. She'd seen him—or at least his silhouette—only seconds earlier. She reached her arm out, hoping to feel him somewhere in the disorienting swirl of white on white. But her fingers touched nothing. She'd lost him. She'd lost everyone. "Emmett! Forrest! Rector!" Were the others still together? Did they realize that she'd lost them? Did Rector think she'd tried to escape during the storm? Was he about to fire his flare through those dark clouds and signal her mother's execution?

A hand brushed against her back. She spun and wrapped the boy in a grateful embrace.

"Oh, Molly! Thank you for finding me," cried Roald. "I thought I was very good at navigating in a blizzard. But—"

"It's okay, Roald," she said. "We're together now." She didn't have the heart to tell him she'd thought he was Emmett. She locked fingers with the boy and continued plodding through the stinging white maelstrom. A moment later, Molly thumped face-first against the dark parka of a grown man; she prayed it wasn't Icepick.

"Good, it's you!" Forrest held his hand up in a vain attempt to shield his face. "Did you see how bright the lights were, right before we lost visibility? We're so close. So be ready to act as soon as this storm dies out. You two need to do whatever you can to keep Rector busy while I secure the Ambrosium. That's the only—oh, frumps, you're the wrong boy. I thought you were the other one. Wonderful, now the corrupt cabin boy knows too!"

"Knows what?" asked Roald.

Molly pulled Roald into a huddle. "Roald, you understand that Rector is a really bad guy, right?" she said.

"Yes, I hate Mr. Rector," Roald said. "He is awful."

"Well, if he gets his hands on that magic space rock he keeps talking about, it will make him incredibly powerful," Molly said. "Wanna help us stop him?"

"Yes."

Molly cleared snow from her glasses and looked around. "The storm is slowing," she said. "We need to find Emmett."

Forrest pulled the flare launcher from his coat.

"No!" Molly cried. "If the guys back on the ship see it, they'll kill my mother!"

"Molly? Molly!"

The snow had thinned enough for her to see Emmett heading her way. "Thank goodness," she breathed.

"Guys, I think we're there," Emmett said when he reached them. He pointed and everyone turned. Without the blinding maelstrom of snow, multihued beams of light could now be seen painting the underside of the clouds. They were shooting up like spotlights from behind the shoulder-high snowdrift directly in front of them.

The wind and snow cut off as suddenly as if someone had flicked an off switch, and Molly realized Rector was right behind Emmett. "See? I told you I knew where I was going!" Rector said. "My Ambrosium is right on the other side of that hill. I can taste it already."

"This is it, kids," Forrest said. He and Rector locked eyes. The only thing separating them from the all-powerful meteorite was one dune of windblown snow. *Yes, someone gets the stone right now,* Molly thought. *Might as well be me.*

She took off for the hill, sprinting as fast as she could through the knee-deep snow. It took Forrest and Rector a moment to realize what she was doing, before they took off after her.

Molly pumped her legs, struggling to ascend the snowdrift. She *had* to reach the meteorite first. But her thighs burned and her breath was so heavy. Forrest barreled past her. "Do the right thing," he huffed as he went by.

No! Molly fell onto her belly and looked up. Forrest was already at the crest of the hill. And Rector would be at his side in seconds. She'd lost the race. She had no chance of beating both men to the rock. But she could still have a say in which of them got there first. She threw herself at Rector's legs, taking him down at the knees. He crashed into the snow beside her.

Glancing back as he began to skid down the other side

of the drift, Forrest crowed victoriously. "You're done, Rector!" he shouted. "You can't outsmart a United States federal aAAAAAAAAAHHH!"

Molly crawled to the crest of the drift and gasped as Agent Forrest disappeared over the edge of a deep crack in the ice that had been invisible from the other side.

"What happened?" Emmett asked as he and Roald reached the top of the snow dune.

"Careful!" Molly yelled before either of the boys stepped too far and slid to their doom. "Forrest fell! Into a bottomless pit or something." From their new vantage point, they could now see the massive crevasse that had swallowed Archibald Forrest; it was over fifty feet long and easily ten feet across, cutting through thick layers of ice, soil, and rock.

"Oh, it has a bottom," Rector said unhappily. "And my space rock is down there."

Indeed, the colorful rays of light were shining up *out of* the enormous crevice.

"You never said the stone was at the bottom of a canyon," Emmett said.

"It *wasn't*," Rector groused as he slowly climbed down the hill, taking care not to slip and become another victim of the gap. "In the time since I was last here, the ground must have cracked open, like one of those, you know, ground-cracky businesses."

"An earthquake?" Emmett said as he, Roald, and

307

Molly cautiously descended to join Rector at the edge of the rift.

"Yes," said Rector. "And the Ambrosium fell in."

"So it is down there," Roald said. He swallowed hard. "With Mr. Agent Forrest."

"That appears to be the case," Rector said. "Oh, by the way, thank you, Molly, for saving my life. Had you not stopped me, I might have met the same loser's fate as our traitorous Archie."

Molly gritted her teeth.

Emmett peered over the edge. "Do you think he's—?"

"Splattered into scrambled eggs? Oh, certainly," Rector said. "Can't see how far down it goes, but it's a hundred feet to be sure. Our Forrest has been turned to mulch."

Molly winced. She'd have been lying if she said she'd miss Archibald Forrest, but she never wanted the man to die. Nor had she wanted to lose an ally against Rector.

Icepick appeared at the crest of the hill and bounded down to join them. For better or for worse, he stopped himself before plummeting into the crevasse. "What did I miss?"

"Nothing much," Rector replied. "The rock is at the bottom of that hole. We need to get down there."

Icepick pulled climbing gear from his pack and tied together every bit of rope they had, but it wasn't nearly enough to reach the base of the chasm.

"We need another way down," Rector said. He marched off.

"There's no back door, Rector," Molly said. "It's a hole in the ground."

"There's obviously a large cavern down there," Rector said. "If we found one crack in its roof, we can find others. Ones with shorter drops. Sheesh, what happened to that Pepper optimism?" He grabbed his pack from Icepick. "I'll hold on to this," he said. "I don't want to lose my stuff if you fall into a pit too."

"Stay close, all right?" Emmett said to Molly. "I thought I'd lost you in the storm and that was way too scary."

"Yes, we stay together now!" said Roald. He stepped in between Emmett and Molly, grabbed each of their hands, and led them off.

They'd hiked another mile when Rector gave a triumphant hoot. "The genius of Ambrose Rector strikes again," he said proudly, gesturing to a small opening between two large black boulders. "I have discovered a tunnel." The tiny hole was barely wide enough for an adult to fit into on their hands and knees, but inside, there was a deep shaft, plunging downward at a forty-five-degree angle.

"How do you know it leads to where the meteorite is?" Molly asked.

"Did you not just hear me say 'genius'? I have a superbrain. I did all the calculations in my head. Compared the angle of the . . . you know, *this*, to the location of the whatchamacallit and . . . well, where else is it going to lead?"

"A dead end?" said Emmett.

"Certain death?" said Molly.

"Monsters?" said Roald.

"Fine, stay out here and wait for the next blizzard," Rector said as he crouched and slipped into the narrow tunnel. "In the meantime, I'll be getting my Ambrosium."

Emmett turned to Icepick. "You're not a double agent too by any chance?"

"I'm double the man that wimpy Agent Forrest ever was," Icepick said. "Now, get in the hole."

Molly climbed into the tunnel, glancing over her shoulder at Emmett. "Why do I have the feeling we're not all getting out of this cave alive?"

The World Below

THOUGH CERTAINLY STEEP enough, the tunnel was no fun slide like the gangplank. The spontaneous spelunkers had to descend slowly, pushing against the walls and fighting gravity in order to keep from smashing their heads on jagged rock protrusions or falling onto sharp stalagmites. Rector was far ahead, as usual, followed by Molly, Emmett, Roald, and Icepick bringing up the rear. Speeding along with the only remaining electric torch, Rector left the others to bang and scrape themselves repeatedly in the darkness. Molly called ahead for him to wait, but the man refused to slow his pace. After crawling for what felt like hours, Molly finally lost sight of their "leader" completely. But there was still dim light ahead. They were close to the end.

Molly squeezed through a particularly narrow stretch

and saw a wide, well-lit opening. But before she could exit, she heard Icepick shout behind her. "Get me out of here! I'm stuck!"

Huffing, she climbed back a few yards to where Emmett and Roald gawked at the brawny henchman, whose thick shoulders were tightly wedged between tunnel walls. "Pull me," he barked, reaching out as far as he was able.

The boys grabbed Icepick's arms, but Molly stopped them. "No." In her mind, she saw the smug, satisfied grin that was on the henchman's face as he threw the anchor that destroyed Robot.

"Molly," said Emmett.

"One less bad guy to deal with, Emmett," she replied.

Emmett paused in thought. "Sorry, Pick, we'll send someone back for you once we're free."

The children skittered down the few remaining yards of tunnel as Icepick yelled behind them, "Hey! Get back here! You can't leave me like this!"

Molly thought she'd be happier about finally getting revenge for Robot. Icepick deserved worse, in her opinion. But she found no joy in the angry cries that echoed behind her.

Those cries finally stopped as the children stepped out of the tunnel and found Rector standing in a rocky clearing, agog at his surroundings. The cavern was immense, extending for what seemed like miles in every direction.

And the Ambrosium's dancing lights were reflected everywhere, their colors twinkling among the myriad crystals that covered the walls and ceiling of the cavern. Between the explorers and the source of those lights, however, stood a vast forest of bizarre, tree-sized mushrooms. The fantastic fungi towered over Molly, both tantalizing and forbidding, in vivid pinks and yellows. Molly half expected to see a talking caterpillar lounging atop one.

"I take it this is a part of Antarctica you have *not* been to before," Molly said to Rector.

"No," he admitted. He clicked off the electric torch, which he no longer needed, thanks to the multihued glow of the Ambrosium. "But you see, Molly? You see the opportunities I give you? Me, not your mother. Not silly old Bell. Me, Ambrose . . . Ambrose . . ."

"Rector," Molly said. Wow, she thought, his brainpower was floundering rapidly. And he seemed aware of it. She could see the fear in his eyes.

"Help me get the stone back," he asked plaintively—a genuine plea. But then he cleared his throat. "I might even consider letting you live, if you do."

"Does anybody hear a stream?" Roald asked, catching the sound of lapping water in the distance. "I am rather thirsty."

"It doesn't help that it's so warm down here," Emmett said. The cave had a completely different climate from the world above. The air was warm and humid, almost springlike. The travelers threw off their hats and gloves, and unbuttoned their coats.

A sudden grunting, banging, and crumbling drew everyone's attention back to the tunnel. Icepick spilled out into the cavern, his beard caked with dust and his jacket in shreds. Tumbling with him was a cascade of rock and rubble that filled the entire entryway. The tunnel was impassable.

"Oh, no," Molly muttered. This was her fault, she thought. If only they'd pulled Icepick free when he'd asked. But no, she just had to get her stupid revenge. And now she'd doomed them all.

"What were you thinking!" Emmett shouted at Icepick. "We're trapped now! That was our way out!"

Icepick stood up and glared, his shoulders heaving. His neck, face, and forehead were covered in scrapes and scratches. He gripped a pickax in one hand and a hatchet in the other.

"Of course, you were stuck in a bad situation," Emmett said, much more softly. "And you, um, solved your problem . . . in the way you best knew how. Bravo. Nice initiative."

"Friends?" Roald said. He was pointing behind them. "Are the giant mushrooms supposed to move?"

Everyone looked to see the tall toadstools rustling as an enormous sea spider burst into the open. It looked just like the hideous insectlike crabs they'd seen at the fishing hole—except this one was the size of a horse.

"Run!" Molly shouted.

Everyone scattered, except Icepick, who rushed straight at the creature. He whooped and swung his pickax at the beast. The tool cracked through the giant crustacean's shell, just behind its head. Its long, spindly legs buckled.

Roaring like a rabid bear, Icepick tugged on one of the creature's twelve-foot-long forelegs. He seemed to be trying to rip the leg off, but this jumbo sea spider was much tougher than its tiny cousins. It snapped a machete-like claw at the man, cutting into his thick arm. But Icepick refused to back down. He bent the leg until it cracked, then landed another blow with his pickax. Then another and another, until the animal released one final wheeze and stopped moving.

"Ha!" Icepick crowed, panting and grinning as he kicked the dead crab.

Molly and Emmett looked to each other, horrified by what they'd just witnessed but relieved that fighting a sea monster seemed to have cheered Icepick enough that he no longer wanted to immediately murder them.

"Well, that was fun," Rector said. He pointed to a spot on the cavern roof, far in the distance, where the dancing lights were brightest. "And since there's no going back, we might as well go forward. To my Ambrosium.

On the other side of this stuff." He marched into the forest of titanic fungi.

"Do you think there are more monsters in there?" Roald asked.

"Undoubtedly," Rector called back.

Icepick pushed Roald from behind, forcing him into the thicket of mushrooms. Before following, Molly whispered to Emmett, "He can't fire his flare down here. First chance we get, we have to break away and rush ahead to the meteorite ourselves."

"Agreed. As soon as we see a good place to ditch them, we run," Emmett said. "We need a signal, though."

"*For Robot*," Molly said immediately. "That's the signal. Tell Roald when you can." They hurried into the shady recesses of the mushroom grove before anyone noticed they were lagging behind.

Lake of Doom!

"WERE THE CRABS that big on your last trip to the Antarctic?" Molly asked, catching the mushroom stalk that Rector had pushed out of his own way and into hers. "'Cause that would've been something worth mentioning."

"Firstly, they're sea spiders," Rector replied. "And, no, the giantness is . . . new. All of this is new." The deeper they forged into the fungi, the softer the ground became, shifting from crystal-specked rock to a bed of spongy pink moss.

"My guess is that the meteorite has something to do with it," Emmett said. "The weird energy it radiates is probably what crystallized the stone and made the mushrooms grow so tall. It seems to have affected the local wildlife too."

"Hrrmph," Icepick grunted. "I will kill anything in my path."

"And that would be my cue to walk *behind* Icepick," said Emmett.

After twenty minutes of squeezing between floppy mushroom stalks, Rector emerged onto a lichen-coated shore. "I have discovered the source of that watery-type sound we were hearing." A vast subterranean lake of shimmering violet water stretched out before them.

"Though I am still thirsty," said Roald, "I do not think I will drink this."

They stared across a half mile of purple-tinted water to the opposite shore. It promised yet more colossal mushrooms, plus a labyrinthine course of rocky ledges that ran up the cavern walls and . . .

"Look way up there," Emmett said, pointing. "There's the crack in the cavern roof. That's where we were! The stone must be right below it, past the mushrooms on the other side of the water."

"Bother beans," Molly moaned. "It's gonna take forever to walk around this lake. Should we camp here?" She checked her pack for the tent within.

"Not when there are giant sea spiders," said Roald.

"Giant sea *crabs*," said Rector. "But I agree, we can't waste time hiking around this water. We're going across it."

"Not me," Molly said, "I can't swim."

"I didn't say swim, I said cross."

Roald crouched by the lake's edge. "Is this purple water safe?"

Rector gave the boy a nudge and Roald splashed into the water. "Well, he doesn't seem to have melted."

"You maniac!" Molly cried, helping Emmett pull Roald from the lake. "What if it had been dangerous?"

"What, you three are friends now?" Rector said drily. "Delightful."

"It is okay," Roald said, spitting purple. "But how do we cross?"

"Yeah, Rector," Molly said, putting her hands on her hips. "Has your genius brain figured out how to build a boat down here?"

"Of course," Rector scoffed.

Long pause.

"The mushroom caps," Emmett said, tired of waiting. "If they're like normal mushrooms, they should float. Um, Icepick, could you get some down for us?"

Fifteen minutes later, they were rafting across the violet lake on two upturned fungus caps the size of dinner tables. Rector and Molly rode together on one, while Icepick took the boys on another. The travelers knelt to keep their balance, while using smaller, broom-sized toadstools to paddle.

Molly found the activity strangely calming. There was an otherworldly beauty to the purple lake and the

319

dazzling sparkles overhead. And not much could be heard beyond the gentle swoosh of the paddles.

Until they were halfway across and a burbling started up between the two rafts. "What do you think the chances are that the fish in this lake are normal size?" Emmett asked.

A slick silver-gray form erupted from the water, sending both mushroom caps spinning off in opposite directions. Everyone threw themselves flat, gripping the edges of their makeshift rafts.

"Holy hagfish!" Molly cried. Twenty feet of ugly eel was jutting up from the water. The ghastly creature arced its titanic body and stared at her. At least, she assumed it was staring—she wasn't quite sure where its eyes were. Or if it had eyes. It definitely had a mouth, though—one big enough to swallow her whole.

"Paddle harder!" Emmett yelled.

The hagfish lurched at Molly, but Rector hurled his mushroom paddle into the creature's maw. The giant eel chomped down on the toadstool and dipped back underwater. Molly realized she'd been gripping their raft so tightly, she'd ripped off chunks of it that now crumbled between her fingers.

"Where is it now?" Molly sputtered.

"Who cares? Just paddle!" Rector shouted. He lay on his belly and began hand paddling toward the far shore.

Icepick, Emmett, and Roald snapped out of their collective stupor and did the same. Still a good fifty yards from land, their raft was bumped from below. The big mushroom cap was launched into the air and when it splashed back down, both Roald and Icepick tumbled off into the water.

On all fours, Emmett looked around in a panic. Icepick was floundering just a few feet away, while Roald was a bit farther off. And the hagfish was circling in a wide loop. Emmett reached out to Icepick and helped him back onto the mushroom.

"Help me with Roald now," Emmett said.

But Icepick placed his size sixteen boot on the boy's chest and shoved him off the raft. Emmett landed with a splash as Roald swam to his side. Icepick continued toward the shore, leaving both boys treading purple water.

Molly tried to change direction, but Rector remained firmly set on the shore. "Help me rescue the boys," Molly said. "Or, so help me, I will jump in too. And you won't have any of us when you need us for your plan."

"Fine!" Rector barked. Together, they paddled to the boys and pulled both onto their raft.

"I am going to make Icepick pay for this," Molly snarled as she helped Emmett steady himself. Then, without warning, the giant hagfish burst from the water, directly beneath Icepick's raft. The henchman and his mushroom cap both disappeared down the creature's gullet.

"Or maybe I won't," said Molly.

The hagfish returned to the lake depths.

"Do you think it is coming back?" Roald asked.

"Who cares? Keep paddling!" Rector shouted. "I swear you children are more interested in asking questions than you are in surviving!"

Finally, they reached the far shore, grateful to be back on dry—albeit squishy—land. They took off their wet parkas and dripping packs.

"Let's just leave this stuff and come back for it," Molly suggested.

But Roald slung one of the damp packs onto his back. "I will carry one," he said. "If we need to sleep down here, I want a tent so I do not see what eats me."

"What do you think we'll run into next?" Emmett asked. "Giant penguins?"

"They could kill us with cuteness!" Molly said.

"Anything could be in there, no?" Roald asked, nodding toward the thick mushroom forest that began anew on this side of the lake.

"Yes," said Rector. "Which is why we're going to avoid it. Look at this lovely arch. It's like someone built a ramp just for us." A natural rock bridge arced upward from the shore, toward the cavern wall. Rector stepped onto it. "Archy here will take us up to those ledges. It's a bit of a detour, but if we can stay high above whatever monsters might be hiding in the . . . you know, the big spongy things—they grow out of the ground and taste like socks?"

"Mushrooms?" Emmett said.

"No, not mushrooms, you ignoramus," Rector snapped. "*Those* things!" He pointed at the mushrooms.

"Those *are*—"

"Not important," Molly said quickly, wondering if Rector had been *this* brain-addled back when he worked for Bell and Edison. Either way, it was time to use Rector's deterioration to their advantage. "That's a good plan, Rector," she said. "We should head straight up to those ledges."

"Indeed," said Rector. He put his hands on his hips and raised an eyebrow. "You're all children. Why are you all children? I could have sworn I had some adults with me. What happened to your nanny?"

"Agent Forrest?" Emmett asked, somewhat gently. "He fell through that crack. Remember?"

Rector shrugged. "Well, that was foolish of him." He turned and marched up the rock bridge.

"Um, this bridge looks very thin in places," Roald said, examining the stone arch from below. "Will it hold us?"

"Don't insult Archy," Rector scolded as he reached the top. "See? Survival."

Down below, Molly and Emmett exchanged glances. This was their chance to ditch Rector. "For Robot!" Molly said loudly.

"For Robot!" Emmett echoed. They spun on their heels and ran for the mushroom forest.

"For Robot!" Roald yelled. And he raced up the rock bridge.

Molly skidded to a halt. "We forgot to tell Roald the signal!"

"Roald! Wait!" Emmett shouted.

But the cabin boy was triumphantly galloping up to Rector. And just as he reached the peak of the arch, the thin rock crumbled beneath him. Molly and Emmett gasped. For a second Roald was airborne, fifty feet above the cavern floor. But his momentum carried him across the gap and his fingers caught the ridge of rock where Rector stood. Molly and Emmett breathed a sigh of relief as Roald clawed his way onto the ledge.

"You know, that kid really is good at a lot of stuff," Emmett said.

Rector scowled. "You broke Archy," he said. "Hey, you broke Archy and I broke Archie! That's funny." He chuckled to himself while Roald stared down at Molly and Emmett, confused.

"Friends?" the boy called.

"What do we do?" Emmett whispered.

Molly bit her lip. Cassandra's words about the Mothers of Invention echoed in her mind. "We have to get the stone first," she said. "Then we hope to help Roald later."

Emmett cupped his hands by his mouth. "It's all up to you now, Roald!"

Roald looked much happier. "I am very good at being up to things!"

Molly and Emmett ducked in among the mushrooms.

"Cutting straight through this forest should be much faster than navigating all those zigzag ledges," Emmett said as they ran amid the oversized yellowish stalks.

"Yeah, as long as nothing gets in our way, we'll be under that crack long before Rector," Molly said as the mushroom directly before her fell over, cleaved in two by a crab claw the size of her head. "I just had to jinx us, didn't I?"

"This way!" Emmett yelled, fleeing in a different direction as the enormous sea spider clicked its pincers at them. "Hurry!"

The children moved as fast as they could, but the fungi had become too dense; they could barely squeeze between them. The creature took a swipe at Molly, but she ducked and the scissorlike claw chopped straight through an oak-thick mushroom stalk.

"Over here!" Emmett shouted. "There's a clearing!" They pushed their way out of the dense grove, onto open ground. Unfortunately, the "clearing" was actually a tight alcove—a barely fifteen-foot nook of spongy pink moss, surrounded on three sides by steep rock walls. There was nowhere to run. Molly and Emmett pressed their backs against the cold stone and gripped each other's hands, helpless, as the colossal sea spider chopped its way through the fungi to face them down.

"Yah!" A figure leapt down from a ledge overhead. The man crashed onto the back of the sea spider, knocking all eight legs out from under it. He rammed a long spear into the beast, expertly piercing it between two plates of tough shell. The big crab gurgled and collapsed. The man—weathered but strong, with ragged clothing and a long, unkempt beard—hopped down from his kill.

Emmett nearly fell over. "Papa?"

Phantoms!

"Oh, Emmett, I didn't see you there," the newcomer said casually, as if there was nothing at all unusual about this situation. He gave the children a friendly nod before pulling his spear from the dead sea spider and proceeding to hack off its legs with a knife fashioned from a jagged soup tin. Could this really be Emmett's father?

"Papa?" Emmett managed to say. "Father?"

"Yes, Emmett, I am your father," Captain Lee said, going about his seafood preparation. "Hmph. I thought you would have something more interesting to say. Who's your friend? She's new."

Emmett said nothing, so Molly jumped in. "I'm Molly Pepper. I'm Emmett's, well, like you said, we're friends. Best friends."

"That's nice," said Captain Lee. "I always wanted

Emmett to have a friend." He smiled at the thought, then hacked off the final crab leg. He had the muscular arms of a man who'd been tearing enormous monsters apart for years. And the paleness of someone who'd been living underground for that long.

"You're really him, aren't you? Captain Wendell Lee?" Molly asked.

"No," he said sadly. "Hard to see how I can call myself captain when I haven't seen the sea in forever." He tossed the crab legs over one broad shoulder and walked off into the mushroom forest.

His sudden exit roused Emmett. "Wait! Papa! Don't go!"

"Ha!" they heard Captain Lee laugh. "Where am I going to go? Hmm, these legs look nice and meaty. Should fill me up for a while."

The children ran after him.

"Oh, you're following me," Captain Lee said. "That's interesting." And then he muttered something in Chinese.

Emmett paused at the sound of his father speaking his native language, but Molly nudged him onward. Captain Lee cut through the mushrooms to a spot on the cavern wall where cracks and protrusions formed natural stair steps. He climbed up to a ledge overlooking the forest, and the children carefully followed.

"Papa!" Emmett called again. "What's wrong with him?" he asked Molly. She shook her head and shrugged as they followed the captain through a door-sized hole in the rock wall.

They entered a cave similar to the one in which they'd found the skeleton—the skeleton of the man who was now standing before them, very much alive. This cave, however, was much more homey. There were stools and tables, carved from giant mushroom stalks, and a mushroom cap bed with a blanket of woven moss. A collection of spears and fishing poles leaned against walls that were decorated with finger-painted stick figures. Most of the images depicted two figures together, one large and one small.

"Captain Lee," Molly said as the man laid his bundle of crab legs by an ash-filled firepit.

"So formal!" he laughed. "What a polite dream-phantom your friend is, Emmett. But didn't I say I'm not a captain anymore? It's just *Mr.* Lee."

"Dream-phantom?" Molly looked to Emmett.

"Papa," Emmett said as the reality of the situation began to dawn on them. "Papa, we're *real*."

Captain Lee expertly ignited a fire by clacking two stones together, and began roasting a hunk of shellfish. "Yes, of course you are real," he said. "I didn't mean to offend you. You are very real. As always." A tear rolled down his creased cheek. "You look older today," he said, his tone bittersweet. "Is this, I wonder, what you might look like after all this time?"

Emmett crouched next to his father. "This *is* what I look like, Papa. Because this is really me. I'm really here."

"Okay, now you're just annoying me," Captain Lee grumped, plucking the seared crab meat from his skewer and waggling it at the boy. "Evaporate and let me eat in peace. Come back and haunt me tomorrow."

Emmett looked flustered, so Molly took matters into her own hands. She snatched the piece of meat from the captain and bopped his shaggy head with it.

Emmett's father fell off his stool. He looked suddenly terrified. "What are you?" He reached out and tentatively poked Molly's arm. "You're real," he breathed. "*Real* real. Not in-my-memories real. Not in my head."

"That's what we've been saying," Molly said.

"Then . . ." He sat up and looked at his son. "Emmett?"

Emmett gave a shaky nod.

"Hug him already!" Molly said.

Father and son threw their arms around each other. Emmett rested his cheek on Captain Lee's shoulder, sobbing openly. Wendell Lee stroked his son's hair, pressing the boy tightly to his chest. "You're real," he repeated. "I can't believe you're real. I . . . How are you here?" He placed his hands on either side of his son's head and looked into his eyes. "You shouldn't be here. This is a dangerous place."

"We know," Emmett said. "But we had to come. We

were looking for you."

"Well, your body," Molly said. "We were looking for your body. And we thought we found it."

"You did find my body!" He gleefully threw his arms in the air. "I'm in it!"

"No, Papa, she means we found another body—a skeleton, in a cave like this, but up on the surface," Emmett said. "But I thought you were dead long before we found that skeleton. I—I never imagined someone could survive here alone!"

"But I did!" He clapped his hands, pumped up with a giddy energy that made it seem like he'd just downed an entire pot of coffee. "Ha-ha! That's your father for you, Emmett! I survived! I survived until you found me!" He got suddenly quiet and serious again. "How *did* you find me? The crabs could have gotten you! There are crabs here the size of palominos."

"We know. We were being attacked by one when you found us," said Molly.

"That was real too?" Captain Lee said. "Well, that puts a new spin on things. I was probably very rude to you down there. I'm much more welcoming to people I don't think are imaginary."

"It's fine, Papa," Emmett said. "You saved our lives."

"Yes, we're alive and you're alive," Molly said. "So, who was the skeleton wearing your jacket?"

"Oh, you must have found Ezra," Emmett's father

said. "See, there was a man on the *Frost Cleaver* with me called Ambrose Rector. He's the one who forced me off the ship. But I suppose I was the lucky one, compared to what he did to the rest of the crew. Such horrible things . . ."

Molly wanted to tell him that they knew all about Ambrose Rector, but Emmett was listening with such silent intensity, she didn't interrupt.

"Ambrose tossed his victims off the ship before he sailed away, and I buried them. But Ezra was still breathing. Barely. I took care of him as long as I could, but he eventually died on me. And then there was the earthquake. And then I ran out of food. So I left the cave and followed the lights—just like Ambrose said *he* had—and they led me to this place. That was my miracle, Emmett. This place has food, water, shelter, warmth . . . If I'd been able to get Ezra here, he might have recovered."

"Are you talking about Ezra *Hopper*? The *Frost Cleaver*'s navigator?" Emmett asked. "In your letter, you said he hated you, treated you awfully."

"He did," his father said plainly. That told Molly all she needed to know about Captain Wendell Lee.

Emmett's father shook his head and blinked a few times. "I'm sorry, Emmett, I'm still so confused," he said. "How did you get here?"

"Here, the cave?" Emmett asked. "Or here, Antarctica?"

332

"Either! I don't care. Just please explain *something*!"

"It's a long story," Emmett said.

"I've got time," Captain Lee said, offering toadstool seats to his guests. "And crab meat. Want some?"

"Yes, please!" Molly said enthusiastically.

"Who are you again?" Captain Lee asked, handing her some food.

"Molly Pepper," she replied. "I'm a friend of your son, remember?"

The captain's eyes got that far-off look again. "Yes, I do remember. I had a son once."

"You still do, Papa," Emmett said, waving.

Captain Lee rapped his knuckles against his forehead. "That's right! You're not just in my head this time. That's going to take some getting used to."

"Papa, are you okay?"

"Never better," he said with a smile. "You have to understand, seeing you and talking to you here in this cave is nothing new for me. It's just never been the real you. That's why you always tended to look a bit different each time. I drew pictures of you so I wouldn't forget what you looked like." He gestured to the stick figures on the wall.

"You've put on some weight, Emmett," said Molly.

"At least your head's not as round," Captain Lee added. He raised a finger. "But wait—how did you get here, again? You children aren't alone, are you?"

"No, we're not," Emmett said. "Which is why we actually *don't* have a lot of time." He sighed. "None of this is going to make sense unless we tell you everything. Even then, it may not."

Captain Lee listened intently as Emmett and Molly rattled off a quick summary of the events that brought them together and led them to that cavern.

"Ambrose Rector is *here*?" he finally asked. "And he's after the glow rock?"

"Is that what you call it?" asked Molly.

"It's a rock that glows: glow rock," Captain Lee said. "It's a better name than 'Ambrosium,' that's for sure."

"Do you know where it is?" Emmett asked.

"Of course."

"Can you take us to it?" asked Emmett.

"No," his father replied. "You stay here. *I* will go confront Ambrose. It's too dangerous for children."

"Were you listening to the story we just told, Mr. Lee?" Molly said. "Emmett and I scaled the Brooklyn Bridge, jumped off a moving train, fought gangsters . . . We've done dangerous."

"Not when I was around," Captain Lee said. "I would not have allowed any of that."

"Molly can take care of herself, Papa," Emmett said. "And I can too. After all I've been through, I'm not the same little boy you used to know."

"I can see that." He pointed to one of the stick figures.

334

"For one thing, you have a nose now."

"Don't be afraid for me, Papa," Emmett said. "Be proud of me."

"We're coming with you, Mr. Lee," Molly said. "Just accept it."

Emmett's father rubbed his temples. "All right, you can come with me. But only if you're definitely real."

"We are," Emmett said. He showed his father the ring on his finger. "See? I even have this."

His father's face lit up. "Hey, I have one too!" He lifted his own hand and wiggled a calloused finger to show off a silver ring with a small green stone.

"You . . . still have your ring?" Emmett said, baffled.

"Of course I do," said Captain Lee. "This ring is my only reminder of your mother. I *never* take it off."

Emmett's eyes moved between the two rings. "Then whose ring is this?" he asked.

"Isn't it yours?" his father said cheerfully before jumping to his feet and gathering weapons. Emmett watched, his jaw slack.

Molly leaned over and whispered, "You're worried about him, aren't you? He's a bit off, but you gotta figure three years alone with crab monsters can do that to a person. Plus, he's been soaking in rays from that meteorite. Maybe—"

"No, I'm worried about *me*," Emmett said. He looked at his hand as if it were some alien creature. "This ring is a little like my father's, but the design, the markings—they're totally different. The gem isn't even the same shade of green. Why was I so certain this was his ring? A ring I'd stared at and studied so intensely when I was younger?"

"Maybe because you needed it to be his," Molly said. "Maybe you needed a part of him back in your life."

He looked at Molly with tears in his eyes. "I can't believe I found him." He sniffled. "Molly, I will never again tell you any of your ideas are ridiculous, or far-fetched, or—"

"Coming here *was* ridiculous and far-fetched," Molly said with a smile. "It's a miracle things worked out like this. Odds were much better we'd end up dead."

"We haven't actually ruled that out yet, you know," Emmett said.

Captain Lee walked up to them with an armload of hand-sharpened spears and homemade daggers. "Shall we?"

Showdown at the Space Rock

THE BOLD, UNFLINCHING manner in which Captain Lee made sudden turns to leap over a certain rock or cut between two very specific mushrooms made Molly assume the man must have gotten to know the layout of this subterranean world inside and out. Which was good, since their stopover at the captain's cave, as pleasant a surprise as it was, cost them a good deal of time in their race to the rock. Still, they should get there ahead of Rector. The villain's head was so loopy when they last saw him, Molly couldn't imagine him finding the pack on his own back, let alone navigating a maze of ledges through a disorienting cavern.

"Keeping up, son?" Captain Lee called back.

"Yes," Emmett replied. "I just keep feeling like this must be a dream."

"Aw, it's not a dream, is it?" Captain Lee moaned. "I was finally accepting the idea that you two were real. Or—wait! Maybe the entire last three years have been a dream. That would explain the giant shellfish."

"No, we're real," Emmett said. "And so is the danger if Rector gets that meteorite."

"Don't worry, son," his father said. "We're almost there." He led them to a grotto in which several stone arches branched up toward the ledges that rimmed the cavern walls. Molly stopped.

"Um, the last one of those we saw almost killed our friend Roald," she said.

"Fear not," Captain Lee said, starting up the nearest rock bridge. "I may have spent the last several years talking to people who weren't there, but I know which paths in this place are safe and which aren't. Do you trust me?"

Molly hesitated. "Would you be offended if I said I wasn't sure?"

"I trust you," Emmett said. They followed his father up the arch.

"That's good after all this time," his father said. "I've missed a lot, haven't I? Given thought to a career yet, Emmett? You'll have to provide for a family of your own soon enough."

"I just turned twelve!"

Molly snickered. And then blushed. She sincerely

hoped Emmett's father wasn't imagining *her* in this future scenario.

Captain Lee shrugged. "I used to think about such things all the time when I was your age," he said. "I couldn't wait to be a man."

"I can," said Emmett. "I'd like some time to be a kid first."

Captain Lee moved briskly along the mazelike ridges, using his spear as a walking stick.

"We should warn you," Molly said, "as evil as Rector was to you and your crew, he's gotten worse."

Emmett's father turned around and raised a stern finger. "All the more reason for you children to let me handle the man when we find him."

"No, offense, Papa," said Emmett, "but Molly and I have more experience with Rector than you do. We know how he thinks. You should let us take the lead on this."

"Young people today," Captain Lee scoffed. "The boy thinks he knows more than his father, just because his father has been living in a hole for years."

He turned and continued along the narrow ledges. The trio inched around a corner and found themselves overlooking a vast expanse of purplish water. "Another lake?" Molly asked.

"Same one," Captain Lee replied. "It fills up most of this place."

The colored lights were much brighter now, the very air shimmering like rainbows on a soap bubble. "We must be close," said Emmett.

"*Shhh!*" His father ushered them past him, around a corner onto a long, triangular outcropping that jutted over the lake like a fang. At the pointed tip of that protruding cliff sat a glowing orange boulder the size of an elephant. Had it been hollow, all three of them could have fit inside, with room to stretch their legs. It had to weigh at least a ton. Molly felt foolish to think she could have "snatched it away" on her own.

"Congratulations," said a familiar voice. Molly and Emmett, in a panic, raced farther out onto the cliff and saw Ambrose Rector, hammer and chisel in hand, on the far side of the meteorite. When he saw them, he slipped the tools back into his pockets. Molly grimaced. *How did he make it here so fast?*

Rector clapped his hands. "Bravo, Miss Pepper. Credit where credit is due," he said. "Kudos to you for figuring out my little secret. Lack of Ambrosium was indeed having an effect on my cerebral processing power. No one else had a clue, of course, because I am such a brilliant actor. But you, Molly—you figured it out. So, cheers to you for that."

"You admit that I've bested you," Molly said. "I assume that means you're giving up and turning yourself over to my superior intellect."

"Very droll," said Rector. "But you are so far from winning, you couldn't spot it with a telescope. See, your one lucky guess about my diminishing brainpower allowed you to get cocky. And like the man who pulls the arms off a starfish only to suffer the creature's vengeance when it regrows those limbs and smothers him with them, you too have underestimated my ability to regain what I had lost."

"Are there giant starfish down here too?" asked Emmett.

"You've already eaten some Ambrosium, haven't you?" Molly guessed somberly.

"Ding, ding, ding!" Rector crowed. "I chipped off and swallowed some of this orangey goodness the moment I reached it." His eyes got wide and wild. "It's working already! Oh, kids, if only you knew what this felt like. My brain is buzzing like never before. It took seconds— no, half seconds—for the ultimate scheme to pop into my head: I now know how I will exact my ultimate vengeance upon the world that rejected me. If you thought the World's Fair plot was big, wait till you see what's coming. The old Rector is back!"

"We've beaten you when you were all hopped up on space rock before; we'll do it again," Molly said defiantly. "You've had your last of that stuff."

"Oh, that's adorable," the villain said. He bent down, retrieved two bowling-ball-sized hunks of Ambrosium at his feet, and placed them into a burlap sack.

Emmett gaped. "How long have you been here?"

"Quite some time now," Rector said, tying the sack to his belt. "But I understand your surprise. I didn't think I'd make it here, either. My brain felt like it was floating in borscht; I probably would have wandered in circles for days without a guide. Luckily, when you two ran off, you left me with the best pathfinder of our sad little group. Roald really is very good at things. I just let the boy run ahead and followed him to the prize."

With horror, Molly's eyes focused on an object lying at the base of the big meteorite: Roald's pack.

"Where is he?" she shouted. "What have you done with him?"

Rector gestured toward a thick rope on the ground. One end stuck out from beneath his left boot, while the other ran over the edge of the cliff. "He's at the other end of this rope. Which I believe dampens your plans for 'stopping' me. See, if you take one step in my direction, I lift my foot and Moldy-Roaldy goes into the grape juice."

"Roald?" Molly called. "Are you really there? Are you okay?"

"The rope is a little tight around my waist," the cabin boy's voice called from beyond the cliff's edge. "And the big hagfish looks hungry down below. But otherwise, I am good. Better than Agent Forrest. He is on the rocks here, halfway down. He is dead. I would rather not be seeing him right now."

342

"We're gonna help you, Roald!" Emmett shouted. "Hang on!"

"That is what I am doing," Roald replied.

"This should be amusing," Rector scoffed.

"You think we can't stop you, Rector?" Molly said, her muscles tensed for action. "It's three against one."

"You're counting Roald?" Rector laughed. "I'm sure he feels very appreciated, but I don't think he'll be helping much in his position."

Molly and Emmett looked over their shoulders to discover that Captain Lee was nowhere to be seen. "He was really there, right?" Molly whispered. "We're not the ones seeing dream-phantoms, are we?"

"Ahem! Hello? Bad guy talking over here!" Rector waved to get their attention again. "Thank you. I was just about to show you what I've built already. Look! It took me, like, ten minutes!"

He twisted at the hips to show them a device strapped to his back. He'd built some sort of machine directly into his pack. Several patches of fabric had been cut out to reveal connective wires and metal panels with toggle switches. "I call it my antigravity booster," he said. He flicked the switch, the pack began to hum, and Rector's entire body began to hover off the ground. The rope he'd been standing on immediately began slipping away, over the side of the cliff, but Rector quickly landed again and caught the cord beneath his boots.

"I have not died!" Roald yelled.

"You see, I thought that if the space rock could make your Robot friend fly, why couldn't it do the same for me?" Rector pointed up to the big crack in the cavern roof and the sunny blue sky beyond. "So, I'll be flying straight out of here and soaring off with a flock of penguins."

"Um, penguins don't actually—"

"Not now, Emmett."

"I hope you enjoy this wacky land of king-sized crustaceans and funky fungi," Rector said, "'cause it's your home now."

"Right," Molly said, calling his bluff. "As if you're going to leave us down here with all this Ambrosium to use for ourselves."

"Good point," the villain said. "I'd better cave this whole place in once I'm safely outside. Thank you, Molly." He put his finger on the switch. "But, look, there's something I like about you kids. So, I'll toss your mother down here for a little reunion before I turn the place to rubble. Not Bell, though. He gets to freeze. It's about time Mr. Telephone Man feels what I felt when I was thrown off the *Frost Cleaver* and left to die."

"No one threw you off the ship!" It was Captain Lee, crouched on a ledge twenty feet above them. He leapt down and tackled Rector.

"Papa, no!" Emmett yelled. He jumped in to stop Rector from falling, but was knocked to the ground right next to the villain.

Molly dove and caught Roald's rope before it vanished over the edge. She lay on her belly, both hands wrapped tightly around the rough hemp, as Roald swung back and forth above the frothing purple lake.

Emmett's father stood over Rector, holding the tip of his spear at the villain's chest. "Lee?" Rector blinked. "You're alive?"

"No thanks to you," Captain Lee spat.

"Really, none?" Rector said. "Because I seem to recall a whole bunch of empty food tins in a cave out there."

"Um, guys?" Molly groaned from the cliff edge, where she strained to keep her grip on the rope. "Roald is heavier than he looks."

"It is mostly muscle weight!" Roald called up.

Emmett scrambled to his feet, but didn't get more than two steps in Molly's direction before Rector whipped his hand out of a jacket pocket and aimed a long silver flare tube at him. Emmett froze.

"One squeeze of my thumb and the boy gets a rocket in his face," the villain said. "Maybe you'd like to move that spear, eh, Lee?"

Emmett's father kept his weapon in place. "Why don't you tell these children the truth, Ambrose?" he said. "No one marooned you. When the *Frost Cleaver*'s engine died, you volunteered to go down to the ice and fix it. But instead you ran off."

"What?" Emmett said. "You said they banished you

because they blamed you for the ship's breakdown!"

"Well, I'm sure they did!" Rector blurted. "They thought I built it!"

"You didn't?" Captain Lee asked, confused.

"No, that buffoon Bell built it. But I couldn't let that cretinous crew know that. They'd taunted me, tormented me."

"Guys?" Molly tried again, pain shooting through her wrists. "These are very interesting revelations and all, but . . ."

"The only respect I got from that crew was when they thought I built the ship," Rector continued. "So when I couldn't fix it . . . Do you honestly think they would have let me back on board?"

"I was the captain," Captain Lee said. "*I* would have!"

"As if they respected you," Rector scoffed. "I had no choice but to run. The joke was on them, though! Because fleeing led me to the Ambrosium."

"Which you then used to kill everyone," Captain Lee sneered.

"Except you," Rector said. "I didn't kill *you*. Which I've been saying all along, and no one can refute it now, because the proof is holding a spear to my throat. Those others got what they deserved, though. They were—"

"They were bigots and bullies," Captain Lee said. "But you turned out to be the worst of all. It sickens me to think that I defended you to them."

346

"Please," Molly begged. "My fingers are slipping." She peeked over the edge and saw Roald struggling to keep his feet away from rows of razorlike hagfish teeth. The enormous eel stretched itself upward and squirted a stream of viscous goo all over Roald.

"The hagfish slimed him!" Molly shouted. "He's gonna slide through the knot!"

"This is unpleasant!" Roald confirmed.

"Please let me help them," Emmett pleaded.

"Tell your father to put down his pig-sticker," Rector said in reply.

"Papa?" Emmett said.

Captain Lee huffed, took a step back, and tossed his spear aside.

"The knives too," Rector said.

Captain Lee removed three makeshift blades from his belt and threw them into the rocks. Satisfied, Rector stood up and nodded, but he kept his flare trained on Emmett as the boy ran to Molly's side and helped her haul Roald away from the monstrous eel. Roald slid up onto the cliff, dripping with goo.

The muscles in Molly's arms were throbbing, but her fury at Rector was stronger than her physical pain. She scooped up a handful of hagfish slime and whipped the goop into Rector's face.

As Rector blinked and spat, angrily wiping the gunk from his eyes, Emmett's father grabbed his arm and attempted to wrestle the flare away. The flare went off. A small rocket burst from the tube and jetted straight up through the huge crack in the cavern roof, where it exploded, a shower of sparks in the cloudless sky.

"No!" Molly screamed. "They'll see the signal! They'll kill my mother!"

"What?" Emmett's father sputtered. He released Rector and turned to Molly, horror and confusion on his face. Seizing the moment, Rector swung his sack of rocks into the captain's head. Captain Lee crumpled.

"Papa!" Emmett rushed to his father's side.

Grinning wickedly, Rector flicked the switch on his antigravity booster and began to levitate off the ground.

"Molly," Emmett yelled. "He's getting away with the stones!"

Molly dove for the fleeing villain, but slipped in a puddle of hagfish slime and slid straight off the edge of the cliff. Acting on instinct, she tightened her grip on the rope that was still in her hand and managed to hang on as Roald grunted overhead and her fall came to a jerky stop.

"Do not worry!" Roald cried. "I have got you!"

Molly's relief was short-lived, though. The rope was covered in slime, and she couldn't fight her slow but steady downward slide. There was a splash from below, and the hagfish launched itself upward. She swung her legs to avoid the creature's toothy maw, but in doing so, she slipped free of the rope completely. Flailing in midair, she grabbed on to the only thing she could reach—Agent Forrest, whose broken body was draped over a rock halfway down the cliff.

"I made it!" she cried out, trying to ignore the fact that she was now dangling from a corpse. She looked down as the hagfish dove back below the water. In seconds, she knew, that thing was going to hurl itself at her again. The rope was too far. And too slimy. She looked up at Roald's concerned, helpless face, and movement caught her eye—Rector flying up toward the exit with his bag of magical rocks.

"Ta-ta, failures!" Rector called. "Never forget, Molly, that you turned down your chance to partner with the only guy getting out of here alive!"

Molly was beginning to lose her grip on Agent Forrest's cold, blue hand. At least Emmett would get to spend his final moments with his father, she thought. Her mother was probably already gone, thanks to that stupid flare. *Flare!*

Fighting the fatigue in her arms, she frantically fished through the dead agent's pockets with her free hand until she found Forrest's flare launcher. She might never leave that cave, but maybe she could make sure Rector didn't either. She aimed the flare at the fleeing villain, whispered a silent thanks to her mother for forcing her to wear glasses, and pressed the fire button.

The rocket exploded against Rector's antigravity pack. Screaming and trying to beat out the flames, he spiraled out of control and crashed into the cavern wall. His unconscious form landed in a heap on a high ledge.

"I did it," she whispered. She heard the water stir below her as her fingers finally slipped free from Forrest's. She closed her eyes and fell . . . onto a cot? She opened her eyes. She was on a sheet of canvas, tautly stretched between two tin poles. The sound of cheering made her look up to see Emmett turning a crank to hoist her swinging stretcher upward on the rope from which it was suspended. When she reached the top and saw the primitive pulley system that had hauled her to safety, she instantly knew whose work had saved her life.

"How did you do this, Emmett?" she asked as Roald and Captain Lee helped her down.

Emmett beamed. "I used the tent from Roald's pack! I separated the poles and poked them through the canvas and used the tie cords to secure them and turned that empty pudding can into—"

"It doesn't matter!" Molly squeezed him in the tightest hug she'd ever given. "You're a genius!"

"He is, isn't he?" Captain Lee said with pride. He nudged Roald. "You see what my son built? And so quickly?"

"Yes, I was here," replied Roald.

Molly finally released Emmett. "Tell me again how you're going to quit inventing," she said, tears mixing with the slime on her cheeks.

Emmett shrugged sheepishly. "Still not sure I can construct us a way out of here, though."

His father patted his back. "At least we are together."

A streak of silver entered the cavern from above. Robot settled down next to his friends, colored lights reflecting from his aluminum chest.

"Robot? Robot!" Molly sputtered. "Where did you come from?"

"The sky," Robot said, pointing upward.

"Now, *this* is definitely a dream-phantom," Captain Lee said. "Right?"

Molly embraced the automaton. "But how, Robot? How are you here?"

"Remember when you asked me how far I could fly?" Robot said. "The answer is *very*."

"You flew here all the way from Barbados?"

"Yes."

"I can't believe it," Molly said. "I thought I'd lost you too."

"Too?" said Robot. "Who else did you lose?"

"My mother," Molly said, her voice catching.

"I can help you find her," Robot said, unfazed. "She is on the boat. I saw her only four point three minutes ago."

"What do you mean? You saw her on the *Aqua-*

Zephyr?" Emmett asked. "Were you able to save her before coming here?"

"Mrs. Pepper saved herself," Robot said. "Several days ago, she overpowered her captors, took control of the ship, and turned it into a snow-crawler, just as she said she would. She and Mr. Bell and I have been searching for you for the last forty-eight hours. It was very helpful when you sent up that flare through the crevice. It assisted us in locating you."

Molly was crying. And laughing.

"You seem confused. I will take you to your mother." Robot scooped Molly into his arms. "Maybe that will help you figure out which emotion to have."

They flew up through the crack in the earth.

"I am a bird," said Robot.

"And an excellent metaphor maker," Molly replied.

As soon as they hit the open air, Molly felt the harsh chill of Antarctica again. But she'd barely had time to register how cold she was when she saw the *AquaZephyr* clomping across the snow-covered rock on six insectlike mechanical legs. Cassandra Pepper stood at the helm, waving.

Molly waved back, beaming. "Of course she made it," she said. "I should never have thought otherwise."

"Because Peppers never give up?" Robot asked.

"Yes, Robot. Because Peppers never give up."

Never Give Up

MOLLY WAS STILL in her mother's arms on the deck of the *AquaZephyr* when Robot dropped Emmett off beside them, and Emmett joined the group hug. Roald did the same a few minutes later, which was only slightly awkward.

"I can't believe you built your snow-crawler," Molly said as Robot flew back into the cavern. "I mean, I *can* believe it. Because you are a genius inventor. And always will be."

"It's incredible, Mrs. Pepper," Emmett said. "Like a mechanical dinosaur!"

"And constructed completely from repurposed materials on the ship," Cassandra added proudly. "Although I must say I had some help," Cassandra said. "From Robot, for instance. And my assistant Alec here." She gave Bell a pat on the back.

"Well, I wouldn't say I was your *assistant*," Bell said.

"Oh?" Cassandra said. "I drew the designs, I gave the instructions . . . What did you do, again?"

"I . . . assisted." Bell cleared his throat. "You've done a remarkable job here, Mrs. Pepper. I am proud to work beside such an extraordinary talent."

"Hey, don't forget about me!" The shout came from Pembroke, who crawled up from a hatch in the deck. Molly immediately hurled a bucket at his head.

"Ow!"

"Molly, no!" Cassandra said. "Mr. Pembroke has been behaving himself, and was actually quite helpful in the construction of the snow-crawler."

"Yeah," Pembroke muttered, rubbing his sore head. "I been assisticating the lady ever since she explained to me how Rector never expected me to survive that explosion. Suddenly-like, I wasn't feeling so loyal to the man no more."

"What about Lars?" Emmett asked.

"I hit him with the coconut Molly gave me," Cassandra replied.

"Is Uncle Lars all right?" Roald asked.

"He's in the brig," Bell said. "He'll recover."

Robot returned and set his next passenger down on the deck.

"Oh, Mrs. Pepper," said Emmett. "This is . . . my father. Captain Wendell Lee."

354

"Please, no 'captain,'" his father said. "It's just Mr. Lee."

Cassandra's eyes were so wide, they barely seemed to fit on her face. "*This*," she said, "I did not see coming."

"I hear you've taken good care of my son," Captain Lee said, shaking her hand. "I can't thank you enough."

Cassandra continued to shake his hand, as if unsure of how to end the gesture. "Emmett's a wonderful boy," she said.

Robot took off again as Bell approached. "I can never adequately apologize for what happened to you, Mr. Lee," Bell said.

"I could consider forgiving you," Captain Lee said, "if you could provide me with a warm change of clothes. It's a lot colder up here than it was in the cavern."

All three children raised their goose-pimply arms. "Us too!"

"Of course!" Bell ran off.

Robot returned once more. He laid down the unconscious form of Ambrose Rector, the singed antigravity booster on his back still smoking. Everybody shifted to the other side of the deck, as if the man had some infectious disease. "Is he—?" Cassandra started.

"Unconscious," Molly said.

"He almost got away," Emmett said. "But Molly stopped him."

"I knew you would," Cassandra said, ruffling both children's hair.

"What do we do with him now, though?" Captain Lee asked.

"Toss him in the brig with Lars," Bell said, returning with an armload of coats that the children and Emmett's father immediately put on. "Once we're back in the States, we'll let the authorities decide his fate. In the meantime, though, do you think Robot would be able to retrieve some bits of that meteorite?"

"Why?" Molly asked with blatant suspicion.

"For experiments," Bell said. *"Carefully monitored* experiments. I know you're skeptical, but this is a previously undiscovered power source! Think of all the ways in which the world could benefit!"

"The world could be hurt by it in all sorts of ways too," Emmett warned.

"Believe me, there will be no similarity between what we do with the Ambrosium and what was done with it by—" Bell turned to where he expected to see the villain splayed out on the deck.

Rector was gone.

"Where'd he go?" Emmett said, looking around in a panic. "He—he was unconscious!"

"Acting!" Rector announced proudly, climbing up from belowdecks. "You people always seem to forget the acting bit. I am a *brilliant* actor." He raised his arm, showing everyone the stick of dynamite he held. Its fuse was lit.

"Ambrose, you're mad! You'll blow us all up!" Bell shouted.

"I suppose I could," Rector replied as he checked the sack at his side. "But what if some of you survived? You'd just find your way back down that hole, grab some Ambrosium of your own, and use it to fight back. Well, not you, Alec. But any of the others might." He flicked the toggle on his antigravity pack and rose off the deck. "Oh, good. Still works." He swooped away and dropped the lit dynamite into the crevasse. "No, I'd rather make sure I'm the only person on Earth with any of this good stuff. I really do wish you had agreed to be my partner, Molly!"

A massive explosion cut off whatever witty retort Molly hoped to shout in reply. The ground shook as flames and smoke erupted from the chasm.

"Everybody hold on," Captain Lee yelled. "Mrs. Pepper, can you operate this vehicle?"

"Of course." Cassandra ran to the helm and started the engine.

The crevasse began caving in. Huge hunks of ice and rock plummeted downward, while tremendous clouds of dust and snow billowed into the sky. The legs of the snow-crawler stirred to life and started clomping away from the crumbling canyon. But the ground was disappearing faster than they were moving.

"The whole cavern roof is going down!" Emmett yelled. "It's miles wide!"

"It's gonna fall out from under us!" Molly shouted. "Go faster, Mother!"

Cassandra slammed the "velocity" lever as far up as it would go. "I hope the vehicle can handle this," she said as the spider-legged ship burst into a gallop. "It's not really built for speed. It is a snow-*crawler*, after all!"

Everyone grabbed the rails, trying with all their might not to be thrown overboard by the tumultuous ride. "I believe in you, Mother!" Molly yelled, though it felt like every bolt on the ship was shaking loose. She prayed the entire thing wouldn't fall apart. She, Emmett, and Roald stumbled, bouncing against the deck. And then, suddenly, the ride slowed. *The engine is failing!* Molly peered over the rail. No, they'd outrun the collapse.

Behind them, the cave-in had turned a huge portion of the landscape into a rubble-filled canyon. Everything that had been in that hidden subterranean world—the giant mushrooms, the sea spiders, the meteorite—was now buried under tons of immovable rock.

Molly looked past the destruction, her eyes following a tiny blot on the far-off sky—Rector, soaring to freedom with his mystical bounty.

"He's doomed himself," Bell said. "He has nowhere to go. He'd never survive a flight to Argentina from here. We were his only way off this wasteland."

Captain Lee stepped out of the wheelhouse. "And he

just destroyed the best source of food and shelter in this place."

Molly shook her head. "He's Ambrose Rector. We haven't seen the last of him."

"Do we go after him?" Emmett asked.

"No," said his father. "We go home."

Homeward Bound

MOLLY AND HER mother stood at the port-side rail, watching the strange, treacherous continent dwindle to a dot on the horizon. They were headed north once more, north to the United States, north to home. But this was not the triumphant return Molly had imagined. She rested her head on her mother's shoulder.

"I'm sorry we never made it to the Pole, Molls," Cassandra said. "I know that was our best chance at being able to reverse our fates once we get home." It had been decided that the risk of Rector seeking vengeance was too great. The man had his Ambrosium. And the rest of Bell's dynamite. The crew set about reverting the *AquaZephyr* to a watercraft that very day. They set sail as soon as they were able.

"We'll figure out a new plan," Molly said. "We always

do." She turned and saw Emmett hugging his father on the ship's bridge. "Besides, we still won."

It filled her with joy to see Emmett reunited with his father. Yet she couldn't help but wonder how Captain Lee's reappearance was going to affect the little family that Emmett and the Peppers had fashioned for themselves.

"Let's go see them," Cassandra said.

"Hey, Captain," Molly said brightly as they entered the wheelhouse.

"Please, Molly," he said. "Can't you just call me Mr. Lee?"

"But you're back at the helm of a ship," she said.

"I suppose I am," he said. "Hmm . . . Captain." He sounded like he was testing the feel of the word. "Okay, yes. You may call me Captain Lee."

Emmett grinned.

"Are you sure you're up to this, Captain Lee?" Cassandra asked. "You've been through quite an ordeal and if you need someone to take over . . ."

"Thank you, Mrs. Pepper," he said. "Perhaps later. But right here, right now, I feel better than I have in years. Just being away from that cave has cleared my head so much. I might still be a bit shaky, but being at the controls of a ship again? This feels right. We Lees are people of the sea, after all."

"Some of us," Emmett said.

His father nodded. "Yes, some of us." He glanced over his shoulder for a final look at the land that had been both his home and prison. "The irony is not lost on me, that I should now be abandoning Ambrose Rector in Antarctica. When I think of all the years that man robbed me of . . ." He lifted his hand from the wheel to wipe a tear. "But we will make up for lost time, won't we, son?" Emmett nodded and gave him another squeeze. "Emmett, why don't you go with your friend? I'd like to speak with Mrs. Pepper for a moment. If that's all right."

"Of course, Captain Lee," Cassandra said. And she waved the children off.

"What do you suppose they're talking about?" Molly said outside.

Emmett let out a long, slow breath. "Me."

"Yeah." Molly bit her lip as they walked along the deck. "Do you want to go back to living with your father?"

Emmett gave a little laugh. "Back where? My father doesn't have a home. He's legally dead."

"But would you *want* to?" she asked.

"I want my family," Emmett said. "My father is my family. But so are you and your mother. I guess it's—"

He quieted as they turned onto the aft deck and saw Roald, staring wistfully out to sea. The cabin boy muttered a halfhearted hello.

"You okay?" Molly asked. "You're probably taking this worse than anyone."

"It is all right," Roald said. "I will be back. It is my destiny." He turned and offered a melancholy smile. "This journey was still a success. I made friends, and I learned things, such as that it is possible for me to make friends. But if you do not mind, I am going to stand here and stare a little longer."

Molly and Emmett left Roald to his musings and turned onto the starboard deck. "He might have a rough time of it when he gets home," Emmett said. "Dealing with his uncle, I mean."

"Home," Molly echoed. She pictured herself in her cramped little pickle-shop bed. It had never seemed so appealing. "It'll be good to be home."

"Will it?" asked Emmett. "We still don't know what the government is going to do with us when we get there. Are we still fugitives?"

"I wonder what happened to the MOI," Molly added. "Do you think they're in jail? Because of us?"

"And what about Nellie?" Emmett said. "We have to tell my father to stop in Turtle Bluff on the way back so we can look for her."

"Maybe she's already gotten the story out," Molly said, allowing herself to get energized by the thought. "In fact, as we speak, the whole world could be learning about our exploits. Maybe we have nothing to worry about. We could be on our way back to a huge heroes' welcome!"

Emmett didn't share her enthusiasm. "That's a big

maybe. Especially since Nellie's notebooks are still all on this ship."

"Don't forget, children, that you have allies in high places." Bell stepped out of his cabin. "Sorry, it wasn't my intention to eavesdrop, but having heard your concerns, I hope I can assuage them. As Guild president, I have quite a lot of influence back home. I promise you, I will do everything in my power to help."

Emmett narrowed his eyes. "Pardon my skepticism, Mr. Bell, but I think you're smart enough to understand our reluctance to trust in one of your promises again."

Bell squirmed a bit. "I suppose I will just have to win your trust back."

Good luck, Molly thought. She'd been through enough to know that the Ambrosium couldn't be trusted in the hands of any power-hungry man. "So sorry you missed your shot at the Pole, Mr. B.," she said, knowing Emmett would catch her sarcasm. "And the space rock too. It's all just so sad for you."

"Yes, well, I . . ." Bell perked up. "By Jove! We still have a sample of the meteorite! The piece inside Robot!"

"Pull the brakes on that train of thought right now, mister!" Molly snapped. "You're not getting anywhere near Robot's heart."

"You made *that* promise too, remember," Emmett said sternly.

Bell cleared his throat. "Yes, of course. I apologize. I

got excited by an idea just now, but I haven't forgotten I gave my word."

"Good, because you can't take that rock out of Robot," Emmett said. "Frankly, I'm worried about how little Ambrosium might be left in him after he flew the whole length of South America to find us."

"Perhaps there's a way we can help each other," Bell said.

Molly didn't like where this was going.

"What if I examined the meteorite while it was still in your friend?" Bell said. "Learning more about it and how it works might help us figure a way to keep it from eroding further. Believe me, I would love to do whatever I can for Robot."

"Can you give me a beard like yours?" Robot asked, hovering down from above. Molly wondered how long he'd been there.

Bell put his arm around the automaton's shoulders. "If it's a beard you want, Rector and his men left a whole selection for you."

"Being alive is fun," said Robot.

"Come, children, let's go make your friend happy," Bell said, leading Robot away.

"You go ahead," Molly said. "We'll catch up in a bit."

"Do you trust him on this?" Emmett asked once Bell was out of earshot.

"Do you?" Molly asked.

"I trust *you*," Emmett replied. "What do you think we should do?"

Molly stared out at the rolling sea. Part of her was so tired of swimming against life's currents. Part of her wanted to give in, let the waves deliver her where they would, and just accept whatever fate the world decided to hand her. Part of her wanted so badly to choose the easier course.

And then there was the rest of her.

EPILOGUE

From the Journals of Alexander Graham Bell

January 17, 1884

Dear Diary,

THEY'RE GONE! Two months of sailing back from Antarctica with them and no word of disagreement, no sign of mutiny, no hint of betrayal. Yes, they were severely disappointed that our return trip to Barbados turned up no sign of Miss Bly, but none of them threatened to abandon the journey over it. In fact, they all seemed generally content on the latter leg of this trip.

Then, today, when I knock on their cabins to tell them that the Florida coast is within sight—they're gone! All of them! Cassandra and Molly Pepper, Emmett, even Captain Lee! Gone! And they took their Robot with them!

How did they even get off the ship? And when? And why?

But I suppose these are mysteries for another time. Right now, I need to go see if that Roald boy knows how to steer the ship. Oh why, dear diary, is life so difficult for a man like me?

Afterword: What's Real and What's Not in 'The Treacherous Seas'

This book is a work of fiction, but many of the people, places, and things that appear in these pages actually existed in world history. So, what's real and what's not?

Nellie Bly: Not only is she real, she's one of the most awesome figures in American history. Nellie Bly revolutionized the world of investigative journalism with her undercover exposé of the Blackwell's Island Insane Asylum (which you may remember from *A Dastardly Plot*). In 1889, Bly also made history by winning a race around the world—and beating the fictional timeframe in Jules Verne's *Around the World in Eighty Days* by a full eight days. See, she's super cool.

Roald: In December of 1911, the decades-long race to reach the South Pole ended when Norwegian explorer Roald Amundsen became the first person to set foot on the legendary geographic location. Is he the same Roald who appears in our story? I'm going to say yes.

Hydrofoils: Yes, Alexander Graham Bell really did invent these funky-looking, super-fast boats. His real hydrofoil was way smaller than the *AquaZephyr*, though. And it never transformed into an awesome snow-crawler. (Also, on a side note, Bell did not actually invent sunglasses or flashlights.)

Tuk Bands: Tuk music is an original Barbadian art form, combining the beats of colonial British military bands with African rhythms. It is accompanied at festivals by costumed dancers portraying specific characters from African folklore. Way back in the 1600s, Tuk band melodies were played on a fiddle, but over time, the fiddles got swapped out for pennywhistles, which were much easier to travel with.

Hagfish and Sea Spiders: Real. The smaller versions, at least. And they're even uglier than you'd imagine. Hagfish really do squirt copious amounts of slime as a defense mechanism. Look them up, but be prepared for nightmares!

Antarctica's Secret Subterranean World: Believe it or not, there are hundreds of lakes buried deep below the Antarctic ice. In 2013, researchers drilled down into the largest of them, Lake Vostok, and recovered samples that suggest the massive, hidden lake is actually teeming with life! Is the Ambrosium waiting to be discovered down there as well? It's not like they're going to tell you.

　—Christopher Healy, 2019

Acknowledgments

On a journey this long and perilous, a writer is bound to hit numerous pitfalls and roadblocks along the way, which is why I need to give tremendous thanks to all the people who helped keep me moving on this leg of the voyage. Thank you to my hardworking editor, Jordan Brown; my tireless agent, Jill Grinberg; and Cheryl Pientka, who helped me first get this boat in the water. Thanks to Jennifer Chu, Barry Wolverton, Shenwei Chang, Martha Brockenbrough, and Christine Howey for the input and advice, and to Kevin Chu at the Museum of Chinese in America, as well. Last, I give endless thanks to the three people I would most want with me on any journey: Noelle Howey, Bryn Healy, and Dash Healy. I'm ready for our next adventure. Are you with me?

Read on for a sneak peek at the conclusion of the
Perilous Journey of Danger and Mayhem series

'THE FINAL GAMBIT'

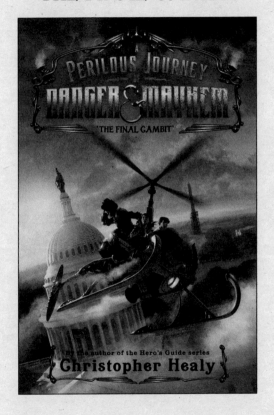

PROLOGUE

Hidden
Buford's Bend, Ohio, October 17, 1884

MOLLY PEPPER HELD her breath and tried to ignore the spider crawling down the bridge of her nose. *It's just a spider,* she told herself. *I don't care about spiders.* This wasn't technically true. Under normal circumstances, Molly *loved* spiders. She once tried to keep an unusually fuzzy one as a pet, an experiment that sadly ended when the creature found its way down the back of her mother's dress. Ignoring this particular spider on her face, however, was proving more difficult by the second. The tickle of tiny legs skittering across her cheek was almost unbearable, but she dared not shake, scratch, or sneeze, because the slightest movement would disturb the sticks and branches piled on top of her and give away her hiding place. The people looking for her would find her. And then it would all be over.

She could hear dry grass crunching beneath the feet of her pursuers just outside the firewood bin, where she lay curled beneath the kindling. But the spider had reached her top lip. Carefully as she could, Molly thrust her lower jaw forward and attempted to blow the spider off. But if there's one thing spiders are good at, it's sticking in place.

"Where is she?" a frustrated voice griped nearby. "We've looked everywhere!"

"Don't worry, she's not getting away this time," came the reply. "Let's check the well!"

As the footsteps outside the bin began to recede, the spider decided to explore Molly's nostril. The sensation was more than she could bear. Twigs scattered and clattered as she leapt from the woodbin, wiping her face and blowing vigorous puffs of air from her nose.

"Drat!" she grumbled, expecting to see her pursuers rushing back to her along the side of the barn where she'd just emerged from the woodpile. But they were nowhere to be seen. She craned her neck to peer down the hill to the circle of stones surrounding the family well. No one. Where had they gone? There was no way they'd gotten far enough away that they wouldn't have heard the commotion she'd just made. It was a trap. Had to be.

She pressed herself against the barn's bright blue wood-plank wall and tiptoed to its rear. Peeking around the corner, she saw nothing but rain barrels. And a clear shot to the house—her cute little yellow house, with its cute little porch and cute little rocking chairs. If she could make it to the house, she'd be safe.

She took another glance behind her. They must have gone inside the barn. That was the only possibility. Her mother was in there. And Emmett. And while Molly didn't like using them as a distraction, she knew it might keep her pursuers busy long enough for her to make a run for the porch. She took a deep breath, rose onto the balls of her feet, and took off at a full sprint.

"Gotcha!"

A figure leapt out from behind the rain barrels, tackling her. Molly yelped as she and her attacker both hit the ground and rolled down the hill in a tangle of arms and legs. They came to a rest by the well and Molly lay in the grass, catching her breath for a few seconds before realizing she was on top of the other girl. "You okay under there, Orla?" Molly asked, unable to stifle a giggle.

"I win!" A small arm poked out from beneath her, raising a fist in victory. "Sometimes it hurts to win."

Laughing, Molly slid aside and freed her friend. Orla wiped her grass-stained hands on her gingham dress as another girl, much taller with a pointy nose and unruly hair, came running down the hill, laughing. "I tagged her, Luddie!" Orla crowed.

Luddie snorted. "You know that 'tagging' is usually done just with the hands, right?"

"Since when do I do things *usual*?" the petite girl said proudly.

"We should hire you out to a rodeo show in need of a

3

bull," Molly said, helping her up.

Luddie gave Molly a playful shove. "You're it this time," she said.

"Okay," said Molly. "But I would advise against hiding in the woodbin unless you don't mind spiders in your . . ." She trailed off as she noticed a wagon coming up the road. "Captain Lee's back from town!" Molly said, running off. "He's gonna have the mail."

"Wait!" Luddie shouted. "Spiders in your *what*? You gotta finish that sentence!"

"Yeah, and I wanna know about that rodeo bull thing," Orla added. "Is that a real job? 'Cause I could see myself doing that."

Molly ran up and around the front of the barn, passing the open front doors and giving a cheerful wave to her mother and her best friend, who were hard at work inside. Cassandra Pepper, the unsung genius inventor, was back to doing what she did best: creating astonishingly imaginative and useful machines. And Molly's more-brother-than-friend, Emmett Lee, was working as Cassandra's apprentice—and looking more confident than Molly had ever seen him. Together, the two were putting the finishing touches on her mother's Daedalus Chariot, a new flying machine to replace the one that had been stolen by their archenemy, the diabolical madman Ambrose Rector.

Cassandra, soldering wires in grease-smeared

4

coveralls, looked up, waved, and proudly flashed the medallion that she wore on a chain around her neck. It wasn't really a medallion—it was the lid to a pickle jar—but Molly had etched the words "World's Greatest Inventor" into it as a gift for her. Emmett, balanced on a stepladder to oil the chariot's spinning overhead propeller, flashed Molly a smile as well. Seeing those two so happy, realizing their mutual dreams of being inventors, gave her warm tingles. (The good kind of tingles, not the kind caused by a spider up your nose.)

The horse neighed as Captain Lee's wagon pulled up to the hitching post by the little yellow house. Molly bounded onto the porch and threw herself into one of the comfy rocking chairs that Cassandra had designed to sway in smooth, silent, fluid motion. She glanced around—at the vibrant paint that she still couldn't believe they'd talked Captain Lee into letting them use, at the adorable hummingbirds hovering around the feeder that Emmett had installed, at the window to her very own bedroom. Molly had never thought she'd be able to live this way. Coming here was something she did for the others, she told herself—an act of self-sacrifice. But she could no longer deny that it was pretty darn nice. Even if part of her wished it wasn't.

Captain Wendell Lee hopped down from the wagon with a wave and a smile. Molly wondered if it was still weird for Emmett to no longer be an orphan, after believing he was for so many years. But ever since they'd rescued his father from that cavern in Antarctica the prior year, Emmett was now just a half-orphan, like Molly. Bonding over their missing parents had been one of the things that initially brought Molly and Emmett together as friends. But Molly always felt worse for Emmett, because she at least had fond memories of her father, who'd been such a big part of her life for her first nine years, but Emmett's mother had died giving birth to him back in China; he'd never known her at all.

Captain Lee unloaded two burlap sacks from the wagon, one filled with flour, the other with iron bolts. "Guess which of these your mother requested?" he said with a grin.

"Did you get the mail?" Molly asked.

Captain Lee furrowed his brow. "A hello would be nice."

"Hello, did you get the mail?" Molly asked.

The captain sighed and carried his bundles inside. "It's on the seat."

Molly ran to the cart, gave the old gray horse a friendly pat on the nose, and grabbed the two envelopes and a newspaper that sat on the driver's bench. Back on the porch, she tossed the envelopes onto a small wooden table—she didn't care about those—and began flipping through the paper, scanning, as she always did, for the name of their long-lost friend, investigative journalist

Nellie Bly. Months earlier, on their mission to find Captain Lee, Nellie disappeared on the island of Barbados. She had gone to seek aid from a man named Grimsby, whom they later learned was an employee of Ambrose Rector. No one had heard from Nellie since.

And this newspaper didn't seem like it was going to change that situation. Molly sighed as she folded back the last page. There, she saw a name that made her breath catch in her throat. And it wasn't Nellie Bly's. It was the name of someone who was supposed to be dead. Someone she knew was dead. And yet, there this person was in the newspaper, talking to reporters.

"C'mon, Molly! We're waiting on you for the next round!" Luddie called from the lawn. "Get educated on your own time!"

"Yeah," added Orla. "Unless you are already playing and you're trying to hide behind that newspaper. In which case . . . we found you."

Molly barely heard them. She couldn't tear her eyes from the article.

"Come on, Molly! You're it!"

"I know," Molly muttered as she reread the sentence for the third time.

There was only one explanation for what she was seeing: Ambrose Rector was back.

Keep the adventure going with
CHRISTOPHER HEALY!

THE PERILOUS JOURNEY SERIES

THE HERO'S GUIDE SERIES

WALDEN POND PRESS™
An Imprint of HarperCollinsPublishers

www.harpercollinschildrens.com

More Must-Read Books from Walden Pond Press

Also available as ebooks.